The Widow's Trial

BOOKS BY JOHN EHLE

Fiction

The Widow's Trial
Last One Home
The Winter People
The Changing of the Guard
The Journey of August King
Time of Drums
The Road
The Land Breakers
Lion on the Hearth
Kingstree Island
Move Over, Mountain

Nonfiction

Trail of Tears: The Rise and Fall of the Cherokee Nation
The Cheeses and Wines of England and France,
with Notes on Irish Whiskey
The Free Men
Shepherd of the Street
The Survivor

The Widow's Trial

John Ehle

1817

HARPER & ROW, PUBLISHERS, New York
Grand Rapids, Philadelphia, St. Louis, San Francisco
London, Sydney, Singapore, Tokyo, Toronto

THE WIDOW'S TRIAL. Copyright © 1989 by John Ehle. All rights reserved. Printed in the United States of America. No part of this book may be used or reproduced in any manner whatsoever without written permission except in the case of brief quotations embodied in critical articles and reviews. For information address Harper & Row, Publishers, Inc., 10 East 53rd Street, New York, N.Y. 10022.

Designed by Sylvia Glickman

Library of Congress Cataloging-in-Publication Data

Ehle, John, 1925–
    The widow's trial / by John Ehle.—1st ed.
        p.   cm.
    ISBN 0-06-016154-X
    I. Title.
PS3555.H5W48   1989
813'.54—dc20   89-45077

89 90 91 92 93 CC/HC 10 9 8 7 6 5 4 3

To
Anne Forsyth

1

MAVIS:

Winnette has always been attracted to danger. She's had twenty-two years of courting it, stretching her life against the bounds, don't you know, not finding much danger even so. Except as a baby she kept pulling her own diapers off. She first noticed Lloyd Plover on the Monday following a long weekend in 1981. "There he comes," somebody called out, and us ladies got busy, occupied, acted as if we didn't even notice, but he knew we were noticing; Plover knew I would be concerned about him for old times' sake, if no other. He came past my packaging station, winked at me—his customary and sole greeting, had been for two years since I shook free of him—bless his mean dear soul. And walked past Winnette, she staring at him openly, went by her, pretty as a calendar, without a notice. Plover was that a way: he would ignore lightning unless it struck him, he was that secure. The report we'd all heard by his arrival—late as usual—was last night a new man on the highway patrol, one of those daily shavers, you know, he'd seen Plover's car drive through the bypass light and go swift as martins up toward Riverbend, and North Carolina's finest had set chase, and, along about Maidenhead, Plover had stopped at Grindstaff Road, where he has a woman friend. Anyway, Plover and Blue Chatham were going to call on her and play the guitar, among other enjoyable sports. Plover was aggravated by the siren and flashing lights. He walked back to the clean-shave and none of that sweet talk about "was I speeding, officer, my speedometer must be broken." He grabbed the clean-shaver by his nice jacket and pulled him out of his car and beat the shit out of him and threw his pistol into the bushes and left him a lump of groans on the road, and he went on to what's-her-name's trailer, where she lives with a woman friend, "catering" so to speak. That's a new word for it I made up. They cater to men friends. No pay, no charge. Surely Plover wouldn't pay. He won't ever have to pay. He's handsome with a Clark Gable darkness, is built well, has strength to spare, and he's got a ball of sexual energy inside, all set to explode, and will explode inside a woman if she's handy and won't take warning for herself. No stopping him, either, with claims of virginity or time-of-month or pregnancy or TB. I was married to him, so I ought to know. Before that I courted with him off and on for several months and learned how he was. Sexual need can come over him most any time of day or night.

Winnette, who already was a divorcée, was getting interested in him, looking at him as he approached, seeing him ignore her and pass on by to move through the swinging double doors, throwing both out of his way, moving into his own section of the factory floor, where he was one of the supervisors.

I'm the one told him Winnette liked the thought of him, which was at her request. I warned her he was hard to tie down, but she and I worked the two packaging machines and had plenty of break times to talk. She was pretty in a small-boned, filly way; nothing was red and orange about her. Mostly she was tans and grays. She had a small face surrounded by a wealth of curls; the hair was an auburn basket for her face to look out of. She dressed feminine, as I call it. No jeans, no T-shirt for Winnette. She wore a clean skirt every day and a blouse too fully cut to reveal her breasts. She was a modest person and had a modest, sweet appearance, even at work.

"That there machine will grab a handful of that blouse and package you with that there skirt," our foreman worried her, laughing with her.

"Maybe not," she told him. She had worked all her life, was smart upstairs, had held jobs at the paper mill, the office at Northcross School, the county register of deeds' office, the Stauton Hardware of a day while she attended the community college of a night, which is one reason I came to like her. I admire a person who's smarter'n I am, and is helpful, is daring—as full of wants as her hair has curls, don't you know what I'm saying, all natural curls. Natural is a proper word for her—a hungry body wanting to be fed by life, not be left over somewhere. She asked me to mention her to Lloyd Plover.

"Why, he's ten years older'n you, honey, if a day," I told her.

"I'm twenty-two."

"Why, he's thirty-one and will eat you up."

"Well . . ." She kept her own thoughts, but later in the day she asked me to tell her more about him. "I hear he needs someone to help him," she said.

"What you want to say?" I asked her.

"I been seeing his face in the machine, asking me to help him," she said. "All day."

"Honey, it'll break your machine," I told her.

Their first date was an experience, from what she told me. She was to drive to his trailer, then they were to go to supper and a drive-in movie. When she arrived at the trailer, which was parked this side of Northcross, the lights were out, but she has spunk enough to knock on the door. The door swung open and he was there sitting on the settee waiting, and he looked at her for a full minute, as if he was evaluating her, all pretty and clean and dressed in a frock. Then he came on outdoors and locked his door. He helped her into the front seat of his car and, never mentioning supper, drove to the movie, asking only three questions, she told me.

"Your name is Willownette?"

"Winnette," she corrected him. "There's no 'ill' in it. I've never been ill a day in my life."

"How old are you?"

"Twenty-two."

"Do you always dress so a man can't tell what you are?"

3

To that she had no answer, she said, but then he smiled, and he does have a wonderful smile, and it's as disarming as sunlight, and she felt comfortable with him.

At the drive-in he chose to park near the rear of the lot, off near the bank, and he went for popcorn and hot dogs and two 7-Ups. The movie was X-rated, and Winnette began to be affected. I assured her Plover must have been, too, knowing him. But he never touched her, except to suggest she take off her jacket, which came about twenty minutes into the story, which was about a girl in Boston.

"Will you let me see what you're hiding?" he asked her. He then unbuttoned the top of her frock and got it down over her shoulders, revealing her bra and two round breasts—at least that's how she described them, and he seemed to accept them as valid, so to speak, and after a while he leaned over and kissed the nipple of the nearest one. This made her more excited, of course. Later he asked if she'd mind taking off the bra, a suggestion that ordinarily would have offended her. He was occupied with the film and was tapping on the steering wheel with his fingertips; she hesitated for a long while before curiosity overcame her and she unfastened her bra at the front fastener and let it fall open, showing what she had to offer.

Nobody except Plover was nearby. There were cars entering and leaving, but no flashes of car lights. Plover's car was in a dark enough place, to be sure, and nobody else probably would see her, even one driving into the place, or see him when he touched each one, held each for a moment in the palm of his hand. "Nicer'n hell," he told her.

So it went, off came her stockings, her dress. An hour after they arrived off came her panties, all off, and she was stark naked sitting beside him, he fully clothed and watching the dirty movie, and she was never so worked up and wanting somebody, just plain wanting somebody, in her life, with the story of the Boston girl finishing up.

He helped her pull her dress over her bare body and drove her home. "Bring all your clothes," he told her. Inside his house, by the time she got her things in hand, he had a lamp lighted and was

4

stripping his own clothes off. He had the TV on—Plover likes to follow the news, all the affairs of the world. He asked her if she wanted a drink or a fix. She did, she said, need something. Back then she didn't know what a fix was. She needed something. He pointed to the refrigerator, and she found a bottle of half-drunk white wine and, needing it but seeing no glasses, she drank some from the bottle, and he took it from her hand and set it aside and embraced her and she felt a rich longing rise in her, then he told her to bend across the top of the table—he has this card table he eats off of and plays solitaire on, and I've known him to use it for sex, mind you. A woman can hold to the far edge and she lays the side of her face against the top.

He had her in among the sheets and pillows, too, and then told her she better get dressed. He watched her dress, which aroused her yet again, she told me, but he appeared to be dull, preoccupied. She asked him to kiss her. He had not kissed her ever. He shrugged, then smiled a welcome, that big smile, and she climbed back into the bed where he lay and asked him to kiss her, please, so he did, but none too well. She kissed him, one might say, and he allowed it. She told me she kissed his chin and cheek and nose. Then he told her she was better at this than he had expected, and he was pleased with her, he said, and he kissed each breast. Then he told her to go on home, but once she reached the door he told her to wait. He went to her, naked as when born, and she said he gently ran his two hands deep into her hair, and kissed her on the lips. Kissed her lovingly until, she told me truthfully, she as well as collapsed. He was left holding her up, his hands in her hair.

Her telling me the events took place in the factory sandwich bar, which has the world's smallest tables and is usually crowded as a sardine can, and is noisy, so what I heard was the best of it. She had to murmur and whisper, considering, since the details being so red and orange. She told me out-and-out, as if she didn't recall it was my own husband, father of my two children.

During a break, one of those where you can go to the toilet if you hurry, or must sit near your machine, I asked her what she would do next, if he ever mentioned another date, and she said, "Lord knows." That's what she said, and began to fuss with her blouse and skirt, pulling it neat to her knees and pulling at her sleeves and lifting her neckline, as if I might be curious about what she carried.

Lord, she's suddenly a virgin, I thought. "He'll ask you by surprise; anything he says has to be by surprise."

"Lord only knows what I think about all I did," she said. "Are you afraid of him?"

"Not because of what he did to you," I assured her. "Might be jealous, since I was his legal wife."

"What—what else is there?"

"Oh, there's his other moods. Not for a wife to testify against her husband, don't you know."

"Does what I said surprise you?"

"Well, now that you mention it, he might have waited for another date or two. No dinner even, no beer."

"No. Take off this and that, and lean over this table."

"He's used to having his way, all right. His mother must have spoiled him rotten—"

"Does it make you—upset with me?"

"What?"

"My being—intimate with him."

"Upset with you? Why, I'm not your mama. How old do you think I am, anyway?"

"I mean, does his being with me make you jealous?"

"No," I lied. A blank, strange denial, really. I'm not a good liar. "Not the strange facts of it, anyway."

"What—makes you jealous?" she asked, as if she really wanted to know, as a friend.

"Tenderness makes me jealous," I admitted. I fluffed up her hair. "But not you." Did she believe me? I wondered. "Don't you tell my children, hear?"

"Tell children about this?" she exclaimed, astonished.

The machine time was called, and we took our work places. The packaging machines were our children, hers and mine. They were automatic, and we corrected their errors, that was about it. Like a nurse attending to four-year-olds, the age of Little Max and Kathy at home.

"What will I tell him, Mavis?" she asked.

"Tell him you can't help him further."

"You know so much more than me."

"About him, I do," I agreed, frowning at her. "Learn from what I decided to do with him."

He passed by. He came in from outside, late for work, and passed by us both with a nod and one of his smiles, the same for each of us.

2

BLUE:

My name is Blue Chatham. Blue was my mother's family name. I'm a musician, not of the blues, but of others. I worked for Plover when he was supervisor of the Number Two Plant at Herndon, making furniture, and when a layoff came there in 1978, him and myself went to work for Silver Spur, making jeans. My job was to wash and distress them, so they looked used and old. We put stone earthenware in the washers is how we done it. Plover was the strongest man in the plant and did my heaviest work for me. I was never stronger than my mother. In fact, she could whip me at most any work till she got rheumatism in her wrists. Even as a boy I was always more of a music man, banjo and harmonica and guitar, and my Uncle Mitch gave me a lick and a promise on his fiddle; however, the banjo is my favorite, it's the busiest and can be made to carry a tune, though it prefers to strum background. I played age fifteen, seventeen, eighteen, twenty, and twenty-one, which was last year, at the music festival at the Thomas Wolfe auditorium in Asheville and won enough acclaim to go to my head—that's all. It doesn't take much.

My friend, Anne, and myself used to double-date alongside Plover, including times he dated Winnette King, who was as smart as she was pretty. Most of Plover's girlfriends weren't smart. I want to say that. She could out-think him and me both, and I'm sure he resented it. Plover was clever, but wasn't educated.

Of an evening we'd be comfortable on the sofas and rugs of his trailer or of Anne's and mine, and drink beer and whiskey and listen to me play music, and we'd all sing. Plover had an excellent voice. Sounded like low notes on a pipe organ. It embarrassed him to be praised for it, but the truth was he could make glasses rattle in the cupboard. Winnette couldn't stay in tune. She was all over the pitch looking for the notes, which was amusing. "Now, let's have Winnette sing by herself," he would say.

She would do whatever he said, except when he brought marijuana. That second weekend she got sick on it and wouldn't use it afterward. "More for me," he'd tell her, and blow smoke in her face. She would sing whenever we did, and he'd try to drown her out, we all would, she was so off-key. Pretty voice, and she was pretty whenever she sang a love ballad, got angelic, like a black-figured nun.

He loved her or he wouldn't have pestered her. That was Plover's way. He protected her from others, and as best he could from life, but he couldn't protect her from himself. I tried to write music about it, put a song on a record, the album he helped me finance. He took up a collection at the denim mill last year, had every man on his shift give four dollars, and in return I played and sang for two hours every day for a while, maybe a month. Better to sing than wash jeans, anyway.

The song was a ballad and told about his protecting her from others, keeping her for himself, until finally he couldn't stand being Mr. Nice Guy. Maybe you know how it is. I mean, a man is a protector, right? But what if he is a predator, too? Like a mother fox on a nest of hound pups—now, there's something to consider.

He had pups at his place, and that was an attraction for her. White Alsatians. Once she moved in with him, she was the one that fed them, for he would not always be home. Plover traveled out and away, left of a Saturday and back by a Monday dawn; sometimes it was merely in time to get to his shift. So he'd be gone from Saturday noon to Monday, and she'd be in the trailer, not answering the bell. "Do you want to get killed?" he told her. She would let Anne and me in. She let me in alone, finally, if I was drunk on alcohol or drugs, either one, for Anne probably told her I couldn't harm a woman if alcoholed up. I could only sing. My papa said Irishmen can talk and sing while drunk, but that's all. My mother's a McIlvenny, my papa about half Scotch-Irish. We can also drink while drunk—but don't expect more than music.

The dogs were white. Did I mention that? They were not for hunting. They tell me Alsatians are sheepdogs. He had three at most, two females and a male named Roosevelt. He had papers on them. They'd foal, or whatever, and it was up to Winnette to care for them and find buyers for the pups, which she done. She got to smelling like puppies, he'd complain, and laugh about his puppy-pussy, but he was grateful to her. The dogs were his, never mind her care. One pup about four months old was noisier than a church clock, and he—well, he shot it with his Luger, as she told me, told the whole wide world, killed her pup. But it was not hers, really. The dogs and guns were his. Once they moved into a house, the one over toward Cannan, they built a better dog house, one Plover could even stand on, and he gave her a dog run—he meant to stop her begging. She sold one pup to her sister and parents and paid for it herself, and there were roars of laughter from Plover at this. That night he took another pup to her parents' farm and sold it to them for cash. Their farm was only half a mile away, and her sister, Clara, lived with the parents, swept and washed and cooked and helped feed their cows and the chickens. She was pretty, too, was mild and tame, very like Winnette; probably had a fire inside her like Winnette, too, but it never had blazed. And Plover told me he had never been able to attract her, though apparently he had even gone into her room while she slept and had begun to rub her up before she awoke. She put him out. Rejecting Plover was cheeky of her, and no doubt was one reason he disliked her.

Winnette twice left him, went back home, and after a few days he went for her. He told me this proudly, as if revealing a surprise. He told me he had missed her in the house, as well as in his bed, that he had come to need her. The situation appeared to baffle

10

him. Then once or twice, as he admitted, he had told her to leave, and she had gone home, but these were mere accidents, he said, him being tanked up on something in his blood. He was a big one for referring to his blood or to anybody's blood, and I believe he would look even for his own soul in the blood. He would talk about blood, rites of tribes and peoples, and making pledges through exchange of blood. This was usually when he was smoking pot or popping downers. He told Winnette any marriage ceremony should incorporate an exchange of blood, which made me laugh, until I realized he was serious. He was offended by my laughing, I could tell, and at once I apologized repeatedly, but to little avail. Whenever he got into a pout over something, no matter how trivial, he harbored it, petted it like he would Winnette, whom he petted much of every day, stroked and rubbed and massaged. I mean, let's say he is sitting on the sofa in their house and he pats the place beside him and she comes there, he strokes her like a pet, a kitten, even excites her, as Anne and I later agreed, both of us could tell, and knew what he was up to. She was not difficult to trigger, anyway, Anne told me. She had learned that from Winnette herself. He knew what a spectacle he was making of her, and why she hid her face from us, buried her head in pillows.

I never saw him hit her and believe he did not, she being willing to please him. I did see bruises twice. Both times she had a black mark on her face, but she said a door in the trailer stuck and was dangerous. Maybe he hit her, but if so, it was drugs did it to him. Pot made him somber, but she told me something was making him cross and irritable. She didn't know what it was. By the time they moved to their second trailer, a big one set off in the woods near South River, she was asking me where he had gone weekend before last, as if I knew, for he had come home early Monday morning in a daze. She had opened the door and found his face a mask, and he had thrust past her and had got into bed, but had not slept, told her to strip and come to him, but he was not considerate of her, she felt, he hurt her, twisted her limbs until she cried, suffocated her, made her sing for him.

Even doubting, confused, she welcomed his saying they were

11

to marry. This was June of last year. It was, I suppose, a sort of victory for her. She said she would marry only in her parents' church, which he agreed to. His own parents' church was out in the sticks. Plover was not given to religion, except he liked what he had heard about Indian religions, at least the stories told him by a Cherokee. For her sake he agreed to their marrying in her church, provided nobody else was present; it was as if he didn't want to be found out. She said her parents would be there, and her sister, Clara, and I, and Anne, so he sweated and sweltered and became argumentative as hell about not being an exhibitionist, but Anne and me jumped in, she with her laugh. She was amused by him. "Six people plus the preacher, seven people," she told him.

He scowled and his teeth chewed on his tongue, seemed like to me, and he had too much spit to swallow, but his threatening looks didn't dissuade Anne.

"You don't have to strip naked, after all," she told him.

He thought Anne was funny. "Putting on the britches, are you?" he told her, and seemed to notice her especially and differently. It was amazing to see his eyes gleam with a new hurt, a search for different entertainment. Anne was my girl, but Plover wouldn't notice priorities. She was big and bony and possessive and not at all pretty, but even so he might take to her.

"And I'll invite Mavis," Winnette told him. Anne and me was sitting there.

All joking stopped then, on the nickel, leaving ragged groans in the trailer, then he went into hiding deep within himself, and denied he had ever considered marriage. "I've got all I want, as it is," he told her.

"That's what I say," Winnette said. She was imitating Anne's example, was standing up to him more than before, which was as dangerous as firearms for a person not stronger than her. Later I asked Anne if she imagined he was going to punish Winnette for agreeing with him. She said yes, he was like that. Anne was a smart person and had a mother's instincts, all right; if she had watched her own weight while young, when she was twenty or thereabouts, she might be an eye-killer today at thirty-five. Yes,

12

she's that age, older than me by ten years, older than any of us, and therefore was more experienced. I liked her very well, her wisdom and even being fat. She fretted and fussed at herself, but hers was one soft body whenever she took me in her arms, let me admit there was wealth of comfort there, as well as wealth of feeling. She could draw out the best in a man, could beckon it with her eyes, her words. Came from Minnesota. I liked her better than anybody else and would have married her, but she never mentioned it.

One evening Plover and Winnette came to Anne's trailer for dinner, and we drank corn whiskey, except Winnette had Cointreau. She hadn't never developed a liking for whiskey. "More left for us," Plover proclaimed. She would only drink liqueurs, and she would bring one with her and drink her share. Anne fried a chicken and made milk gravy and biscuits. She had homemade ice cream for dessert, not churn-made, sorry to say, but freezer-made, good. Better than Sealtest. She offered slices of cake, as well, but only Winnette took any at all. Winnette kept thin mainly because she ate only nibbles—I had noticed this before. She would sample everything, that's it. Only sample it. She was by nature modest.

Plover was on edge tonight, even more than usual, resenting her comments, her trying-to-be-of-help notions; he kept reminding her that his invitation for her to marry him had been refused. Her denials were not acceptable. He became so furious he pulled a pistol out of his pocket—this will seem extraordinary—and aimed it at her and said he would hear no more from her.

"He's proposing!" Anne chortled. "Look at Plover's proposal!" She shouted and laughed, though she was scared as I was.

I dared to laugh, and so Plover's anger became deflated, and he was left holding the useless pistol, and he seemed to arrive back into reality. His eyes, his awareness changed, and he hid the pistol in his hip pocket and sat down across from Winnette, there at our coffee table, and said he was a fool to act like that. Anne began to talk about plans for their wedding, saying she would book the church for three o'clock on a Sunday, and she would pay the preacher as part of her gift, and she would give invitations to Winnette's sister and parents.

"Now we do hope you'll be there, Lloyd," she told him, using his formal name, flashing on him the superior smile of an older person.

"I will," he said, which surprised us all. "I will, Anne, for your sake," he promised her, and appeared to be grateful to her for affording relief of his awkwardness.

"You won't need to bring any of your firearms," she told him.

This time Plover did not pout, did not threaten. Indeed, he became content, as if the wedding, even compromised by visitors, was what he in truth wanted. He asked for ice for his whiskey and proceeded to get contentedly drunk, listened to me play the guitar and sing. He asked three times for "Tennessee Birdwalk," a song I thought he had tired of, and roared with laughter. On leaving, Winnette had to help him down the steep steps of Anne's trailer. There are only four or five steps, but they are inconsistent and wobbly, made by her and myself of a Sunday. He hugged Winnette possessively, seemed to care about her, best we could tell, and she and him toppled off the steps, muddied each other, happy that evening as they left, the two drunk and floundering about in the wet, moving in awkward embrace to his car. I've known Plover to drive fast as birds while so drunk he could not stand up alone, as tonight. Off they went, horn blowing his salute and defiance.

3

MAVIS:

My invitation to Winnette's wedding came not from her, though she stood each day six and a half feet away, but from an Anne Bailey, whoever she is. I knew some of the Baileys in high school, but not Anne. This was a Woolworth's-type greeting card, mailed to me at the factory, can you imagine, with the date and time of the wedding inked in, using a felt pen, and done in blue, not black, which I know to be fashionable. "What do you want to do this for?" I demanded of Winnette, so overwrought I could scarcely speak. "Is it because of the pill?"

Winnette turned to stare at me incredulously.

"Well, you complained of a rash," I told her. "It's my own husband you're marrying, you know."

"Well, you don't have him, Mavis."

"My children are involved."

"Well, they can come, too, Mavis."

"Come to see their father marry a girl young enough to be his daughter."

"I am not young enough."

Both our machines were clanking and churning and slapping, and I had to shout and bite my words, speaking over them. "Obviously I'm not rec-com-mend-ing this. It's one thing to have a bit on the side, an-other to marry legally."

15

People were turning to look our way. Probably they couldn't understand the words because of the clatter, but must have known we were upset. "You went to living with him, which was bad enough, but you can walk away from that any time. Take my word for it, marriage is legal."

"Well, he's the one wants it," she said.

That caught me unawares and stirred me up. It's a wonder I didn't box her ears. "Why?" I asked her. My experience was different. I had been the one to drag him to the town hall. He was high and was feeling friendly to the world. Our living together wasn't going anywhere and it was my crazy notion that a baby would restore our relationship, the newness of the baby could be rubbed all over us, so to speak, and he would stop shopping around for variety. Then the second baby followed eleven months later and then I was trapped for certain, and there he went about his flaunting and courting and carousing. It was me who maneuvered him to the ring.

"You're telling me he wants it? Then it's for a reason," I said. All day I fretted, sweated about it, so that my stomach went sour and I spit up phlegm. At noon break, I couldn't eat a bite. I gave her mine, and she ate it, not realizing how upset she had made me.

"Such as he has is to come to my kids," I told her. "Now, you'll take it, won't you?"

"Why, he's not going to die," she assured me.

"The way he drinks and drives, don't tell me." I dosed an Alka-Seltzer and drank swallows of Diet Pepsi, and the two together gave me a rumble inside, which scared me, actually. "Oh, honey, I don't know why I dislike your wedding so much." She allowed me to hug her. She wasn't stiff about me at all, as I was about her. "He's all I ever loved," I told her, which is so. I'll gouge her eyes out, so he won't want her, I told myself, rip her ears off, rip the nipples off her breasts, pollute her with stinks and bleed her coloring, throw ashes on her . . .

She and I bought new frocks at the same time, a coincidence, but it suggested mystic powers at work, deserved taking better warning. My dress was dark blue and had a white blouse and big bow, which made me feel younger. Winnette chose a white suit, it not at the peak of good taste, seemed to me, for a bride. Made her more a mole than she ought to be, or than she was. At my suggestion she put down enough money to hold it on layaway—Plover took her check each week—to give time to think about the choice, and reconsider. This was a Thursday and the store would be open Saturday till six P.M.

As matters turned out, Plover vetoed the suit, or any white clothes at all. Virginity, even if inferred, embarrassed him. "What you want all that white for?" he asked her. "It's not your first round." He encouraged her to buy a blue dress and a white scarf and black belt, all this on the Saturday before the wedding. She told me him and his friend Blue and this Anne Bailey were at the shop in attendance, Blue and Plover sprawled on customer chairs watching Winnette model outfits. "She should want to look like she was ready to escape on her honeymoon," Blue told Plover. There was to be no honeymoon, wasn't mentioned otherwise, not even a day off was offered, not even a visit to an Asheville hotel, nothing. Plover didn't volunteer to pay for her outfit, either, even after taking her paychecks, and he bought a new sports shirt for his part, that was all.

Flowers must have been supplied by the church. When my kids and me arrived, ladies were doing three flower arrangements. At two o'clock Plover and that friend Blue and the so-called Anne Bailey arrived at church, all together, but when Plover saw our son and daughter, Max and Kathy, age four—overlapping age four—he went mellow, his strength ebbed, and he left the others and came close enough. The two had not seen him to know for the better part of a year, and he had only seen them twice, both times by coincidence at Ingles grocery store.

As for me, he noticed me not at all. Only Max and Kathy. Well, I had scrubbed them to a shine and dressed them up, had slicked Max's hair, and they didn't know to be afraid, were at ease and smiling, the youngest, Kathy, not even aware he was her father.

Winnette's parents and sister and four or five other family members arrived. They took seats the other side of the church. I ought to sit with them, the thought occurred to me, since this was the side for the groom's, which did not quite suit me, especially when his parents and half-wit sister came in and sat behind me. A lady of the church sat down at the electric organ, and the preacher came in from the Sunday school building and shook Plover's hand, Plover feeling so ill at ease and out of place he actually left the nave, or whatever it's called, and must have retreated to the lobby or vestibule, to wait there for advice from that Blue nincompoop. And the bride's march, with Winnette coming out, was a surprise to me, for he wasn't to be seen. Her father went to find him, then the nitwit friend Blue came forward, and soon the groom did, and so the service was performed, though he never answered the questions, even when repeated. When they was announced married, the organist went through an anthem, or whatever, again, and Winnette came over and sat by me to give me a hug and receive my "Better luck, honey, than me."

Meanwhile, the groom and Blue were already outdoors, and the pastor, a Mr. Collins, went outdoors, too. When he returned he let the doors slap shut, so we all turned around, as if shot. He beckoned to Winnette, who hurried to him, then she beckoned to the others of us, and we all followed. Plover had put himself in the driver's seat of his car, and he motioned for Winnette to get into the seat beside him, and he directed Blue the banjo man and Anne Bailey into the backseat. Then he and Winnette were married there for a second time, the pastor outside, beside the open car windows, going through the entire ceremony. Plover answered for his part and swore allegiance. That was the way he was; he liked to have his way.

4

WINNETTE PLOVER:

I loved him very much.

We meant to find a house soon as we married. The trailer was too small in every direction, and it had never been underskirted. The wind would whistle under it terribly and knife its way through cracks in the floor. I bought a rug at Cooks. He resented the money lost, as he termed it, and threw the carpet into the yard, so it lay there for a few days till I went ahead and rescued it. Meanwhile he bought himself guns he fancied, so that the trailer came to resemble an arsenal, and bought supplies of whiskey and pot for himself—I rarely took either. Also, other things, such as Angel Dust, which I had never known about until our wedding night. He said it was heaven sent, the angels had combed it out of their golden hair and it had been gathered in vials by a man he knew in Tennessee, near Elizabethton. He had a silver medicine box, maybe two inches square, which he gave me as a wedding gift. My only one. Actually, the ring he gave me at the two ceremonies was one my mother loaned me. Inside the box I expected to find my own wedding band, maybe even a diamond engagement ring to match, for Plover always had plenty of money; having money and spending it are two different things, seems like—not with me, for I'd rather enjoy spending it on beautiful gifts than keeping it. He had money in mason jars buried here

19

and there, two that I knew of buried in the dog lot, another under the rickety steps to the trailer door, so that you had to crawl even to uncover it. He had marijuana in buried jars, too.

I opened the silver box and found seven capsules looking like the cod liver oil capsules Mama used to take, which as a child I took-one of and chewed it up, to my distress and disappointment. These were supposed to be filled with Angel Dust, and one was to be swallowed now, to make my wedding night happy. So I took one and drank a measuring cup full of brandy, and directly the effect was of being above myself, outside my worries. It did make me lovely, I felt, and successful and loving, and we made love as tenderly as Persian kittens.

Often he was tender, more tender than before, but whenever he was on drugs his mood would be enhanced. It might be happy. Then it might be sour and even belligerent. One Sunday afternoon about four-thirty, he had been drinking since breakfast and doing speed to pick up his spirits. His eyes got so glassy that I decided to give him plenty of room, but there is only so much room in a trailer. He couldn't find his motorcycle key, so I began to help him look. He decided I had hid it from him, and when I denied it, he took his thirty caliber carbine and fired it—not at me, of course, but fired it in the trailer, a sort of warning shot. I ran. There must have been smoke coming off my footprints. Three times he fired, shouting Father, Son, and Holy Ghost, and by the Holy Ghost I was behind the car. This happened one more time, and every time he refused to believe he had done it. I had to show him the bullet holes. He never would believe it, even so, and told Blue I had made it up. He told Blue he couldn't do anything like shoot a pistol inside his own house. That's why I laid no special attention on these violent displays, because they were not directed at me and were mere puffs of temper brought on by pills, which he must have bought on his weekend jaunts. I knew he was getting deeper into drugs because the number of phone calls had steadily increased, and he would leave packages with me for people to pick up, and several times he brought home on Sunday evening so much marijuana—about five pounds—I agreed to help him weigh it out and package it, and these he took away late Sunday night, or hid.

Our marriage went smooth as silk, so long as he got his way. There was the carpet incident. There was the hapless, silly shootings. Then came the dog incident. This occurred, like everything, on a weekend. Most Saturday mornings before I rolled out of bed, I'd hear Plover's new motorcycle start. I would be listening to it put-put, then purr, and once Plover had it warmed up, he would roar away, to be gone a few hours or a few days, leaving me to answer the phone and say when he'd be back, the same men's voices asking for him. Then, too, I had the dogs to feed and tend to, including the new litter, which had been seven pups in number, and now was down to two. One was to be ours. I petted both, couldn't pet one without the other. When Plover was away, I would take the pups to bed with me and would read to them, practicing for my babies yet to be. Lovely and lonely these Saturdays, having time enough to lie about, read, listen to music. Plover liked only rock, so we had that on during the week. I liked country and show tunes and jazz, and most of what was on the college radio channel.

Often he would return maybe Sunday morning. The roar of the cycle could be heard as far away as the bridge at the Mason Road, about half a mile away, so that'd give me time to switch the radio program, straighten the sheets, put a drop of toilet water on myself, take a quarter-inch of toothpaste and swish it about in my mouth. Or I would take a swallow of brandy. He liked to think I was learning to drink. Then I would hide one of the pills, pretending to be high, which would please him, for he would usually be high on alcohol and some dope or other and didn't want to be alone in his celebrating.

One Sunday he came back in the afternoon and, bored, began trying to teach the two puppies to walk on a leash. One would do well, but the other would bark at him and complain. Both were cute as pie, but anything challenging Plover was asking for trouble. He kicked the dog and slapped it, which made me cry, and that upset him all the more. He started cussing, using all the words he knew, words I cringed at, that I had never heard before age

21

sixteen, and he got one of his rifles from the house and came out and actually shot the puppy.

Even so, she was still alive and was able to yap. So pitiful she was, pleading for saving from an assault she couldn't understand, and I was crying, too.

He told me to get more bullets. I could not, simply could not move, and he struck me in the side of the head with his open hand, which made my ears ring, my head go dizzy, and he grabbed me by the hair and pulled and pushed me roughly up those trailer steps. I got two handsful of bullets and showed them to him, for I didn't know one lot from another. He would have hit me again, I knew, even without having ever been hit before, he wasn't a knowing person just then. He made me take the bullets outdoors and stand there while he shot the pup over and over, repeatedly drilled her, but after all his shots she still lived, so he told me to bring him some more bullets.

Half blind, I found my way—I don't think I could see for crying, and got the bullets and brought them. The pup had crawled under our car, and Plover got dirty and bloody pulling her out to shoot her again.

I dug a grave and laid her in it on a bed of leaves, he watching me, leering at me, tottering, grimacing, his eyes glassy, as strange and foreign as in a stained mirror. Suddenly he knelt beside the grave, motioned me back, and he gently stuffed the dead puppy's tongue into its mouth and with his own bloody hands pulled the dirt in over it. He mounded the grave and, with the help of his rifle, managed to get to his feet. He asked me to take him indoors and help him wash up. He laid a big bloody hand and arm across my shoulders and shared his weight with me, and I got him to the steps and he fell forward into the trailer and crawled forward and lay on the carpet. His clothes had blood on them, too. I got them off and pulled him and the rug to the trailer's bathroom and turned on the little bitty shower, and he couldn't stand, so I used a washcloth to clean him part way and rubbed him dry. I wasn't too careful with him. It was on feeling his body, I came to feel the heat, and I took his temperature, using a rectal thermometer because his teeth were chattering. He had a temperature of 102. I woke him up, slapped at his chest and shoulders; finally he heard me pleading with him and got to his all-fours, and I put an overcoat over him and, him to that extent, took him to the hospital, where the doctors pumped out his stomach and put him in Room 401.

"Can you make him well?" I recall asking the doctors, the interns.

"Whenever he wants us to," they assured me.

"I want you to," I told him, "before you let him out of here. Please. For God's sake, find out what makes him—so violent."

An intern took from a plastic bag two crumpled labels which had been found in my husband's overcoat pocket. "Valium is one, Dexedrine is the other," he told me. "Does he take other drugs?"

"Yes. Pot, Angel Dust—"

"What else?"

"I don't know. Alcohol, of course."

Plover awoke. I was nearby, sitting on the chair beside his bed. He awoke and asked me to ring for the nurse. He felt better, he said. "Why did you bring me here?"

I told him how sick he had been and what he had done to the puppy, and he had no memory of any of it and denied ever doing harm to an animal, much less his own. He told me to tell them to release him from the hospital. I don't know what your game is, he told me.

At the nurses' desk I approved the doctor's order to keep him in the room till he was dried out, about two days, they said, and the intern named Robert was sent for, and three others assembled, and they entered Plover's room together. A great commotion ensued, even bureau drawers flew through the air and I fled from being seen, went to the cafeteria and sat there telling myself to stay calm, and I drank a cup of tea. I prayed under my breath for my husband. It did not occur to me, was not possible even then, to leave him. It never occurred to me. That would hurt him further, deeply. I could not leave him now most of all, because he needed help, and that required Blue and Anne and me, and maybe Mavis. It meant those who had learned to live with him. For me, leaving would be desertion.

My father came in response to my call. That I had phoned him from the hospital added urgency. He came along, leaving Mama, who knew nothing of the call; she was out in the garden, he told me. My father is a kind man who was once the pastor of a small Baptist church in the Roan Valley, one of the oldest churches in the county, but he stopped preaching at age twenty-seven and went to work at the Cranberry iron mines. He told me he found a minister's life restrictive. In all my life I've never known him to be unkind or knowingly to hurt anyone. He was so relieved to find that nothing was wrong with me, the illness being only with Plover, that he was content to listen without interrupting to my history of the day.

"One long day," he said, moaning. "Not a proper Sunday." It was he who asked if I wanted to leave Plover. "I only meant it would be better now than afterward," he explained.

"He needs me," I explained.

"Does a man who can't be helped ever need anybody?"

The question phased me out. The idea that Plover could not be helped was beyond me.

"Been married only a short while," he mentioned, clearing his throat, adjusting his body on the chair. My father is modest in manner and tastes and feelings. I heard him once, answering how are you today, reply that he felt *medium,* and so he did, no doubt. Just now he was speaking of medium adjustment . . .

"You'll not risk living with him, will you?"

"Who else will?" I asked.

"Think your mama and me have better sense," he said, with the twinkle of a smile.

"I'm his wife, and bound to."

"Your mother left me one time. Do you recall?"

"Did you ever hit her?"

He looked up, surprised.

"Or slap her?"

He shook his head solemnly.

I shook my head just as solemnly.

"If you want to take a trip some'ers, Winnette, I can let you and

24

Clara have the money, up to a thousand dollars apiece. A type of prize for my peace of mind."

"A peace prize," I told him, smiling gratefully. "But, no thank you." Why did I refuse, I wondered. The need for being held, being loved was not the end-all of my life. I had come to expect a nightly bout with him, the burst of emotion and energy with a strong masculine being, assertive, dominating, cleansing of my own emotions. But I had lived without that.

"You're twenty-two," Papa said. "Difficult to tell me anything when I was your age. About then I got a call to preach. My father poo-pooed it, said God had better choices, other chances, said I was too mild a person anyway, ought to take up hunting. I was too much a fisherman, he told me. Took me five years of anxious listening before I was willing to admit he was right."

"It's not because of my age I'm deciding," I assured him. "I love him, Papa."

"I loved God. You know how a man loves God?"

"No."

"Like Plover loves a gun. A form of respect for power, for silent unleashed power. It's called reverence." He ate a cup of custard, and both of us had tea. I remember him pouring three tiny containers of half-n-half into it. He invited me to come home with him. I said for the one night only, but that he must come with me first of all.

We walked the flights of stairs to Plover's floor, my father being unwilling to risk himself to an elevator. As we entered the fourth floor hallway I could hear my husband crying out, asking for me. The nurses at the station were relieved to see me—they were at their wits' end. I rushed to him, leaving them and Papa behind, and watched as his eyes focused on me and his mouth closed, the awful sounds stopped, and a baby gurgle replaced it as I took his hand and held it between my two hands. Tears came to his eyes.

He wanted me to untie the cords that the interns had knotted, but I could not. I tried, but could not, and he was not insistent. He seemed to understand that he needed help and was willing to be treated. Once the bonds were to be removed by the orderlies, he promised to be cooperative, and he proved to be. For all of two

25

days, up till he was released, tests were made on him, everything inside and out, and the doctor didn't find anything out of the way. "He's healthy as an ox," is the way one put it to me. "It's dope he takes, that's the problem, isn't it?" he said. "Heroin, I imagine. That's the worst."

"No, he doesn't take that," I told him.

"He denied it, too, but then, he denies Angel Dust, Black Beauties, bennies, speed, marijuana, cocaine—"

"He doesn't take cocaine."

"Denies Valium, Quaaludes, Librium. He says he takes a beer from time to time."

The doctor let me rest with such comfort as I could get from that. His name is Doctor Robbins. I used to think of it as Robin, as in the bird, but he puts two *b*'s into it. He was as nice as if I wasn't merely another common problem, a woman hoping for a cure for her husband. A nurse told me there's not a week go by but some bloke, as she called him, is brought in shivering and sweating from the pills.

He liked me, this Dr. Robbins. A woman can tell. He didn't say so, of course. He's much too aloof for that. But, I could tell by the kindness in his eyes, and the one time he took my hand and squeezed it. I noticed he wore a wedding band. Suppose he might have children at home, and I told myself not to daydream, not to dream of having a husband who was well. Faith would make Plover well. Love and faith.

"You are going into service," the doctor told me, "much like men who go to combat. It's dangerous, and I'll worry about you, Mrs. Plover." He pressed his card into my hand. "Call me any time, day or night," he said.

I memorized his numbers, office and home, then tore the card up and flushed it away in the women's room, afraid of what Plover would do to me if he ever found it.

5

MAVIS:

Winnette asked me to allow my two, Max and Kathy, to visit Plover, but I told her no-sir-ree, it's not in the cards. He was not given any visitation rights by the divorce court. She thought this would bolster his morale, now that he had been set free by the medicine men. My diagnosis of his illness was that he had never grown up. As I told her, he was a boy even yet, with a man's strength.

Winnette reminded me of his sexual prowess, which I had to admit was mature enough. "That's why he likes a trailer," I told her.

"Oh, he's promised me a house," Winnette said, overlooking the remark. But on our break, she came up close enough for me to smell her shampoo, and she asked me what I meant about the trailer.

"It used to shake with me," I claimed. "Now and then the *TV Guide* or pot of flowers would fall off the set, or a dish off a shelf." It was all true, there was a glass shelf on wall brackets that I had found in the shop at Northcross, and I had screwed it on the wall myself, and we would try to make knickknacks fall off of it, especially books. He was easily put off by books. "Plover is so dyslexic he can't even read," I told her.

"Why, I've seen him read."

"No," I told her, "he can read a few of the psalms, because his mother helped him memorize them, that's all. He can memorize fast as lightning, but not read words. It's a foreign language, English is. So when I made a bookshelf for the Bible and the library books, he was annoyed. I mean, if we were making love in the trailer's living room on the sofa, they very likely would fall off."

At lunchtime we could talk for up to thirty minutes, if we liked, and one day—this was a month or so after his hospital stay—she talked about his improving; he was letting her change the TV channels or select the radio music, he was not drinking or popping pills there at the trailer, and not doing so much of it elsewhere, not going off on trips without a word. Now he took her with him in the car, and though he bought marijuana in bigger lots, he never appeared to have the other drugs to weigh and sell. She wasn't so worried about marijuana, she told me. Then, too, she had dolled up the trailer, and he had repaired, had steadied the steps, and she had been given a book of checks to his checking account, and she had registered for a night course at Orchid Tech in bookkeeping, with his paying the school tuition. Of course, she told me proudly, he had put his car in her name just recently, had given her the car, so to speak. She answered the telephone for him, made appointments, took orders, and she did help weigh out the pot, but she did not smoke it, nor did he smoke it in the trailer. He agreed to get to work on time and stay a full shift. She had put the bullets up on the closet shelf, and he had sworn to her that none of the guns was loaded. He had, she told me, acquired a few more pistols and rifles and shotguns, but only as a hobby, he enjoyed trading for them.

Whenever they went off on Saturday together, they'd drive into East Tennessee, or sometimes to Blacksburg, Virginia, and buy the pot in lots, up to ten pounds. It would take three to six hours for a round trip, then they would stop to shop at one or two of the farmers' markets, and might stop for lunch at one of the Hardee's or at a Wendy's, which she preferred because it had a salad bar, or they'd choose a Pizza Hut and order the sixteen-inch pizza and she would get a salad to boot. That and a Pepsi-Cola—

she told me everything—and would be full of food and the car with gas, as she told me, by the time they picked up the package. She never referred to it as pot, but as a package. Once that was on board, she would take the wheel and drive home directly. They had enough gas, had seen to that. They'd not exceed the speed limit, once the package was aboard—or the packages. Plover would often lie down in the backseat, which amused her; this was so he wouldn't be seen, as if the police might have spotted him before, or be looking for a couple. She was the one who broke the law transporting it, seemed to me; I suppose that had something to do with the title of the car, but I never told her anything critical of him, for she was on the high road of trust and love, so that her pretty mouth drooled on telling about him, her little voice would choke up, her eyes would sparkle and her tongue would keep moistening her lips. She made me proud of her, and envious. I mean, what if she succeeded, what if she made a gentleman out of Plover? What if he came to be dependable and sober? She was talking of a house—they were going to buy a house. Every week they went out to look at houses. She had two houses in mind, both on gravel roads affording car access in each direction, which Plover required, she said. Two houses to choose from, and with money enough for the down payment, provided Blue did find a buyer for the trailer, as promised.

Plover without a trailer? I could scarcely imagine it. The trailer was his shell, the fitted, metal container he would make rattle and shake by moving through it or grabbing his wife inside it. The trailer was clothing that was too small, that was bursting from having him inside it, his body moving, the music loud, reverberating. He was not only king of his castle; he put on his castle like a coat. "How big are these houses?" I asked Winnette.

She drew their floor plans on a napkin, even marked the windows and the fireplace. Each was off to itself, in a stand of oak trees, set back from the road, and each had a porch and a number of sheds and coops, plenty of hiding places. And each had a spare room, which he said would be for the guns, until, as she told me, the baby, once it came.

That news chilled my blood, it really did. Thoughtless of her to mention such a prospect to me, even before it happened, to diminish my own children and my own marriage. "Well, there's bound to be more water under the dam first," I told her.

"Under the bridge," she told me. "It's over the dam or under the bridge."

"Oh, go to hell," I told her, upset to think she would have such grand ambitions. She was my student, so to speak, a joke I began playing on life once upon a time, an entertainment. She was accepting the big challenge and was educating Lloyd Plover. She didn't know how angry and hurt I was, for I can hide it very well. That's one thing marriage teaches you, to be two-faced when you must. "Many a slap first, let me tell you."

"Slap?" she said, looking at me searchingly.

"That big hand knocks the senses out of you, now don't it?" Oh, I could tell now that she knew.

"I never thought he'd strike a woman."

"His own papa does it even yet to his wife and that daughter."

"No, I don't know," she said fiercely, meaning she wouldn't believe me.

"So you mean to have your baby? Well, good luck, honey, if he slaps your baby before it's born."

"He'd never—never hit me there."

"No, that's safe for baby-dear, is it?" I told her, suddenly hating her prettiness and youth and good hopes and goodness, and the sweet smell of her shampoo, and the innocence in her eyes, which were staring at me frank with assurances.

I took his two children by to see him, couldn't do less now that she was taking him over, so to speak, making him her own. They were in their house on Tom Smith Road. We three, his first family, so to speak, dropped by and found him dressed in wool pants and a colorful sports shirt, first time I had seen him dolled up that way, out of dungarees and the tan shirts he had worn for years. He looked like a Florida tourist's body with Plover's head. She had done all this to him, of course. The new furniture, the six-by-eight-foot rug, the coffee table, for God's sake. He was not surprised to see us and asked Max and Kathy to sit on the sofa with him, then called off toward the end of the house, told wife number two to bring the children a cold drink apiece, and bring something for Mavis. He mentioned having beer about. I never drink beer, as he knows. I asked if he had any of that peach or apple brandy McKinney makes every year, and he said no, he sometimes wished he had. It was my pleasure to take out of my bag a handful of those two-ounce bottles of vodka and I gave him two, and he snatched them, dropped one and retrieved it in a flash and hid them between his legs, grinning like a possum, got them hid as she came out of the bedroom fastening her Yves St. Laurent belt. She had told me most every day for a week that he had given it to her as a twenty-third birthday present. Whether he had or not, I don't know. She was, in my opinion, becoming a little optimist, which is the same as a liar, changing the world around. She was a child, too, so to speak, the two of them were playing house together, playing loving husband and wife, and I was the one with the losses to remember, and the two children living in an apartment small for the three of us, and having loneliness, God knows, and already thirty and burdened with a ready-made family and plenty of debts, and no prospects in sight. And this pretty one sitting with her blouse coming unbuttoned was drinking soda pop and had my husband. "Now you children stay and get to know your papa," I told them. "And your stepmother." I emphasized the "step" a bit more than intended, so that the word rolled in my mouth. So I drove off to Ingles and grocered for the week, and by the time I got back the four of them were out in the yard under the oaks throwing a soccer ball to one another, a ball she had bought in case it were to be needed, and she had even bought a little pump to blow it up with, so she doubtless realized I would relent and drop them by. "I decided a baseball might be too hard," she told me as Plover took the children off toward the dog lot to see a litter of puppies, leaving her and me to admire the cool, sunny, lazy day in her yard.

I left the children there another time, at her suggestion left them overnight. She had two pallets for the spare-room floor. They were in among the gun collection, but she swore they were all unloaded and on lock, and it so happened the trucking company owner, Mr. Zaphrin Fletcher, himself had asked to take me to dinner to the seafood house, his favorite restaurant, and this would save having the children and a baby-sitter about my apartment when he arrived. Years ago Mr. Fletcher had started out owning one truck. This was as soon as World War II was over, and he added trucks as if they was strawberries, until now he was number fourteen in the Southeast; he had told me at the wash-and-dry, where I helped him once.

I dared to leave Kathy and Max there. Listen, it was a new form of madness for me. It was giving him more than visiting rights, which the court had refused him because of the fights and the drunkenness. Nothing like what she was after now, which was to keep them overnight. Clear as anything what she was planning.

I got them next morning, so lonely for them I could die. They had not needed to be away from me, anyway, not for overnight. Mr. Fletcher had eaten his supper in a flash, talking about tie-ups in Nashville and Atlanta, and my own neck didn't appear to interest him until he took me home. Then he became a one-minute marvel. Talk about tie-ups. He came in my apartment and sniffed about and asked me for my consent. There were no preliminaries. I allowed him to go home soon thereafter, satisfied. He left a fifty-dollar bill on the television. He was out of the driveway before nine o'clock. Next morning I went for the kids, and they were crying to stay, not to come home. I had to box Max's ears to get him to hush. Plover was pleased they wanted to stay with him. On the way home I side-roaded the car and told them I'd take them into the woods and leave them unless they hushed. They hushed, for they knew I would and that a tramp would get them and kill them.

"And say you're sorry."

"I'm sorry, Mama," each one whispered, though getting Max to obey is worlds harder than Kathy.

"I know that other wife plied you with cookies and chocolates, for I saw the cups. Just hush, Max, while I'm talking to you. Hush, entirely, Max, or you'll turn out wrong. Last night I suppose she was getting the puppies out for you to play with, now wasn't she?" And so on and so on, blaming them for what she had done to eliminate me. I can see myself plain, as through a mirror, and it's not my best role, being a single mother, for it's too much of a set of rules and blaming the children. They tell me a woman ought to have her own work life and to rear her own children, that way she can be in-de-pen-dent. Well, I've worked since sixteen and know the inside of it, and the outside, and for part of the years I've had two to raise alone, and it's not the way God intended. I'm too cross, too afraid they'll do wrong, too lonely, too God-damned mean, left with nobody to balance me and share the horrors of it. Even Plover, cantankerous, obstinate, insulting as he was the last year I lived with him was better than nobody. "Get out, leave me," he used to yell.

Being with him again stirred up many a tide inside me. He seemed not to notice me particularly, except when I gave him two of the vodkas, and when he hid them and he winked the wickedest joke, so to speak, as if having them in his crotch gave him pleasure. When he drank them, I don't know. On Monday morning she asked me if I had seen him drink anything while I was present, so I took it for granted he had shown signs of being onto a swig or two, or that she had found the bottles, or that he had fallen off the wagon completely and drunk other stuff. Never meant to set him off his pledge, of course. Don't see how a few ounces could affect Plover, after all he's had to drink. In South River, at Harrison's house, he and Harry sometimes drank a case of wine, that's six bottles apiece. And often I've known him to drink a quart of whiskey between noon and supper, and then dig out one of his canning jars of brandy, a pint of that, so he'd be sitting on the front steps and now and then you'd hear the screw-top unscrew on the mason jar, then directly hear the screw-top screw on. An evening with Plover went that a way until finally he'd come indoors smiling like a Cheshire cat, and I'd help him undress and get him into bed and caress him without any fear of him, with him unable to do more'n try to sing and suck. These nights were pleasant because I thought of him as being my Sampson, shorn of hair, and I could hold him and fondle him and might even arouse him, and I could kiss him tenderly and he would moan and groan, and then maybe sometimes, he would respond as best he could. And then sleep, both of us, soundly as newborn.

33

I didn't mind his drinking because that disarmed him, kept him from hurting me with get-out-of-here orders.

Later, once everybody in the county was asking questions about him and Winnette, they'd ask me did you like or dislike her, Mavis? Did you still love or hate him, Mavis? And I told them, honey, a woman like me with two children and myself to support, has no time for all that. I have to survive, that's it. But I guess I loved him, even so, even after, and I loved her, too, in my way.

6

?

WINNETTE:

I invited her children, Max and Kathy, to come with us on a Saturday to pick up the package in Virginia that Plover had telephoned about. Mavis was invited, too, but at the last minute she said she would rather not be away from home on her own cleaning day. Also, my car—now that it was in my name I could call it mine—was small in the backseat. I told her I would sit back there with Max and Kathy, but she wouldn't have that. We left Mavis's place about nine o'clock and stopped at two flea markets before we even reached the state line. Once in Virginia, Plover took the wheel, he not having been there enough to be known. We stopped for Sunday dinner at a place near Bland, at a farmhouse that had been made into a restaurant, with more good food than we could ever eat, and we reached Blacksburg about one o'clock, where Plover filled the car a quarter full of fuel—all he ever put in before a pickup. A full tank was extra weight, he explained.

The package was to be left in a big trash can beside the road, and the road was Red Fox Road, that was what Plover had told me. He told the children nothing, not even that there was to be a package. It was merely a hunt for a house site where the house had burnt down in a stand of big trees. We found it quick as not, and Plover drove up into the yard, to near the wounded house,

35

and jumped out and picked up the package, left the mason jar in which I had put the money, and we were off and running.

However, two cars appeared on the road and blocked the drive to the house, and four men got out and came up the drive toward us. They were maybe a hundred feet away and coming closer, men dressed in regular suits, and the four came up closer, and when they were near our car Plover gunned it and roared right past them. Before they could get out their pistols he was going cross-country and crashed through a wood fence and over the ditch onto the road and was away, gaining speed. He crossed over the Interstate and kept going at a hundred miles an hour until the sirens were lost, away off, one probably going south and the other north on I-81. Then he cut south on a paved road. At Wytheville, Virginia, he rented a Hertz truck at a service station and left my car to have it serviced, and in the Hertz van we crossed the state line at Twin Oaks. There were two N.C. patrol cars waiting on the right, waiting for my car to come through, I suspect. I had the children in the back of the van playing cat and mouse.

Now, none of this they could figure out, not about the old house or a package or the police or the chase, but they were impressed with the excitement and with their father and agreed to keep it all a secret, or else not get to come on any other jaunts with us.

Truth was, I never meant to come on any more jaunts, either.

Next Saturday, Plover sent Blue with the van. He turned it in and brought back my car, which Plover parked in the woods in back of the Elks' Club campsite.

Monday morning policemen arrived at the plant and asked questions of the manager. They wanted to question me, but Mr. Starnes said they would need to wait until the noon dinner hour, for he had nobody to work my machine. That was a polite lie, but he told it. The sheriff's men asked about Plover, and they went into his part of the plant and tried to ask him questions, but he told them his car had been stolen, he had turned in that information as soon as he realized it on Saturday, and he was as interested in who had been driving as they were.

"You have children?" they asked him.

"No. My wife and I live alone."

He got out of it. That evening Blue had a neighbor report finding the car in the woods. The police came and took fingerprints, but they found ours and probably those of the garage people, whom they didn't know about. Of course, the police knew very well they were being fooled. They were being outfoxed at their own games, that was all. All they knew to do was return my stolen car to me.

At work next day Mr. Starnes sat by as a Mr. Henricks, a company lawyer, talked to Plover about a supervisor ever doing anything, anything at all, even remotely that might embarrass Silver Spur in the press, and how even the appearance of law-breaking was too much, and so he droned on, and that Plover had often been late to work, was seen often leaving early, and so forth, and Plover quit. It was, he told me, what was expected of him. He might do more, but never less than was expected of him. He accepted Mr. Starnes's written recommendation saying he was leaving on his own after six good years of service, and he told me he would look for another job, one which wasn't insulting to a person's character.

He encouraged me to stay on, for we did need to have income. That night he left home without a word, was gone two hours, came in complaining about being followed on his way home from Mavis's, although they had not stopped him. The sheriffs were onto him, that was proof, which annoyed him and gave him excuse for being drunk. And not only drunk, but glazed over, his eyes vacant, as if his mind were distant, as if he had taken something more.

This was one of the most important nights of my marriage. It really was, because I began to cry, and I told him through my tears that I had not had my period start on time and had hoped I was bearing our baby, but if he was going to go to Mavis's and get lost to the world I couldn't stand to bear his child for him, and he slapped me then, and I shouted in fury that I would lose it and he slapped me to the floor and kicked me in the belly and stomped me and dragged me out into the yard by my hair and left me near the dog lot. That was the place I lay, to consider the state of my

37

failure in life at twenty-three years of age.

I got in my car to leave, go home to my parents. He must have heard me slam the car door, for he came running. I locked the doors. He said he would kick the glass out, if I didn't open it. He kicked the door so hard, he fell back onto the ground, got to his feet cursing. "All right, you asked for it!"

I opened the door, all the while pleading with him not to hurt me, and he slapped me so hard I recall lying sprawled over the hood of the car, and then I felt his hand seeking to tear down my panties, and I managed to roll off the hood and run, and I ran fast, but he tackled me and dragged me by my hair into the house and locked the door and got his Luger and fired it close to my head and told me he knew I had given Virginia cops notice and was trying to destroy his business and was rude to his suppliers on the telephone and wanted him in prison, that he was in danger enough without me interfering and molesting him, yes and criticizing, persecuting him and dressing him up to show him off and inviting his children over so I could tell people what sort of sacrificing wife I was, and forever embarrassing him. He fired the pistol again, the bullet ricocheting off one of my stainless-steel pots, and told me to strip naked and show him what I had to offer to him, which I did, stripping fast as I could, though he said I was delaying, and he told me to show him while I sang. Then I leaned over the table, as he ordered, and he made love to me, if love has anything to do with that trembling exercise. He slept while I lay in bed beside him, afraid to move.

I was all night awake, and next morning I decided to get out of the house, and I sneaked out, tears rolling down my face, and drove to Papa's, where I asked him to protect me. About ten o'clock Plover came for his legal wife, as he called me. Arrived on a new-looking motorcycle, one that roared. Plover himself was contrite and Papa let him inside the house, but at once dialed the sheriff's office, put friends there on notice, so Plover was scared and went outdoors to stand in the yard, then soon left on that big motorcycle.

Mama took me to Dr. Robbins, the one who had doctored Plover, and he was gentle with me and told me he wouldn't believe the lies I had told him. And they were lies, too. I had not necessarily lost my baby, he told me. "That man of yours ought to be in the Russian Army," he told me. I would say he was upset, as I was, because of my face and body bruises.

I didn't go to work that week, and Mavis said Mr. Starnes's girlfriend worked my machine herself. Mildred Hancock is her name. She is Starnes's number one friend; Mavis had told me that, and she had held my job before he took her into the office. She hadn't liked standing up all day. First two days Plover came by twice, Mavis said, sheepdogged, walked about the machine, she said, was gentle as a lamb, and Mavis told him to look for me in the hospital where he had sent me.

When I was a little girl Papa, with Mama holding the ladder and me back out of tool-falling distance, built me a tree house in an elm tree, one favored by entire families of squirrels. My tree house was three feet by five feet. Many times I measured it with Mama's sewing tape. The roof was a single piece of tin with the edges crimped by Papa, so they could not cut me. The ladder could be raised and hung on two big stobs, so that nobody could follow up, nor see me, even, if I huddled my body and lay against the trunk. It was my place for escape, my treasured hiding place, my lookout from which I could see the house and yards and drive, and far-off road and village, but could not be seen. It was a secret. Of course, Papa and Mama knew about it, but they were members of the secret, my coconspirators in favor of privacy.

I had my sister, Clara, go with me now. Carrying a comforter, I climbed alone to its safety once more and wrapped up, making a cocoon of my injured self.

"You all right up there, Winnette?" Clara called to me.

I called back, yes.

"Don't you dare flirt with the bears," she told me. She walked carefully down the hill to the house, afraid of slipping. Our own mother had fallen at age fifty, had broken her hip, and has never been quite the same since, is always afraid of falling and, indeed, of everything else. She's an excellent cook and keeps the house spotless, but only inside the house does she feel confident.

The squirrels came to accept my being here, began welcoming

me with chatter. I'll bet they had heard from their own parents of my visits as a child; today the parents' stories were proving to be true: a child huddled up in a comforter, her face was resting on her arm, the eyes full of tears, of hurt pride and hurt body. See the tears on her cheeks. She's known a disappointment too cruel for sound. A loss so severe it steals all riches away, robs even itself, leaving the ball of melting flesh and bone. And now a sound. Listen. A moan. A plea. A prayer. A little cry unto itself, to seek company.

Got so during that week of bruises that Mavis would come to see me, got so she would call every evening after work, would ask me could she do anything for me, could she get me my clothes, could she talk to Plover on my behalf, try to reason with him?

Blue and Anne came by, too. She told me, "He's become so moody nobody knows what he's doing exactly, or what he will do next." One time—I believe Blue was off talking to Papa, looking at Papa's new Chevy—Anne told Sis and me that Plover had last night been blaming her, Sis, for breaking up his marriage. Sis, who is twenty, is a secretive, sweet person who has never dared harm a soul. "Of course, when he's drunk he might say anything," Anne told us, "and we never believed a word of it."

"Well, I do say." My sister stared about vacantly, trapped by surprise. "I never would interfere."

"No, he's not best at thinking," Anne told her. "Logic is not his long suit these days, he's so lost and unable."

"What's he best at?" Sis asked, suddenly showing her aggravation.

"Oh, he's best known for needing help," Anne said, then smiled coyly at me, as if that might explain my interest in him. "He's made for women needing men to take care of, to serve."

"Oh, I don't think so," I told her, knowing what she said was true, but I couldn't accept, couldn't bear to accept it.

"You can find you a man to raise," Anne told Sis, "if you want one. Plenty of little boy–men about."

Babying Plover—well, that was not so. He didn't lend himself to that. Any soft fingers laid on Plover only made him want to bite the hand. He was as unnerved by a woman's gentleness as he was

40

his own. Anne couldn't be expected to understand that. A woman had to ride out his storms of passion with him, not try to alter them, or even tone them down.

Anyway, from Anne, as well as Mavis, I gathered that Plover was suffering, and my being away was contribution to that. He was complaining about finances, too, condemning the monthly house payments as being spawned by me and the devil, another of my afflictions, like the dishwasher he could not learn to use. It broke dishes and glasses, the way he stacked them. Anne said his refrigerator was empty, except for a few cold drinks from my days there, and a big jar of dill pickles—which didn't need refrigeration—and he had a box of pretzels and bag of chips, Anne said, and half a pound of liver pudding, "or maybe it was livermush, but he'd never know how to fry it."

"No, he can't cook," I agreed with her. "He burns himself and kicks the stove." That made both Clara and Anne laugh. I recounted the time two flies had bothered him while he was trying to nap, and he took a flyswatter to them and pretty well broke everything in the trailer swatting at them.

"Wonder he didn't shoot them," Anne said. Plover recalled slapping me and was worried about the unborn baby, too, she told me. He did so want it to be born—that was his anguish on Monday night; he wanted it safe and protected and wondered how I was caring for it. Anybody who harmed his baby would have to answer to him, and that included the baby's mother. All right for her to take all the money out of his checking account and steal his car . . .

"What's he good for?" Sis asked Anne.

Amusing to watch Anne's face: she started at once to reply with good evidence, with assurances of Plover's worth, but she hesitated, became frowning and resentful, slowly retiring. Sis laughed at her, then at me for claiming to have found many good values in him.

"Did I miss them?" Sis asked me, putting her face up close to mine, her lips pouting as she waited for my reply, "him and Mavis? Why you little fool," she said to me, her older sister by three years.

Our charades and analyses were all very well, but there was likely to be a baby born in August, by my reckoning, this being December fifteenth. That gave the baby the sign of Leo. My mother is a Virgo. She is one of a twin, so really ought to have been a Gemini. She married a Sagittarius, which I've read is not recommendable, the two being contrary signs, but my mother and father have not had a dozen cross words ever, and he has never struck her, nor she him, and he's never threatened her or her baby with a gun, either.

I decided to go to work again. Mavis said Mr. Starnes offered to put me in the office till I recovered from my "motorcycle accident." Plover would not come near me there, if I wanted to return.

The first morning several people came by to welcome me, including Mr. Starnes himself, who was relieved to death, said he had missed seeing me. All that week Plover let me be. "Might be off on a trip, making a purchase," I suggested to Mavis, carefully watching her. Sometimes I think Mavis, for all her claims of friendship, which are genuine—I wonder sometimes if Mavis wanted him herself, if she harbored the notion of reconciliation. Yet, also she was my friend and my relationship with Plover was like a sore gum for her, was painful pleasure. Sometimes I wondered if she confused herself with me.

The week went by, a week without seeing him except once across the parking lot and once at the steak house as he and Blue were leaving tips for the waitress. My anger pretty well cushioned itself, got so I could enjoy it, so to speak, and the Christmas carols on the radio and in the stores made me forgiving, I suppose. Anyway, I'm forgiving by nature. I bought him a birthday present, his birthday being December twelfth—a colored shirt made by Liberty of London, a flower garden of colors. Sis and I had gone shopping at the Asheville Mall, and we saw it and liked it and bought it, thinking of it as a funny gift for our dad. It was a large size, too big for Papa, but with colors so flagrant and bright it might be that the bigger it was the better. My friend Anne thought I should give it to Plover. "Why not at least be friendly?" she said.

Mavis advised against it. "Better let sleeping dogs lie," she told me.

But, I was his wife, after all was said and done, and our baby was inside me. What would the baby advise me?

I mailed the shirt to him. I didn't even admit whom it was from. This was the first time in my life I had ever written out my own house's address, now only his address, and writing the words, even Tom Smith Road, did make me cry.

Anne arranged Christmas brunch and invited Sis and my parents and me. Sis didn't want us to accept, but I argued that circumstances had reduced me to two girlfriends, Anne the more dependable of them, and I simply had to go. Papa decided he must accompany me, so the four of us agreed to go to Anne's. This made Sis unhappy, and she even made up a little song: You behave or you'll have to visit Winnette's friends on Christmas Day.

Christmas morning my family unwrapped gifts, so many we felt warm from love and giving. Sizes were generally wrong, and the colors were a mischief for us all, but we feasted on nuts and candies and cake and had laughs to go around.

My last three gifts had been mailed in, one from Aunt Sophia and another from Aunt Matilda, whom we called Matey and who lived near Ridgecrest. She sent me a toy, a colored top with a scene, a railroad that went round and round inside the top's dome and made a train whistle. "I wonder if Aunt Matey knows how old you are," Mama said, which made us all laugh afresh. The third package was mailed from Asheville. I opened it, expecting it to be from Mavis, for she had not given me anything except a Maidenform bra this year—it too small. Inside the black wrapper was a plastic box, taped at its edges. I cut it free with Papa's pocket knife. All of the family were watching as I opened it.

A ring. Two rings. A big diamond set in one of them. An engagement and wedding ring. It didn't need a card. Not a sound from my parents or sister.

That afternoon Papa stood up the entire time we were at Anne's trailer. He wouldn't take his hat off, either. It was a gentleman's felt hat I had given him only that morning, one that made him look like a lawyer. Blue wasn't present, not when we arrived. We had our Diet Pepsi and Papa had an Orange Crush, Anne having bought it especially for him, and about three, to my joy, Mavis and her two arrived, filling the trailer with commotion and laughter. Anne had a big pan of Chef-Boyardee spaghetti sauce, into which she now chopped two onions and a sweet pepper. She had me chop up three firm tomatoes, as well, for adding later. We tasted it time and again. Sis grated the cheese, far too much, I felt, but it appeared to be of no concern to anybody else. Mama, while sitting on the couch, broke up lettuce for a large salad, and the children took turns dropping spaghetti into a pot. Blue arrived. Nervously Papa called me to the door's window to see him. Something was peculiar apparently. I saw that Blue had Plover in tow. The two were coming toward us.

My first instinct was to leave, step out the back door to go to Sis's car, but the trailer had only the one, the front door. My next thought was to quickly take his rings off, but haste confused me. They seemed to be smaller than earlier and would not slip off.

I felt exposed, as if naked and displayed before my friends and family, and I actually turned from the door and was examining one of Blue's calendar pictures of motor cars when they came in, so that my back was to him. The rings slipped off now, but fell out of my trembling fingers, fell to the hard trailer floor with a racket and rolled noisily toward him and Blue, who retrieved them while Plover and I stared at each other across days of pain, of lost dreams, across distances with sculptured thoughts, broken arms and legs and bosoms, like Grecian statues.

I dashed past him and out the door, rushed away, sat in Sis's car until she had time to get our coats and the rings. She took her time starting the car, which made me tearfully exasperated with her, but start it she did, even as our parents left the trailer. Sis speeded up, once we were on the straightaway. "Well, there you have it," she said, exhaling deeply in relief. "So much for your friend Anne." When I didn't reply, she asked, "Where to, Madam?"

"To his house, to Plover's and my house," I told her. "I will get the rest of my things."

44

Sis waited in the car, listening for sounds of any other car motor. I had my key, thank goodness, and hurried into the kitchen, where I got my English blue platters, and into the bedroom, where I noticed the bed was a rumpled mess. I opened one of the drawers in the chest and it slid far out and onto the floor, dumping all its contents, so I tried to get the coins and fingernail clippers and receipts and other small items off the floor and into place again. Some had gone under the bed and had to be crawled for. Some of the items were mine, but a piece of costume jewelry was somebody's new to me—maybe new to him, I thought with a cringe. I was trembling so much I could scarcely think. In the closet I found a dress, one I believed might be Mavis's, something she had worn often to work. I was engrossed, trying to recall, when his shadow flashed across the wall. I closed the closet, swung around, frightened, but it was my sister who stood in the doorway. "You about ready to go, Winney?"

I was so weak from the fright that my steps were uncertain and my vision was blurred. Then I heard the gunfire, somewhere off in the woods. One shot, then another, and I thought, Oh my God he's shot somebody. I pushed Sis into the living room and looked out the window. No one in sight. We were halfway out the door when I remembered my cashmere sweater and returned to the bedroom. "Only a second," I told Sis. The sweater was not on the closet shelf where I kept it, folded up. I pulled out one of his, of Plover's dresser drawers and it came off its rollers, and I had to wrestle it back inside, Sis calling to me all the while, her voice finally cracking with fright. "He's here, a car," she called.

It was not Blue's car, I told her, my own body trembling. "My Lord Jesus," I whispered. The car parked in the yard near the tree Plover called the delivery tree, but Sis and I stayed hid until the driver left, then she and I left, too, she carrying the platters and my food processor, and I carrying the underwear and blouses and two skirts and the pair of designer shoes Sis had given me, and the key, which I used to lock the house. Then, dear freedom, free at last I followed Sis to the car and threw my things and myself into the rear seat as she ground the starter.

"Oh, do get it fixed, Sis."

Out the drive we went and away to the west, the way Blue was unlikely to travel, Clara driving carefully, so as not to have a mishap at this dangerous place.

Once we were home and safe, I went out the back and stood behind a tree and bawled, and Sis, who followed with a cold Pepsi, didn't ask why, thank the Lord, for I wouldn't have been able to tell her. Mine was a bleeding hurt, and had to do with so much that was half-known, such as Plover being so scared when he faced me, and Mavis having some of her clothes there, and my cashmere sweater having been given to somebody, and the gunshots off in the woods terrifying me in my home, sharp blasts that had moved through my entire body, up from my groin through my head. And Sis holding out even now the can of Pepsi. And my sense that if I had done differently, the day would have ended better, with all the unknowns known and straight as arrows and adjusted, all of us would have related better, so that maybe my life would be answers and not so many questions and wondering.

7

CLARA:

Winney actually paid me—insisted on it—to drive her to work every day, and come for her at four-thirty sharp, including pay for every minute I had to wait in the drive outside the office doors. I felt I was being watched whenever I parked there. One afternoon as we left, a motorcycle followed us, but only far as the intersection, where it turned north and we went straight, toward home. Whether it was Plover or not, I don't know. Winney told me Plover was rarely at the factory, so she thought it was not he, but once the helmet and goggles were in place even she can't be sure.

Also, she offered to pay me for my Saturday, to drive her out to the country to visit Plover's parents. She felt she owed this to them. In fact, it would be the second time she had seen them, the first visit to their home. Maybe she had a notion that in their environs she would find clues to their son's character. I mention this because it showed her thinking remained on him, and her duty to him and to their unborn child. It was as if, just maybe, a magic potion could solve his tangled instincts. She was to be the fairy princess to bring this about.

Fairy princess she was in appearance, anyway. She was relaxed, she had her rich, full coloring back. Best I could tell, she was sleeping better. Of course, better is not saying much, because she wasn't sleeping when she arrived from the lair. She doesn't like my calling his house the lair, either, but I do so anyway. It's one of my little signs of independence, like refusing to charge for waiting time. A sister who charges for waiting time is pretty close to the line.

The elder Plovers lived Back of the Beyond, as it's called, secluded even from bears and birds. They own a section of land, six hundred and forty acres, most of it too steep and rocky for farming, in a windy cove, Pisgah National Forest bounding on three sides. Deer, even as we drove up the last rutted tenth of a mile, were grazing in the topmost field. As we got out of the car Winnette and I could see down the cove opening, could see Mount Mitchell and Clingman's Dome, the Black Brothers and other peaks of the Blacks, the highest range in eastern America.

The older Plovers stayed indoors, they and their severely demented daughter, age twenty. We knocked on porch posts quite a spell before a curtain rustled, and soon thereafter we heard a back door open and close, then later still footsteps on the frozen ground made a crunch, crunch, and there at the tree some thirty feet away appeared a bent man, fifty-some, although his beard confused his age, dressed in blotched suede jacket and worn corduroy pants, a Penland Funeral Home cap on—I had never seen an advertisement for a funeral home carried as daily patter, a reminder. "What you want?" he asked us.

"We're looking for you," Winnette said.

"You the census?"

"No."

Then after a pause, "I don't have anything for you."

Winnette went closer to him, so he might recognize her, and at that moment a woman called out from the house, "Is that Winnette?" to which the man angrily replied, told her he was "a-handlin' this myself," and when she called the name again, he angrily told her to mind, then moved toward the house dismissing us. "The road's downhill," he told us, "as everything else is." He moved behind his house as the woman spoke to him again, and we heard him say, "I don't give a damn who she is. We don't have anything for her."

"But it's Winnette," the woman whined at him.

"He put her out, he told me." A door slammed and we were left in the yard, and after our surprise melted away we foot-crunched our way to the car. I was glad to be away from there, to tell the truth, but Winnette was serious as Baptism, and quiet, so I let her be until we reached the pavement, where I stopped at a shack of a filling station and bought her a Brown Mule on a stick. Lord, she had not even got to tell them about her baby, which was in my mind the secret she wanted to share, telling others in the family about the baby, therefore forcing her to decide not to lose it. Any slip-up Mama was hoping for, casting her own vote that way, even admitting to her and me that she had lost three to a doctor's poking about—three.

"Thought it was a sin," I told Mama.

"Well, I think it might be," she admitted, "but everybody did it."

"And a worry," I told her. Winnette was listening, absorbing the confession.

"Well, it was. You can take my word for it," Mama said. "Miss what you don't have more than what you have."

That comment made me laugh out loud, which was thoughtless, of course, rude considering the serious subject. "Well, I wouldn't have an abortion," I told Mama and Winnette, "no matter." That was easy for me to say, of course. It was not my present lot to be married at all, much less married to Plover and carrying his baby, but I felt the baby had not wronged anyone, after all.

One night I crawled into bed with Winnette and held her in my arms for a precious while. Several other nights I had done this, too. Sometimes she would go to sleep like that, but tonight she asked me if she must lose the child and gain her own freedom. She told me she had asked this friendly doctor, Robbins, if it would require booking into a hospital, and if she would have the fact of an abortion on her medical record, where Plover might find out about it. Robbins said no, it could be done in an office, almost incidentally, and the act kept secret, provided she didn't wait long. She had talked to Mavis about it, had asked her what Plover would want, and Mavis had mentioned actually asking him, herself, which made my bones cold to think about.

8

MAVIS:

Her asking me if she should have this baby, the idea—when I have his two children already. Max and Kathy had whatever rights and privileges, such as it amounted to. He had come to know them; he at least felt at ease with them now. That was her trait, Winney's—her sister calls her that—that she keeps creating responsibilities until it all tumbles.

He really is a sensitive person, but in his own brash way, so to speak. No man wants to be loaded down. That's natural for them, just as some women enjoy being noticed and made dependent. Listen, anybody who can ride a motorcycle at over a hundred miles an hour—listen, he took the two children on a ride—Kathy confided this to me—on that dreaded pavement road where the new highway bypasses. They went at ninety-five miles an hour, and they without helmets or any experience. They held on, that's it. They were scared enough to pee, and their wet pants only made him laugh, once he wiped his leather seat dry. And they thought he was God ever after.

Now, so long as Winnette worshipped him and did what he said, he the older man, experienced, a supervisor, a lover by reputation, why he favored her. Nowadays she lets it be known his sheets needed washing, and so did his three dishes—all he had when she first went with him, she says. I don't know what happened in that case to the set of six him and me bought at the flea market before Christmas three years ago. Once she let him sense that he ought to like books she liked and not smoke pot and not drink so much and not drive so fast, and not eat so much meat and do sit down at a table to eat, and use the silverware as tools, not weapons. Do not belch and do wear this shirt not that one, and fix the step, like you said you would, and on and on till he overflowed. I told her so yesterday when she asked me about bearing the baby, whether or not—as if she's not eager to have it and mold it the way she couldn't mold him, and make it into one of these mother's boys with maybe a ring in his ear, discussing his clothes and hair style and whether to prefer satin over linen over muslin sheets. He'll have plenty of dishes in his kitchen, I imagine.

She drove Plover to the wall, so all he was sure of was his brute force and guns and his bravery, which made him seek dangers to go into, to live with. All he had was animal stuff, survival. And what she had that attracted him was only what every woman has, basic equipment, but she's trapped him with it, or did for a while, used it most effectively; she almost civilized Plover, almost had him eating out of her hand, the smooth-skinned handsome ape eating his salads out of her pretty hand.

Till wham! Bang! Return to himself with a bang! Leaving her with a baby in her womb.

She asked me if those were my things in his bedroom. I denied it. She asked where her sweater is. I told her he gave it to me; which is true. That's all I told her. The gift was on a Sunday. The children had been with him overnight and now were out washing my car, using his hose and attachments, and he asked me to use it. Then he asked me to make love with him. He didn't bother to kiss me or apologize for two years of estrangement. He said he had this desire, an old one, and for old times' sake. All the arguments I had rehearsed before, ready to say if ever he dared touch me, went out of my mind in a flurry, and I stood there like a Belk mannequin while he unbuttoned my blouse and stripped me, lifted me onto his bed and arranged me as nice as could be, all in such an effective way I felt I had never been laid before. Say what you please, there are no experiences to compare with it, and once a woman gets used to it, then she's hooked as surely as drugs. I know. And Win-ney knows, probably can't swear off, either, can't shake the urge, can't walk away cold from Plover, not when laid by Plover at his best.

Funny thing, the children two Sundays in a row washed the car while him and me were bedded, and then this past Sunday it was raining, and that made Plover and me all the more eager to cuddle, but the children said it was raining and did they have to wash a car in the rain, and I said yes, indeed. No umbrella. Their mackinaws were Plover's, I suppose; each could barely see out. Him and me had a laugh as we peeked at them, Plover's arm around me, his hand beginning to find the buttons.

Then Winnette asked me to advise her about the baby in her own body—does she think I am Ann Landers in Chicago? Does she know he has me put on Winnette's sweater whenever I strip naked, and that he stores it under her pillow? Does she know he carefully, oh so carefully, rolls it up in order to bare my breasts, and runs his hand into it, even as he feels my softest hair, and sniffs it even as my body floods open for him. No, and she'll not know. I told her so far as I can learn he has forgotten her.

And I told her he said to me he expected she had decided to abort the baby, and that she had better or he'd kill it himself.

The words spoke themselves—they came up and left me breathless, weak, limp as a newborn. I'll never forget the anguish in Winnette's eyes.

"I think she likes that doctor," I told Plover. "I know she thinks he likes her."

"Why?" he asked, trying to appear casual. A twitch came to the nerve beside his right eye. "How do you know?"

"Well, why do you stare at me like that? I'm not doing it to her."

He left the house and returned in an hour. He came back indoors, mumbling about that doctor and threatening his health, and I saw the glaze over his eyes that spelled trouble for everybody who was close enough to grab, so I rounded up my two and quick as I could get my car key I left him, saying I was going to

53

the store for him. So he still is jealous of her, that's the point. She has something out of the ordinary, all right, something precious. Showing jealousy is as close as Plover comes to revealing he loves a woman.

"No," I told her Monday morning—yesterday. "No, Winnette. He never seems to notice, even when I mention your name."

9

DR. ROBBINS:

She came to the office and asked me about an abortion, to advise her on it. At that time I had appointments all morning, meeting with ill people. I had no time to deliberate. There was my lunch break, of course, which I could give her, but at a sacrifice of my private time, the hour set aside to pay my housecleaner at home and read my morning mail, watch the stock reports on Financial News Network, and, incidentally, eat one of the slenderizer TV dinners, usually one of the ones with Chinese vegetables. My home is only a six-minute walk away, so it's a chance to walk— and I walk swiftly, as recommended in the *New England Journal of Medicine* in order to get my pulse up. I walk one-third of a mile each way, enough to get the motors ticking away. Rain or shine—I keep several of the large umbrellas at home and office, for umbrellas do get left about.

Now, as for the operation, itself, it could be inserted between patients' appointments, requiring only a few minutes. The nurse could do the set-up, could even sedate her should she be alarmed at the time. However—and this is the point—my policy is not to talk a woman into the decision to abort. Her mental health, also her religious health, are complex as she moves into an area of no return.

Simply no return. My wife, when she was living with me those sixteen years, had two abortions, and she subsequently heard babies cry in her sleep. Now, she was not a practicing Christian, was not more religious than the average college graduate, but she was troubled for a long time afterward. After her first operation, performed at two months by Dr. Ab Bolton here in Emerald Mines, I decided not to do abortions myself without a firm resolve on the woman's part. "No, I don't have time to talk to her about what's involved," I told my nurse, who told Winnette Plover, who, however, even when informed, didn't leave, and when I started home she followed, telling me how important it all was to her. I do walk fast. I don't believe in jogging. Bad for the hips. And the day was rainy so she was trying to keep up and share a bit of umbrella. She came right home and into the house and into the kitchen, claiming the baby was a result of mistreatment and was it going to be deformed? She had come to suspect so in a dream— all such nonsense. We sat down in the glassed-in porch and ate our lunch, while I let her rattle on, I reading only one letter, that of my mother in Maine. Everything's cheaper in Maine, she told me, but it's too cold to live there.

"It's cold here, too," I commented aloud.

"How's that?" Winnette asked, interrupted in her recital of dreams and half-doubts, which apparently made up her life these days, which seemed to be drastic days, indeed. She was frightfully attractive, even about her dilemma, I must say.

I turned the TV on, told her I must see after the stock market. I asked if she knew how to operate the TV satellite dish. She did not. I selected satellite F3, Channel 11, and waited for the one o'clock report on the Dow. "All my stocks are on the Dow," I mentioned to her.

Unhappy, she stared at me.

"I told my broker to buy for the long-term and not to trade off, back and forth, which brokers do sometimes. I said to stick to the thirty stocks on the Dow. If there are no obvious bargains in the Dow, buy Merck or Schering-Plough I told him. You see, I send him so much a month to invest. He puts it in the cash account until he has enough for a hundred shares, then SOCK-O."

She was staring at me strangely. Well, women do get distraught

56

over abortions, let me admit. It's taking a needle to their own life, entering their holy of holies, the temple where life is enthroned, where softness and toughness intertwine.

The Financial News Network has an irritating series of commercials, repeated ad nauseam, plugging precious metals options, which I've heard a hundred times. Speaking over these noises, she was saying, "It's the creator of life, or the creating forces. You understand, I can create life, and it's inside my body, his child, well protected."

"So you have debated whether to have this done, have you?" I said, speaking loudly, over the TV.

"Yes."

"Gone back and forth." The Dow had gone up seven that morning and had fallen three, and was now plus four.

"Will you do it?" she asked me.

"Mrs. Plover, I hesitate to do an abortion if the woman is hesitant."

"It took lying awake all night to get up courage to come to you."

"Did you talk to your husband about it?"

"No," she blurted.

"It's his baby, too. Is he—unfeeling?"

"Yes."

"I see," I said, jotting down the latest quote on Merck, which had just rolled by on the TV screen. "Would you talk with your pastor? Is he relevant?"

"My pastor?"

"Your mother. If your husband and mother were to encourage this, then if you make the appointment—leave at least an hour for you to have the operation and have a brief rest afterward. Your husband and mother might come with you. Now I mention both because mothers are sympathetic, and husbands see that schedules are followed."

"Doctor Robbins, you have met my husband."

"Have I?" Once she reminded me, I put it all together. "Of course I have. The dresser drawer—"

"You want me to bring him?"

"No," I said at once. Fumbling about, I clicked on the mute

button, turning off the TV commentary. "I see your problem."

"As for my mother, she wants me to have it done."

"Yes . . . What does your husband think?"

"He has not been asked. I left him. We're separated."

"All the more reason . . . for me to be concerned." I nursed that thought. "Man from beyond Kola literally persecuted Dr. Ralph Patton for three years because he 'killed my baby,' as this man termed it. Dr. Patton tried to get bullet-proof glass installed in his car, found it could be done only in Charlotte and would cost three thousand dollars for the windshield and two side windows, which he agreed to, but once done the added weight of glass and frames made his car sluggish on hills." I rather hoped she would smile, accept some relief from this concern, but she appeared to me to be dazed, a lost sheep looking for its lamb. "How long have you been married, Mrs. Plover?" I clicked the mute button so that I could listen to the closing report, which so often foretells accurately the Dow's afternoon performance. "The Nikkel also went up," I told her. When she appeared to be confused, I added, "last night."

"Last night?"

"The Nikkel. And the FTSE this morning."

"Oh."

"Now then, on we go with it."

"We do?"

"On we go back to work. So we've said it all, you and I. Make an appointment for you and your mother, and if not your husband, then could you get a notarized letter from him authorizing me—"

"Oh, he won't sign anything. When I began living with him, he wouldn't have a checking account for the longest time, then wrote out checks in pencil."

I clicked off the satellite system, then the set itself and sat staring at my own mother's letter, which would require one or two phone calls. Before me was the sticky remains of the half-eaten TV dinners. She had eaten none of hers. "Mrs. Plover, it's often better to go to a large medical center, where anonymity—where sheer numbers make personalities less important. I can make you an appointment at Duke. Also, there are doctors in Asheville who have no acquaintance with you or your husband, who would scarcely recognize you later, who come into a small room where you are behind a drape from the waist up, the lower part elevated, and they do the service, the operation, which at your stage, two months, is simple and causes little bleeding, no pain."

"Except the memory?"

"Not of pain. You will attach little importance to the operation, itself."

"Of the baby."

"Of the missing one, the nonbaby, the not-anything, really, at two months. It's not a baby, actually."

"I will miss it, anyway?"

"Predictably, yes. Many do. Nature is a taskmaster. But if you and your husband have separated—do you expect to divorce him?"

"I've—I never make plans about—not ahead."

"Then it's wise to proceed on that possibility first."

"I thought you will help me."

So gentle, so frail, so vulnerable. Ah, yes, that's the word—vulnerable. "I will make you an appointment elsewhere," I told her.

Sometime that afternoon she wrote me a note and slipped it under my house door, and it troubled me all through the CNN seven o'clock news. I kept reading it over and over.

Dear Dr. Robbins,

Are you a fixture? A fitting? I played the fool and followed you home. That was rude of me. But my plea for help blended with your TV and your frozen food. You need a warm person to live with you and care about you and help you find yourself, for you are at present behind the TV flicker somewhere. I needed help so much, and you never even knew, never heard.

Your friend,
Winnette Plover

Normally I go to the movies on Wednesday evening. Even if on call at the emergency room, I will go to the movies, leaving the ticket booth phone number with my service. We have a pleasant, though small, movie house. Tonight I canceled out on my intentions and sat at home measuring myself, not only now but during early days of my practice and marriage, before my wife, Nita, went flouncing off with the flower wholesaler. How long she had been seeing him, I don't know. In that sixteen years I did care, did risk my own health for my patients, did spend countless hours in personal conversation, encouragement of sick people, it being foresworn that the patient's willpower is an influence in the struggle. Compared to today, I was, while Nita lived with me, a more caring person. Also, I totaled up my present situation: thirty-nine, approaching the critical age of forty, home paid for, practice thriving—why are practices said to thrive instead of prosper, I wonder. Too difficult to pronounce? No wife present, legally separated. Childless. This isolated, hard-working male now has nothing to love, not a person, not a pet, and not himself. Smokes moderately, most often pipes, for which he has four meerschaums and three favorite briars. He has his grandfather's tobacco humidor and pipe rack. Owns two cars, a BMW and a four-wheel-drive Land Cruiser for use on back roads and in the snow. He has a TV dish that receives two hundred and seventeen programs at any given time, broadcasts from all parts of North America. Owns a microwave, dishwasher, clothes washer and dryer, a Cuisinart, a copy of many southern cookbooks, including *The Joy of Cooking*, owns fourteen French-made copper pots, tin lined, with lids; this person has the iron skillet his aunt willed to him, who is, who was her favorite nephew. He owns his home and his fourteen-hundred-square-foot office building. He is in excellent health, recent medical checkup at the Greenbriar clinic confirms this. Blood pressure of 140 over 70, weight one hundred eighty-six, which is not bad for a six footer with big frame. Eyesight is twenty-forty, near perfect, and has not worsened since the sudden change from twenty-twenty fifteen years ago. Can swim thirty laps of the community pool at Cascade Park, or could by the end of last summer. His father is still well at age sixty-four. This individual has no alcohol or drug or tobacco afflictions, works six full days a week. His mother is well, helps with seven grandchildren. Prospects for a long life are excellent. He will live a long and prosperous existence without variation and without children or a wife to love, so he is in that respect, in those human terms a failure. In most others, ones which lend themselves to management, he is a success.

I wrote two letters, one to my wife, saying I would go forward now with the divorce. Secondly, I wrote a letter to this pretty young lady who had sat just there, and who had suffered concern enough to write me.

Dear Winnette:

I risk being allowed to call you by your friendly name.

Thank you for your letter. It has started me to thinking about myself, my insistence on personal privacy, which you took to be callousness. I do have ever so many hundreds of people bringing their cares to me that I have built defenses, which is necessary, but I have of late years built walls instead of fences, and maybe for a while that also was necessary.

Therefore, pardon my preoccupation during my home-time today. Since I lacked personal contact, I'll try to balance matters by inviting you to go to dinner with me. Please give me an evening to become acquainted. We will, in this case, drive to Marion, to the Crossbow Restaurant, if that suits you. It has the best buffet and desserts in the region. Do let us give it a try, and meet me when we have time for a chat.

Winnette, we will of course discuss your problem. I do not encourage prospective mothers to abort their babies, especially their first; the operation, itself, is of little consequence medically, but usually there are other considerations which friends can advise on better than doctors. Let me, since that's so, take you to dinner and try to listen as a friend.

Sincerely,
Chuck Robbins

I did not have her address, but next morning my secretary dug her form out of the files. Reading its boxes and blanks, I saw that she was twenty-three years of age, of legal age for decisions. She was not on any medication at all. She did not smoke. She drank moderately. She had no dietary restrictions. She had not borne children. She was 5'4" tall, weighed 110 pounds. She did not need glasses. She had had no operations in her lifetime at all, no accidents except the motorcycle accident she had come to me about when this form had been filled out—if, indeed, that battery of bruises was from a motorcycle accident.

We went to dinner, she and I, the following Monday evening. The drive to Marion required forty minutes time by my BMW's clock and required going down a quite twisty road, one which forces its way along the side of the Appalachian escarpment, affording views of lighted towns below for many miles, and affording views above us of the ridge crest, with lighted houses and motels, yes, and high above us, seen through the BMW moonroof, the clear winter sky full of stars. She drove my car. She had arrived at my office in her own. It was she who had suggested we meet there, and once she began to ooh and aah over my car, impetuously I said, "Here, you drive," handing her the keys. Gleefully she took them and ensconced her pretty body in the big leather seat, turned on lights, started the powerful motor. I helped her buckle her seatbelt, then read off the titles of my car's musical library and picked out with her help a tape to play, discussing several. I told her my car collection was chosen by me personally. "On trips I prefer musicals for traveling, for one can measure distance by the stories. Here I have *My Fair Lady* with Rex Harrison, *Evita* in its London performance, and this is New York's cast of *Evita,* and you'll be surprised to find the London production is rougher, ruder, more—more dissonant than the American. At least, that surprised me. Then here's *South Pacific.''*

She smiled, scrunched up her shoulders, admitted to indecision among so many delectable offerings.

"I like Lloyd Webber's work very much, although he has not in this case chosen a worthwhile hero to present, which creates hopped-up theater. Two thousand people come together every night to bear witness to her tricks and plots."

"Evita . . ." she began. By now she was sailing along nicely, driving expertly. "Evita is a hero. Or a heroine."

"Yes, if you like dictators."

"Bigger than life," she said.

"Damn monster, really."

"Evita?"

"Evita. Had bloody hands."

"I've never hurt anybody, myself," she boasted, making the claim abruptly.

"Never will then."

"Yes, I will. I certainly intend to."

"Oh, my goodness. Not me, I hope."

"No."

"Who, then?"

"Don't know yet." Then she said, "But I mean to try everything."

"Oh, hell," I said, laughing. "One of those, as if human experience had only Hollywood endings."

Frowning, she said, "I like the idea, to try everything in life."

"For me it's rubbish philosophy," I told her and enjoyed the wide-eyed astonishment on her lovely face. "You do express yourself in wonders," I told her and laughed. "You are expressive, Winnette."

"Do it all once or twice," she murmured, none too pleased about my laughing at her.

I assumed we had chosen *Evita.* I had, in any event, inserted *Evita* and now sped fast-forward to her final song, where she is explaining herself, her tyrannies. "Now, listen to this," I told Winnette and turned the volume louder. "You hear her. Don't blame me, I was poor. I had to do it, she tells us, because I needed my chance. Damn nonsense, isn't it?"

"What?"

"Look at the road, Winnette. We're going down a mountain. One error and we're sailing off in space together."

"Together. I like that," she said.

"You won't have that experience but the one time."

"I like your saying 'together.'"

"Well, that would make it better," I admitted, "but it remains unacceptable."

She laughed, outrageously gleeful, as I told her.

"Outrageous and gleeful?" she said impressed.

"Awhile ago, Evita said she did it because she had to."

"Yes, think of the depth of that philosophy. Hitler explaining he had to be Hitler because of who he was. Or Caligula. Never mind the death and suffering of thousands of people, excuse their pain for reason of my childhood poverty, as if being poor bestows moral privilege. Or being crippled is a social blessing. Or being black or white or red excuses street attacks . . ." I got going and she drove faster, maybe hoping to scare me into silence, and once I was through, the *Evita* tape had reached its triumphant, heralding close: the damn empress was dead and so was my argument, or so it appeared for all the effect it had had, for Winnette was humming the melody and didn't seem to be listening.

She winked at me. "Glad you're not driving," she told me, apparently a friendly comment about my exuberance when I'm arguing a point.

Oh my, she was rather dear, a sweet thing, as they say, terribly winning, her confidence particularly impressive. I put *Gigi* into the tape player, and Chevalier and Gingold sang their piece about remembering a dinner date years ago, and Winnette and I had a fit laughing. I told Winnette we would remember ours.

"Why? How do you know?" she asked.

"I'm sure of it," I told her.

"And when we're old—Chevalier must be seventy in that song. He can't remember anything."

"I'll be seventy. And you will remind me."

She wasn't opposed to the idea, but wanted assurances.

"I can't prove the future," I told her. "Do look at the road occasionally, Winnette."

"I never knew a doctor to tell the future," she admitted, "in my whole life."

"And you'll be fifty when I'm seventy, and still be pretty, I predict. You're of the type that stays young."

"Oh, I do hope I'm prettier," she said. I recall her exact words and wondered if she didn't realize how pretty she was that moment, with the moonlight and starlight lighting her, highlighting her I might say, and me feeling helplessly enthralled by her enthusiasm and youthfulness.

After dinner and a satisfied, contented drive back, we went to my house for coffee and music, and we watched a movie, one of thirty offered by the TV dish, and it never seemed right to me to kiss her. On leaving, she paused for a moment at the door, and I did venture. I am more restrained ordinarily. Indeed, I'm older than she by most of a generation. In any event, rationale aside, we did kiss briefly good night, and her lips were soft, the softest lips in my experience, limited though it may be. I tried the kiss again, which seemed to surprise her. "Research," I told her.

"What sort of research?"

"Serious lip research." I told her how remarkably soft her lips were.

"I suppose that's true of everything about me," she said and moved out the door.

Her car needed repairs, I decided, not only body work. The motor rasped heavily. "Might need a clean air filter," I told her.

"Me?" she said laughing.

She backed into the street. I caught a glimpse of her dear smiling face as the car bolted forward, leaving me alone and ghostly, a body with its spirit leaving.

I wrote that very night:

Dear Winnette,

Do remember all I said about heroes and heroines. It occurs to me that *Gigi* also is a celebration of everyday people—at least of average girls growing up. So where does that leave me, liking both?

I miss you.

You have been gone less than ten minutes. I came indoors and turned the TV set off, in order to feel my loneliness.

65

Delicious. Complete. A likable pain, necessary, no doubt. Therapy.

Lovely people cannot keep going away like this.

> Fondly,
> Chuck (I've never used
> Horace since being ridden
> like a horse in the fourth
> grade.)

There is no fool like an old fool, and even though being in your late thirties is not old, in this case it seemed to qualify me. I carried a pad in my shirt pocket on which I wrote only notes to her, and I would mail the sheaf every day or so. I could not telephone her because she had asked me not to; something about the phone might be listened to. Also, she mentioned her sister's opinions. But after three packets of my notes, with ideas for choosing where we might go next to dinner, she phoned me at home early one evening and told me she was at the phone booth in Emerald Mines, at the taxi stand, and had a dressed pheasant to cook, and was I busy.

I drove there for her. She had a car, but she explained it would be better not to park it at my house. We cooked the pheasant and two yams. She made a salad, and we opened a bottle of French champagne, one from a case, payment by a patient who, sorry to have to say, passed on. Six of the bottles remained. I did have a slice or two of cheese, so I supplied cheese and apple slices and the champagne. So we were friends close together for those wondrous two and a half hours. I remember asking if I might judge her soft lips again, and she consented "for science sake," she said. "All parts of me," she had said, and so it was. We rather forgot the oven and did overcook the pheasant, not that it was too done, too dry to be edible. We ate it with our fingers, thinking up words to describe emotions and mysteries, we having gone through a garden of both.

At nine-forty she insisted on leaving. Reluctantly I gave her up, agreed to drive her to her car. "We have not once talked about your baby," I told her.

"I'm going to have it for my own," she told me at once.

"Very well. That's the safest way."

"It will be handsome," she said, "whatever else it is."

I drove her to her car. Let me recall—at nine-fifty, or within five minutes of that time. I remained inside my own car, the BMW, watching the taillights as she drove along upper street. I heard a motorcycle start its motor. In my memory, a motorcycle was associated with her, with her accident, and for that reason the sound unnerved me. I swung my car into the road and followed. On the way to her house, I saw the motorcycle only once, and her car merely as a flash of taillights as she rounded a curve going very fast. Of course, I speeded up and could easily have overtaken her, but I passed the parked motorcycle at Mans Peak and so knew it had abandoned the chase.

What a—perfect, miracle evening. Nothing predictable, nothing unexpected. Couldn't have been better. Most welcome. It reassured me of myself, which is always helpful.

At home, while I was reflecting on my satisfaction, the phone next to my elbow rang. No one spoke to me. "Winnette," I said, thinking it might be she. "Good night, Winnette," I said, and regretted doing so, for I could hear the gentle, controlled breathing of a caller. Slowly, finally, I hung up. The phone rang again, this time also without a speaking caller. I hung up, then laid the receiver on the table, and fixed myself a stiff drink. "For the run of the play," I toasted my reflection in the mirror.

10

MR. MACMILLAN:

My name is Harold MacMillan, the same as a past prime minister of England except for the capitalization of the second "M." I was appointed by Judge Sidney Blackington to represent the defendant in the Plover family murder trial, which became the most talked about trial in the North Carolina mountains for years. Indeed, it was written up in magazines, as well as newspapers. I've often read about myself, became common practice to read about myself while my wife and I had coffee and a kaiser roll apiece, breakfast under her diet regime. No butter allowed, none for me, anyway. She can have it but usually does not. Three to four ounces of orange juice, the roll, two cups of black decaffeinated coffee, and my pills as first prescribed for me by Dr. Horace Meredith after my heart attack at age sixty-five. That came in the fall of last year. Papers reported I said this, I did that, and the defendant refused to say anything except guilty. That was not quite true, although admittedly one problem of our defense was to wrestle with the client's insistence that she was guilty. Readily she confessed to killing her husband. This was not done with pride. It was simply announced that yes, the killing was committed as described, which left me to explain why, to show that in this case her action was justified and deserved no prison term. The newspapers told me at breakfast that Mr. MacMillan tells us "this was done in self-defense"—that was one day. Mr. McMillan (spelled differently) tells us the defendant acted irrationally, "under foreign influence or insanity." I never said any such thing, but so it was sometimes reported, leaving me to savage my kaiser bun and read on.

On being appointed defense attorney, I went to Assistant District Attorney Abel Juicks, a young man who dressed in three-piece suits and wore cuff links, signs of his ambition, and asked him to test for drugs in the body of the deceased. He is required by statute to test for alcohol, but this old statute, passed long before drugs came into the region, does not oblige him to test for drugs. The nature of this case suggested drugs were involved. I also asked the physician doing the autopsy for the state, but he wanted official notification and pay. Juicks told me his own office could comply. Now, he did not say he would, only that he could, and as the date of the trial approached, my request of him, as well as of the autopsy doctor in Chapel Hill, never did gain a response of any sort. Juicks was not wanting those tests to be made, apparently. Also, he was going for first-degree murder, even the death penalty. A pity.

Meanwhile, I was meeting with my pretty little defendant, who refused bail, refused my orders and entreaties, and stayed in her cell. I was seeking to find out the details of the case, the motivation, the possibility of a plea of insanity, which did not sit well with the defendant, who claimed to have total recall of the events leading up to the fatal shots, and to have acted sanely. In other words, I had a client who was more than willing to be punished, and a district attorney who was letting me believe he was pursuing the truth, while in fact he was pursuing conviction, even to the extent of prosecuting to the gas chamber a young woman carrying an unborn child. I am sixty-six and have practiced law forty-some years in Florida. Most often civil law has been my work, representing major companies, usually not going to a courtroom, much less jury trials. This case was a departure for me, a break with the boredom of retirement. I was ill prepared for the Assistant DA, a young lawyer with no more background than law school and a flock of political relatives, and a year as Assistant.

I could not believe his tricking this child-bride in this way.

At any rate, one week before the trial date, I filed with the court:

MOTION

Immediately upon being appointed to represent the defendant, I, Harold MacMillan, had contacted the physician doing the autopsy at the State Hospital in Raleigh, and specifically had requested that a test be made of the deceased to determine whether or not there were drugs in the blood and the system.

That it is important to the defense of this case and to the interest of justice to know whether or not there were drugs present in the deceased leading up to the fatal shooting.

WHEREFORE, the defendant prays that an order of the Court issue requiring the State of North Carolina to furnish the defendant with information, if such can be made available, relative to the presence, or lack of presence, of drugs in the system of the deceased at time of death.

Respectfully submitted this 2nd day of September, 1982.

C. HAROLD MACMILLAN,
Attorney for Defendant

The *C* stands for Crawford. As a young lawyer I used it as yet another step to standing, suffering the misuse by some of my clients who would address letters: See Harold MacMillan. Once I was elected Secretary of the Florida State Bar in the 1970s, the *C* was dropped.

When, in spite of the court's issue, there was not a peep emanating from Juick's office, and not a whisper from the autopsy, I filed a Motion for Continuance, which was denied; therefore, on the appointed day I was ill prepared when questioning began of the citizen peers, the mountain men and women who would pass jury judgment, now that the press had had its way with her.

One of them was a school teacher, Rachel Famous Turner, who has taught for thirty years at the Middle School. I believe she teaches English. Or maybe it's social studies. A month or so before the trial, I encountered her class visiting the county courthouse; about twice a year she and twenty-five would show up, the clerk of court told me, all towheaded and blue-eyed and looking intelligent. "You can all look intelligent, whether you are or not"—that was what she told them. Look intelligent, you bunnies. Miss Famous, as she was called, was a gem. I eavesdropped on her lecture on the building her children were standing in. "This room is the room where court is held. It's on the top floor, one flight up from the street, and is twenty feet high to the ceiling. Six twelve-foot-high windows to a side. The thirty visitors' benches are pine, stained to look like walnut. They are quite comfortable. Each seats eight people. That makes how many visitors, class?"

Somebody ventured an answer.

"Mr. MacMillan, do you know?"

I choked on my pipe smoke, so surprised to be called on, and that she knew me.

"Each of you children report tomorrow your judgment, your total. You, too, Mr. MacMillan."

I laughed. What else could I do?

"Up here is the jury box, seating how many jurors, class?"

"Twelve," I called out at once, which caused general laughter.

"Seats up there are oak, are hard as a rock, but are said to be comfortable. You children try them. Don't crowd. Are they comfortable? I would enjoy being on the jury, but only twice have I been called, and both times I was dismissed by the attorneys, men, of course—after being asked what college I had attended. The mention of Chapel Hill told them I was too educated for their argument."

I must admit to flushing red with embarrassment, as all the children turned their sharply critical gazes on me.

"When you get to be attorneys, you must do better," Mrs. Turner told them. "Now who wants to sit in the judge's seat? Who first? Now careful of the high steps. See, you are up above the throng. Up high is where Justice sits. And the judge can see the thirty benches at the back and, oh, yes, the little balcony, which affords standing room for about forty people. It rests on top of the courtroom's vestibule. *V-e-s-t-i-b-u-l-e.* The word means entrance hallway, receiving area. It's just beyond the two swinging doors. Now, Joshua, you let Katherine sit in the judge's seat.

Move along. And in front of the thirty visitors' benches is the bar, where the lawyers sit with the clients. *C-l-i-e-n-t.* One or more clients will be defendants. They and witnesses will testify. Who wants to sit in the witness box? Only one at a time. You see there is only one witness chair. One person at a time faces justice. There are never two at a time, are there Mr. MacMillan? For instance, you have read about the Plover murder. The murderer will be seated first there at the bar, with her attorney, whoever that is to be. Then on call, she will walk alone to the witness chair and sit there where Katherine is sitting now. Yes, you'd better jump away. But in a real trial there is no escape. The morning sun will fall through those six east windows, the afternoon sun through the southwest six, and the light will strike the witness, and her attorney will stand here at the bar. In a North Carolina court the attorney usually does not move closer to the witness than the bar. And he will ask her to tell why and how she killed her husband at noon on a certain Sunday—or was it afternoon, children?

A babble of voices told her afternoon.

"Three shots or two, children?"

"Three shots," they replied. All knew.

"Alone she'll sit where Phillip is sitting now and her lawyer—who will he be, Mr. MacMillan?"

"Not appointed, yet," I replied.

"The attorney will help her through the recital, the light falling on her, the men—mostly men watching from the benches and probably from the balcony, the smell of tobacco in the air, the ceiling fans on, I imagine, stirring up the heat and odors and sending it all back down on the visitors, and of course, the press. And Mrs. Plover will walk out a free woman, or she will be incarcerated. *I-n-c-a-r-c-e-r-a-t-e-d,* locked up in prison. And the twelve of you still sitting in the jury box will decide—unless you attended a university. Look alive, look especially bright, you twelve. The woman's very life is in your hands. Death now lies here, freedom over there. See how she cringes as she faces the light. Justice reveals all, remember that. Do look alive, children. I know it's awesome, this room, and smells musty from old trials going back generations. Many a guilty and innocent victim of life has been in here. What's that, Henrietta?"

"Awesome?" the child said.

"Spell it? *A-w-e-s-o-m-e.* Two *e*'s in all, one at a time. Means full of power, means humbling, means historic."

So much for R. Famous Turner's courthouse lecture. Imagine my own surprise on seeing now, here and now, on the opening day of Superior Court, with me the appointed defense attorney, that she sat here in the same courtroom, apparently called the third time in her life for jury duty. The thirty benches were full of visitors, and there were, even as she had predicted, about forty men and women crowded into the little balcony. Judge Sidney Blackington himself, ancient relic of mountain justice, looked down from his high box, his white hair, assisted by a hairpiece, needing trimming and brushing. Also his mustache. The witness stand was just now empty. I sat beside Winnette King Plover, the defendant, who was tense as strained wire, her hands clenched in tight little fists, bloodless, or so they appeared. It would not be proper for me to take her hand and try to calm her, soothe her. Of course, I did not. We were just now finishing our jury selection, and Miss Famous, as she was generally called, was in the jury box answering questions. Assistant DA Juicks asked if she had "any predisposition" toward the case, and she paused, and I thought she was about to spell the word. She replied, "No, none." When I was recognized, I asked her where she had studied in college. She replied Chapel Hill, and I abruptly said, "No further questions," which startled the court and audience. There was a titter among them. The young DA—a dapper dresser, as I mentioned—must have thought I meant certainly to reject her; in any case, I did not. I favored the chance to have a forceful woman, preferably an opinionated one, among the twelve.

It was late in the morning before the first witness was called. An elderly man dressed in faded overalls, an untidy hat on his head, took the witness stand and was routinely sworn in by the bailiff. Mr. Juicks asked him his name.

"A. W. Plover," he replied.

"Would you remove your hat."

He did so. He gave it a quick dusting with a few swipes of his hand.

"The visitors and press should not laugh, nor otherwise participate," Judge Blackington announced without rancor, and without much hope of convincing anybody, I felt.

Solicitor Juicks said, "Where do you live, Mr. Plover?"

"Phillips Road, the gravel part of hit," he added. "Have lived there all my life."

"You work at what occupation?"

"Farmer."

"Are you married?"

"Why, yes."

"How many children?"

"Six."

"And the youngest son was named what?"

"Lloyd Ernest."

"And did he live near you?"

"No, sir. He lived near the tech school."

"Was he married?"

"Married to that there woman on the aisle, name of Mavis Huntington, and later married to that woman there, name of Winnette King."

"You see Winnette King in the courtroom?"

"There she is. I told you."

"When did you last see your son, to speak to?"

"I saw my son about eight weeks past. He was on one of the upper Streets, waiting."

"Did you speak to him?"

"Yes. I said hello, and he said hello, papa."

"Was he in good health?"

"He appeared to be. He was standing near the taxi pickup."

"When next did you see him?"

"At the funeral house, laid out dead."

Once the DA was finished with him I was able to question him.

"Did you, Mr. Plover, have your youngest son and his wife as guests in your home anytime during the year before he died?"

"Some—no, I don't think so. It was about a year."

74

"On that visit Winnette looked like she had been beaten, didn't she?"

Juicks: "Objection."

Judge Blackington sustained him, and I entered an exception. "Did you or your wife have need to treat any bruises about Winnette's body?"

Juicks: "Objection."

Again the court sustained his objection, and again I excepted. Then I asked, "Was it unusual for your youngest son and Winnette to visit you?"

"Yes, you might think so."

"It happened frequently?"

"No."

"Was this their first visit?"

"Yes."

"Was the purpose of the visit to have Winnette's bruises doctored by your wife?"

"I suppose so."

"Objection, Your Honor," the assistant district attorney said.

"Sustained. The jury will ignore the witness's reply."

"Exception, Your Honor." That was number three.

"I have no further questions of this witness at this time."

Winnette, seated beside me, whispered to me, "He knows why I was brought there. He had to lock me in."

"So do they," I whispered to her, and nodded toward the jury. "They know, too."

Judge Blackington called Juicks and me closer by and warned me not to take the court's time by using prosecution witnesses to establish my defense. I told him, one person is dead, that's true. I respect that. However, another is in jeopardy, and that makes me extremely anxious in her defense.

11

"I am Anne Marantha Bailey and live in my silver-top trailer on Belbuckle Road. That's between Rooftop and Emerald Mines, in Altamont County. I have known the defendant, Winnette King Plover, for four years, and I knew Plover for six or seven years."

"Plover?" the judge asked her.

"He went by that. The deceased."

"Yes, but his name was Lloyd Ernest."

"I know it, myself, but never heard him answer to Lloyd or Ernest."

"Are you married?"

Anne cast a wary look toward Blue sitting third row back, just behind Winnette, and then shook her head.

"Please reply," Juicks said.

"No."

"Tell the judge and jury, Miss Bailey, in your own words, what happened on the last morning you visited Winnette and Lloyd Plover, the fact of that morning only."

"It was a drizzly day and rain was predicted and the car races at Wilkesboro had been called off, which—"

"The bare facts of your visit, Miss Bailey," Juicks said kindly. "Your arrival at their home on Tom Smith Road, Route 3—"

"I did."

"For what purpose?"

"I did arrive. To help her clean up."

"Clean up the house?"

"She never really needed help, but she was worried about Plover, who had started drinking the night before, and she wanted company. She told me on the telephone to come help clean the house, and she picked me up at my trailer about ten o'clock. Plover—Lloyd Ernest Plover—was in the yard working on a new dog run he had promised her for four months—since she went back to him. They had been separated for a while. He was building it with a black man name of . . ." Anne paused, stared fearfully about. "I've forgot his name," she told Juicks.

"Was it Carvel Morrison?"

"There's been so much emphasis on names," she explained.

"Carvel Morrison, was it?"

"Yes."

"Go on with the account."

"He—Carvel was helping Plover—helping Lloyd Ernest Plover. Winnette and I vacuumed and dusted and furniture-polished the living room and the bedroom, and we got the kitchen counters clean, and she called to Plover did he want his gun room dusted. It was off limits, you see. He was draped in fencing, the six-foot chain links, and never answered her, but he came inside finally and opened up the gun room, went inside it. He was in there maybe five minutes, then came out and said to dust it all. 'And why are you resting?' he asked. 'Did you work ten minutes, or was it twelve?' There he stood in the middle of a sparkling, pine-scented living room telling us all that, and he was morose, not joking, so I knew he was in trouble, himself. Even his speech was slurred."

"Miss Bailey," Juicks said, "Lloyd Ernest Plover is not on trial. We are simply trying to establish that he was shot on this certain morning. Now, did you actually see him drinking?"

"No."

"Tell us what you did see and hear, yourself."

"She asked him did he want anything to eat. It was now about noon, and we were thinking about making sandwiches."

"Yes, and he said what?"

"He never answered her."

"Yes, well what else did you hear?"

"She asked him again, 'Do you want anything to eat?' "

"And he replied?"

"He never said a word."

"Very well. What happened next?"

"He seemed to hear her, all right, but he had a glassy look to his eyes, not as if he had only been drinking, but the pills would make him glassy."

"Miss Bailey," Juicks said unhappily, "did you see him take any pills?"

"No, I never saw it. In my life I rarely saw Plover take—"

"Now then, he returned outdoors, and does he resume work?"

"Yes. I think so. Winnette was very nervous by now and talked of leaving the house and hiding, because of the glassy look, and she asked me to stop my car down the road and she'd come to me through the woods, and she was halfway out the kitchen door when he was suddenly there, at the kitchen door the other side of the house, and he came in and she tried to show him affection by hugging him, and he didn't respond, was not stiff but was distant. Winnette King Plover kissed him, kissed Ernest Lloyd Plover, but he ignored her. I asked him why he wasn't helping Carvel Harrison with the fencing—"

"Morrison."

"What?"

"Was Carvel's name not Morrison?"

"I don't recall."

"It was Morrison, for the record."

"Was it?"

"It is. We've been trying to find a Carvel Morrison. Please continue."

"I asked him, and he said nothing to me, but he went into the bedroom. Now, their bedroom has a double bed and a chest of drawers and nothing else, no room left over for a chair, so he had to be lying down, and Winnette whispered she would go out the back way and I was to drive down the road, but right that minute he called to her. She went into the bedroom and I heard him ask her if I was still there. He told Winnette to tell me to go. She came back into the living room and said, 'Well, did you hear him?' I told her yes, but that I wouldn't leave her alone, five to six months pregnant, with him in the house, and she became scared and said it would make him furious to be disobeyed. So I left, but stood out in the yard with Carvel Harrison, who was stretching fence, which is easy with the fence stretcher, but not if you're working alone, and he was nailing, that is stapling it with the power stapler, and we worked for maybe ten or fifteen minutes. He needed to know where the gate was to go, so I used that as an excuse to go see how Winnette was faring. I knocked at the front door and there was no answer. I tried the door and it was locked. I joined the Carvel man and said we must decide, and we set the gate against the corner post nearest the house's front door, and that took about twenty minutes, so in all I had suffered half an hour or more worrying. I left Carvel to do more stapling on the fence and started to the house. Then the stapler seemed to go off, explode, and then I realized it might be the noise from a gun, a single, loud noise. I couldn't decide where it was from, and then after a minute I rushed to the house porch and called to Winnette King Plover to unlock the front door."

"Now, then, Miss Bailey, did she let you in?"

"Nothing."

"And did you go inside the house?"

"No, she never unlocked it."

"And what did you do?"

"I opened the storm door, which serves as a screen door in summer, and I shouted for them to come let me in. Plover appeared. I saw he was holding a towel to his nakedness, and he told me to leave them be. And I said, 'Plover, let me in.' He told me to leave. Nothing ever got the better of Plover, don't you know. And Carvel came along, and Plover was standing there telling Carvel to get me into my car and see me to hell. Then he went back into the innards of the house, and there was a shot, another shot."

"What did he wear at this time?" Juicks asked me.

79

"A shot, then another shot. Then I began screaming, and Plover appeared with the towel on his chest, all bloody. Above the waist, nothing. He had on nothing. No socks or shoes. He unlatched the door and pushed past me and fell onto the porch steps. As Plover fell Carvel caught him and got blood all over his shirt and pants front, which made him complain. Either he was surprised by all the blood or worried about his clothes."

"Yes, and was Winnette the only person left in the house—"

"Might be his only clothes with him, since he had come up from Rooftop."

"Yes. Was Mrs. Plover the only one in the house?"

"She and I. Not Carvel. And Plover had been in the house."

"When the shots were fired?"

"I wasn't sure they were shots, or had come from the house. I still thought the noise might have been the stapler blowing up. The noise and the blood were two different things."

"So what did Mrs. Plover do, now that she had shot her husband?"

"Did she?" A rustle of objection moved through the courtroom, but Winnette's attorney remained silent.

"She came out and asked me if an ambulance was needed. And Plover said, 'Damn the ambulance,' or words to that effect. She went indoors and called an ambulance. Carvel helped Plover to his feet; they moved slowly toward Plover's car. He fell again, sort of crumpled at the legs from weakness or dizziness. I called Winnette to bring towels. Carvel was bent over Plover and told me he needed help in breathing, for he was unconscious, but being a—a black he didn't want to become involved. I didn't know whether Carvel would do that or not, would risk contact with a white man, so I knelt and did the breathing. I was aware of Winnette's towels arriving and a blanket and later of her father arriving and the ambulance, its lights flashing. The two ambulance attendants put Plover on a stretcher and got him into the ambulance. Police arrived, and two officers asked me my name. I was still sitting on the ground, was wiping my mouth out with the corner of a towel. There's no telling what diseases a person can get—"

"Where was Mrs. Plover?" Juicks asked.

"She was with the officers, standing there looking down at me. I couldn't remember my name I was so frightened. So Winnette told them."

"No further questions at this time, Your Honor," Juicks said.

12

MR. MACMILLAN:

I had a whispered conference with Winnette, who appeared to be composed and competent, and then sent forward to this same witness, Anne Bailey, a number of pictures of the Plover house, to establish identification of house and yard and rooms, and even sent forward a floor plan. "When Ernest Plover—when Lloyd Ernest Plover came into the house about one o'clock, he was unusual in appearance, you say?"

"He did not return her affection nor reply to questions," Anne Bailey told me.

"Anything else?"

"He walked sort of sideways."

"His eyes were glassy?"

"And dilated. They were watery."

"Thank you. Now you say that Winnette King Plover planned to leave the house?"

"Yes."

"To escape."

"Yes."

"You were to park your car on the road and she was to come through the woods?"

"Yes."

"There was reluctance on her part to stay in the house with him?"

"Yes."

"She was frightened of Mr. Plover?"

"She was scared to death."

I thanked her and returned to my seat. Juicks came to the bar, once I sat down, and in a loud voice asked Anne Bailey, "When Mr. Plover unlocked the front door, you say he was screaming? Was he in pain?"

"He wanted me to leave."

"What was in his hand?"

"A towel."

"Could you see both hands?"

"I—think so."

"Did you that day or at any time hear any arguing between Mr. and Mrs. Plover?"

"No."

"Thank you. No further questions at this time."

For the record I then asked, "Did Mrs. Plover help with the artificial respiration?"

"Why, she did, to relieve me. Yes."

"So she called for help, then called for the ambulance, and she helped with the—"

"She did. I remember now. Until her father got there."

"When did she phone her father?"

"I don't know."

"Does he live nearby, within a few minutes drive?"

"I—it's fairly nearby, Mr. MacMillan."

"So perhaps she had phoned him earlier."

"I suppose so. Or he happened by."

"What was Winnette wearing?"

"It—it was—she had on a blue jeans short skirt."

"What did Winnette wear on her feet?"

"While we were working?"

"No, once you heard the two noises, and—"

"She was barefoot."

83

"And above her waist?"

"She had slipped on a bra."

"How—how many dogs were in the dog lot, Miss Bailey?"

"They had three big ones."

"What breed?"

"Alsatians. White Alsatians."

"White. Three German police dogs?"

"Yes."

"And the dog lot was how large?"

"The new run was to go from the dog houses to two oak trees, a distance of thirty, forty feet. So it was a nice fan-shaped area. Winnette wanted it because the dogs until then had to be kept in small dog houses, with no chance to exercise, except as she took them out, and that was, had to be one at a time."

"Why one at a time?"

"They were large ones for her to handle."

By now Winnette was showing interest in the proceedings. The dull reluctance, the withdrawal characterizing our visits in the cell and the psychiatrist's visits, was breaking up. Time after time, while Anne Bailey testified, a sharpness came to her manner. She was after all, I decided, a bright person. In the cell she had not cared, for instance, what I would say, but she became interested now, perked up during Anne Bailey's testimony, of which she approved, and at the close had me ask the questions about her dog trot. During the trial the dogs were being fed by her sister, Clara, she told me. "She's living in my house now."

During the break for lunch, Winnette and I remained in the courtroom. She ate half the sandwich Anne passed to her. She had eaten all too little in the jail, seemed to have consigned herself to wasting away, so I was pleased. Anne brought a big orange drink, too, and I passed that along to Winnette, who drank several swallows, then burped—all rather ladylike, politely. I have no doubt her digestive system was in chaos at this time.

An ambulance attendant, Art Young, walked by. He was expected to testify about the condition of Plover in the yard. I caught a glimpse of Highway Patrolman Burnette; he was shadowing the back of the courtroom. He had refused my request to testify as a defense witness. Everyone knew Plover had beat him up so bad he had been hospitalized, but Burnette had never publicly admitted as much and would not do so, preferring injustice for Winnette to embarrassment for himself. Of these, Art Young was the first called.

"My name is Arthur, sometimes Art, Thomas. I work for the Altamont County First Aid, which operates out of the Mans Peak Fire Department. There are two of us men on duty at all times, day and night. I was at the station at Mans Peak when a call came in, a woman's voice needing an ambulance. She was extremely nervous and had trouble telling me how to reach her house."

"How do you know she was nervous?" Juicks asked him.

"She was crying. Her voice was trembling."

"Was her voice trembling, or was she crying?"

"Trembling and crying both. She told me how to reach her house. Please hurry, she told us. I asked her what the problem was. I have to know that, you see, and I have to know her name. And she said, 'I shot my husband.' All calls are recorded, and the tapes are kept, and that's on the tape. I listened to it yesterday evening. So we went out there at once. Her name was Winnette King."

Juicks asked him how long he had worked for the First Aid Service and where he had trained.

"I am a medical technician, IV. That allows me to start intravenous fluids and give emergency aid. I had a nine-week course in 1980. Afterward, I had a two-term course at Orchid Tech. Some time ago I had four years service in Vietnam as a medic."

"So you and your partner went to the address?"

"Yes. In response to the woman's appeal. It was eight minutes away. As we turned into Tom Smith Road a car pulled in in front of us, somebody else, and that car led us directly to the house. In the yard I saw a man was on the ground naked and was stretched out on his back, and a woman who was—I was told to be his wife—was administering artificial respiration. There was another woman kneeling beside the body, and one of them Rooftop black men was standing nearby. We checked the patient. He was in shock. His flesh was clammy and was cool. His respiration was shallow, and was only eight, while normally it would be sixteen or eighteen. So he was critical, and quick as we could we lifted him onto the stretcher and took him onto the ambulance and got an airway established. I started the artificial breathing. At the hospital we turned him over to the emergency room personnel."

Juicks leafed through several notes. "What was the patient wearing?"

"Nothing except spare towels."

"Had he been injured?"

"He was bleeding from his chest. There was a bullet hole in front and the bullet had exited or entered through his back. Not much blood was coming out. It was just about seeping out. The holes were small."

"Did you get his name?"

"Oh, yes. The scared woman said it was Lloyd Plover."

"Did he say anything to you?"

"Not a word. We administered advanced life support by getting an airway established and started to breathe him artificially with a bag mask. I started the oxygen on him and rushed him to the hospital."

"Were officers present?"

"They arrived as we ambulanced the patient. I told them he had gunshot wounds from a pistol or rifle."

"Did you stay at the emergency room?"

"For an hour my partner and I helped that there woman doctor who works weekends, her and the nurses, until we got a call to take Casswell Roberts to the hospital."

"Who is Casswell—did you say Roberts?"

"You don't know Casswell? Dairyman. Brought the first holsteins into Altamont County."

"Does he have anything to do with this case?"

"No, not that I know of."

Winnette had been squirming on the bench during the time Art told about the phone call; she was showing some of the anxiousness she must have felt at the time, on that afternoon. She was casting off some of her lethargy, all right, which was a relief to me. In my examination I asked Art if he still owned the billy goat that had lost a hind leg in a dog fight. I'd done enough research on Art to hear about that. He replied that the goat was still bossing everything in sight, except Art, himself. The diversion gave him a chance to get a laugh, and the jury a chance to relax and me a chance to defuse some of the weighty worry of his testimony. I asked if there had been many calls in his local experience pertaining to accidental gunshot wounds.

"Oh, yes, Mr. MacMillan. One a month. That and power mowers."

Juicks must have been annoyed by my use of the word *accidental,* so he stressed it by asking Art if Winnette had said she accidentally shot her husband. That gave me the opportunity to ask if Winnette had said she had shot her husband intentionally, which made Art and the jury laugh. "You didn't believe that the woman was trying to explain the circumstances of the shooting while on the phone, did you, Art?"

"No, sir."

"She was eager to have an ambulance sent, is that so?"

"Yes, sir."

"And that was the purpose of the call, to save her husband's life."

"Exactly so."

"So far as you knew that Sunday afternoon, she had shot her husband accidentally?"

"Yes, sir."

"Did the wife in your presence hinder or harass you or seek to delay you?"

"No, sir."

"Or to harm her husband in any way?"

"No, sir."

"I'm sure of it," I said, and sat down.

Winnette ate the other half of her sandwich while the pathologist began his report. He explained that a pathologist is a physician with an M.D. who has gone on to specialize in causes of death, and he had practiced for eight years, performing autopsies. "My duties are mostly in Wataupa County, but the local man, Dr.

Swasie, was away, so I covered for him and performed the autopsy on Ernest Plover."

"Lloyd Ernest Plover," somebody, a woman, said, correcting him. I realized with amusement it was the schoolteacher speaking from the jury box. She turned scarlet from embarrassment, once she realized what she had done.

"I often do cover work in the mountains," Dr. McClure told us. "On this certain day I went to the Emerald Mines Hospital and examined Mr. Plover, who was dead. The body was in the hospital morgue. The body had suffered a gunshot, noticeable in the left side of the back below the shoulder blade and the left side of the breast. The body was not clothed. The body was of large frame, adult, Caucasian, male, about thirty to thirty-five years, brown hair. He had the start of a mustache. The back wound had the characteristics of a gunshot entrance wound. It was smaller than the exit wound. It was circular. The chest wound, evidently the exit wound, was larger and was not round, the bullet having tumbled as it passed through the body, or had been smashed. There was no other external injury to the body, save for a cut on the right hand, the knuckles, but what had caused it I cannot say." The doctor testified he had cut into the corpse and had found the left side of the chest full of blood. The heart had not been injured. The left lung had been punctured where the upper and lower lobes of the left lung overlap, so the bullet had made a hole about an inch in diameter through both. The hemorrhage in the chest had been massive. There were no other wounds on the body, and no organ damaged except the left lung. On examination, I judge that the man's health had, up to the time of the wound, been good, and that the cause of death was the gunshot wound. It was not instantly fatal, but he could not have lived more than fifteen minutes, once his lung was shot through."

When my chance came to question Dr. McClure, I asked if he was related to the McClures in High Falls, who had helped years ago to develop two or three mountain resorts, and he explained that he was a David, not a Cummings McClure descendant, so was not closely related.

I said, "Looks like you've covered everything—and clearly, too, Doctor, very clear report. I admire that. The toxicologic analysis is of interest to us. I requested that a sample of the blood be retained and sent for an examination for alcohol and drugs."

"Objection," Juicks interrupted.

The judge looked from Juicks to me, then to McClure. "Well, let me have counsel come to the bench."

We held a whispered conversation, Juicks and Blackington and I. Juicks was of the opinion that I was trying to influence the case with drug charges. The evidence of drugs would so inflame the jury against the dead Plover that the jury could not fairly judge the case, he told us.

Of course, whether Plover had been using drugs, and what drugs he used, was vital to an understanding of the situation, as I explained.

Juicks was adamant. Further, he said, the testimony of McClure, who did not carry out those drug tests, was hearsay.

"It is the best evidence available, due to your not supplying any other, or any at all, in spite of repeated requests from me," I told him.

"It's not for me to do your work."

"It is for both you and me to find the facts in this case."

The judge intervened, said he would allow McClure to answer the question, let it be called hearsay for the record, for the purpose of argument in connection . . ." He paused, looked at the gathering storm afflicting Juicks. "Well, let's have it given, damn it, Mr. Juicks, but outside the presence of the jury."

I said, "It's hearsay from one professional to another, in an official report?"

Juicks continued to object, did not want anything said about drugs, considered the word itself to be inflammatory in this part of the world. The judge continued to insist we would hear the evidence, then later determine whether or not to expose it. First we needed to know what the finding was. Therefore, the jury was dismissed, the visitors excused, and McClure remained on the stand. Of course, Winnette remained beside me.

At this point the court found that McClure did have news of

a drug report, but no report. Somewhere there was one. He believed it had been sent to Dr. Goforth, the County's chief medical examiner, and he understood Dr. Goforth had the report at home and could possibly look for it at one o'clock, once he went there for lunch. Angrily I made clear to the judge that this series of delays, amounting to evasiveness, was damaging to a woman's defense of her life, that I had repeatedly requested such test be made and had, when they were not forthcoming, filed a motion and had been heard on that motion before the Superior Court, that I had received not a whisper of cooperation from Mr. Juicks's office. In Florida such tests would have been made. I had twice used the toll-free number of the chief medical toxicologist for the state, had asked him if the specimen remained and had asked for a report. He wanted to know who was going to pay for it. I told him it didn't make a cent of difference, I would pay for it, that a woman's future was at stake, and I wanted it done. And he told me, "Well, don't worry about it, I'll see to it." Then he called me back and told me on the phone that his first results usually needed further checking, if specific drugs were to be identified. For instance, Quaaludes was a family, and he asked if I wanted more specific tests, that one does need to make specific tests in case of those, and the tests add to the cost. I told him yes, by all means, and he said he would try to make such tests and send a report. He assured me on the telephone of a report, and maybe that is the report that's over at Dr. Goforth's house. Your Honor, I will put every one of these doctors under subpoena and bring them in here if necessary to get the truth of this."

Mr. Juicks tried to defuse my anger. He had the gall to say he had wanted all along to know the truth of this matter but had not seen the report. "The tests are not of a type usually done. If Mr. MacMillan had a Superior Court order to get such a report, he might have called Chapel Hill, where I understand the blood sample would need to be sent, and would have it by now. My office has done all we could, but I certainly don't feel that my office needs to run down something we don't normally have that's uncustomary in this part of the state where drugs are seldom found. Alcohol must be tested for, but Mr. MacMillan wants drugs. The state does not require tests for drugs, nor does my office, and I'm not going to stipulate that I allow this report into evidence. I might, but don't know what it says."

The judge waved aside considerations. "Well, will you agree, Mr. Juicks and Mr. MacMillan, that we allow Dr. McClure to testify to what the report is, since he knows, even if he has not seen it?"

"What—will it be in evidence?"

"It's voir dire, Mr. Juicks. Nobody's here."

"Very well, sir."

I said, "Your Honor, the comment that the DA's office had done all they could to be helpful needs attention."

The judge waved that aside, as he should have. I do become sarcastic when upset. "All right now, shall we have the doctor answer your question about the tox—toxicomy—the toxicology simply for—outside the presence of the jury?"

Dr. McClure had remained on the stand, had been engaged looking from judge to Juicks to me to judge and was now tucking his notes into his tight fist, preparing to begin. I asked him, "Dr. McClure, on April the nineteenth you had completed your medical examination, had you?"

"No, sir."

"I mean—excuse me, on the twentieth. I'm sorry. Two days after the shooting you had completed the autopsy?"

"Correct."

"Do you recall my telephone call—this was before you had completed the autopsy, asking that you send toxicology specimens to Chapel Hill for drug studies?"

"Yes, sir."

"Now, do you know whether—did you make such a request?"

"I sent the request along."

"The man to do these is a Dr. Milton Monroe?"

"Yes, sir."

"All right, in making up a report on cause of death, in reaching conclusions, do you rely on information received from Chapel Hill? I am referring here to cases where the cause of death is suspect."

"Yes, I do. Usually."

"You usually do. Now, in making your report this morning did you rely on information received by telephone or in an official report from Chapel Hill?"

"I relied on their toxicology information because we can't do it ourselves. Sure I did."

"So it usually is part of your testimony, the toxicology information."

"I—normally, we don't have it, but provided we have it, it is."

"Why wasn't it presented?"

"Because the only report I have I got by phone yesterday, and . . ." he glanced worriedly at Juicks, "that won't do, will it?"

"Dr. McClure, do you have this verbal information from Dr. Monroe in Chapel Hill relative to drug studies done at my request?"

"Yes. From on the phone is all."

"What are the results?"

He turned to his notes. "There was methaqualone, also known as Quaalude, in this—in Mr. Plover's blood. And there was cocaine."

I was so relieved, surely I had to have shown it. Up until now I had been trusting only to what Anne Bailey and her friend Blue had told me, and what Winnette had not denied. "What quantities?" I asked.

"Methaqualone at 0.5 milligrams. Cocaine not ascertainable."

"Why is it—was it not—"

"Dr. Milton Monroe said it's impossible after a short while to measure the amount used of cocaine. He told me this yesterday."

Once I was done with Dr. McClure, the judge asked Juicks what says the state as to whether or not it will object to this testimony being given the jury.

"If I might ask Dr. McClure some questions," Juicks said. "Dr. McClure, what does 0.5 milligrams of methaqualone signify?"

"That's per hundred milliliters of blood."

"What does it—how much is that, in effect?"

"Little to be said as to effect. Depends on the person. Some more than others, and any estimate is complicated by the presence of cocaine, too."

"Did you call it methaqualone?"

"It's one of the sleeping pills. It's a hypnotic."

"Now listen here, tell us if 0.5 milligrams per hundred—is that a normal dose?" Juicks asked.

"No dose is normal in my experience. I don't know."

"Is that what one would take as a dose?"

"I asked Dr. Monroe if—and let's see here . . ." He referred to his notes. "That's equivalent to no higher blood level than one would have with a three-hundred milligram Quaalude."

"Is that a small, or medium, or large dose?" Juicks asked.

"It's what he referred to as a normal, large dose."

"I see. Mr.—Dr. McClure, did he try to measure the cocaine?"

"I don't know how to answer that. I don't know."

"What is cocaine, a depressant?"

"No, sir. It's a stimulant."

"Would it counteract the sleeping pill dose?"

"Might. Or it might result in bizarre reaction. It's almost impossible to guess as to that."

"There are legitimate medicines that contain cocaine?"

"It has been used as an anesthetic to local areas of the body. Usually this is in the nose, such as that. If a person has a painful nasal passage, cocaine might be used to deaden pain."

"Even though it's a stimulant, it will—"

"Yes, it will deaden pain locally."

"Is there any way to determine if the cocaine in the body was enough to affect his actions?"

"No, sir. Not by me."

"From the report, based on Dr. Monroe, is there any—do you conclude, can you, that Plover was under the influence of any drugs at the time he was shot?"

"Suffice it to say, they were present."

"With what influence, Dr. McClure?"

"It's—too late to say."

After Juicks's questioning, I asked Dr. McClure if cocaine dissipates rapidly, if that was why the measurements were necessarily inconclusive.

"That is the case," he replied.

I asked him if Quaaludes dissipate, too.

"I don't know the speed of their dissipation," he said.

The judge asked Juicks if he had anything more. He did not. "All right, what do you say, in that case, as to your objection previously entered?"

"Your Honor," Juicks said, starting off at once, "I contend that all this drug business is inflammatory. It is highly so here, where drugs have only begun to creep in and people are terrified and angry. Cocaine particularly is a drug that has a flagrant reputation here. The evidence is not conclusive. Also, it is emotionally charged. We are—are not concerned with the reputation of the deceased; these matters are merely inflammatory. We don't know that they had anything to do with his actions. If we knew they did, I would agree they're relevant, but we have no such evidence. This testimony is hearsay, that's another thing. It would tend to inflame the jurors against the deceased Plover, who is not on trial, and tend to lead them astray from the facts of the case."

He was perspiring, was wet as a toad. He was in trouble with his own mind, I judged. "Your Honor, I think the evidence is substantial," I argued, and that the fact that the deceased was under drugs contributed to his death. If I get Dr. Monroe up here from Chapel Hill, he's going to testify the same as McClure."

"What say about it being inflammatory?" Judge Blackington asked me.

"It's more important that it points out the truth, Your Honor. I hate to hear a district attorney say the truth is inflammatory."

"Well," Blackington said, "we can try the district attorney's office another time."

"In a trial for murder, it's the full truth we must seek. Murder itself is inflammatory. If drugs are inflammatory, then drugs might have inflamed the deceased."

Mr. Juicks retorted that I kept blaming his office for not doing investigating I should do. "He is upset because I did not go to Chapel Hill as his errand boy—"

"Not at all. Not now," I assured him. "We have heard the report in full. I accept the report."

"We have done nothing to block Mr. MacMillan from the information. If we had received the report in the normal course, we would have handed it to him."

"I have heard the report just now," I assured him, "and it is acceptable to me."

"It is hearsay and inflammatory," Juicks shouted at me—literally shouted.

"It does seem to have inflamed you, but not me. If you want Dr. Monroe to come under subpoena from Chapel Hill, I will subpoena him."

The judge tapped his desk top with his knuckles, gaining quiet. For a full minute he stared off at the back of the room, where several visitors were returning to their seats. "It is hearsay, Mr. MacMillan," he told me finally. "I will have to agree with the district attorney on that. As it stands the evidence is insufficient to have probative value. Therefore—let me see—I rule that Mr. Juicks's objection is sustained.

"Your Honor," I said wearily, "the defendant excepts."

"Exception is noted," the judge murmured.

"Exception number four," I murmured, sitting down, burning inside. This judge, who the hell is he, anyway. He was serving his thirteenth round with this court, has his home near Asheville, somebody said. The idea of denying the truth in order to satisfy decorum, this in a blood murder. Unfair to me and this young woman. Now she was to be presented, or so Juicks hoped, as a wife who has slaughtered her husband while he, dear lad, was stone sober, hadn't had a drink all day and wasn't under the influence of drugs. A family spat that had gone strangely awry, with the wife irrationally killing him.

The jury filed back, the visitors returned. I asked the good doctor, who was still on the stand, to describe the hurt place on Plover's hand. "Tell the court what might have caused the injury," I suggested.

"I don't know what caused it."

"Is it the type of mark that might have been left if he had hit a wall with his fist?"

"It could be."

Juicks was on his feet. "Objection, Your Honor, to this venturing about."

"Overruled."

"Or if he had hit somebody."

"Yes. It could have been."

Juicks did not want that to remain in the jury's mind. "Dr. McClure, could the hand injury have been caused by a fall to the ground?"

"Yes, it could have."

13

MAVIS:

I was sitting in the courtroom even before lunch. Mr. Juicks told me to be there by one o'clock to testify. My two children with me, looking at the scene, they as nervous as me. My two were to be in school; I allowed them a holiday since this was their own father, a scene they would remember all their lives. Of course, they knew Winnette, too. So I phoned their teacher. "Their father's trial comes up," I told the teacher. "Rather his second wife's trial comes up, and I'm to testify, and the children are needed, too."

Not with any sense of pleasure or glory was I there. The loss of Plover was a shock, believe me. Unexpected. You never know the value of a hand till you lose it. We were not related, don't you know. We were too close to be broken apart abruptly. I suppose I was closer to him than he was to me.

A short, dumpy man in uniform was called to the witness box. A policeman of some sort. Just at that moment I caught a glimpse of her, Winnette, sitting beside her tall, slender-as-a-reed lawyer, him wearing a tweed suit that looked tailor-made. He looked like an Englishman. He had a long face for a man, a quince smile, which appeared to be always on the verge of laughter, whether kind or mockery would depend, I suppose. Winnette was snatching glances at him, as if measuring him—one of her future conquests, no doubt she was wondering about that, even though he was forty, fifty years past her age. She's oversexed, that Winnette. That's what I've decided. And she's told me she has multiple orgasms.

A heavy-set man I used to know at the Northcross School store was on the stand. For the life of me I couldn't recall his name. "I am Strother Clay, an employee of the sheriff of this county, that's Altamont County, have been for thirteen years and was employed on the eighteenth day of April of this year. We received a call at 1:32 in the afternoon, and I rode with Deputy Burleson to Tom Smith Road, which the defendant told me is also called the River Road, to a house one mile beyond the pavement. The call came from the First Aid Service. We drove the Lab Van, which is used to do our lab work and the field work both. Officer Burleson is in charge of the van. He's not able to be here today, being in Ohio. He's sorry for his absence. In the yard we came upon the ambulance with its back end to the road, and two ambulance men were trying to load a subject. I didn't recognize the subject, who was on a stretcher, till we had approached close on foot. There were four people there, three whites and a black. They were standing between the house and the ambulance, well away from the ambulance attendants, who told them to stay back. In the yard, as we ascertained after routine questioning, were Anne Bailey, Winnette King Plover, the wife of the subject who was being ambulanced, the black, by name Carvel A. Morrison, Jr., and Mrs. Plover's father. I approached the four subjects and asked what happened. You know, as anybody would, I asked what was the matter. And the one who was Mrs. Plover said she had shot her husband. I just asked the whole group, and she replied. I went over to the ambulance as they were shutting the doors, and I looked in and saw Plover's face. It was the same Plover I'd known in high school, when he was into football, was a fullback for junior and senior years and I was with the newspaper, writing about him. He got to be a senior but dropped out of school after the last possible football season. He was a terrific fullback, let me tell you, and Carolina wanted to recruit him, and Wake Forest, too, and the University of Tennessee, Appalachian State, even though he was such a bum student—"

"Mr. Clay," the DA said, "is this pertinent?"

"Only to establish that I recognized him to be Lloyd Plover."

"We don't question the identity of the deceased," the DA said.

Irritated, Officer Strother Clay twisted about in his chair. Strother—how could I expect of myself to remember Strother? I wondered. Old Virginia name. A Strother surveyed the Tennessee line between North Carolina in about 1800.

"The woman who said she shot her husband is in the courtroom today," he told the court, told us in the visitors' section.

Juicks asked him to point her out.

Strother pointed a long, lean forefinger at Winnette Plover.

"So then," Juicks said, "you are standing in the yard and the ambulance drives away."

"And Mrs. Plover told us to come inside and she would show us where the gun was. I followed her and she pointed it out in back of the TV set, and I stayed with it while Officer Burleson went to get equipment to pick it up and mark it. She had put it on a shelf, on the bottom shelf behind the TV. When we got it out, I saw it was a P-38 from the German Army, World War II."

"Is the weapon present?"

"Yes, sir. It's on the table."

"Have the gun marked state's exhibit number one."

Used to have old dresses and plenty of furs at the Northcross store, sent by rich people to help us poor Appalachians, and Strother Clay knew I liked old styles of clothes and would put back a few dresses and hats, veils and handkerchiefs.

"Officer Burleson put the pistol in a plastic bag," he told us in the courtroom. "I advised Mrs. Plover of her constitutional rights. She said she didn't care about anything and didn't want to have a lawyer or have any rights. So she replied to me, saying 'now or never.' Officer Burleson did a handwiping test on Mrs. Plover to see if she had fired a gun recently. The test was negative, but Mrs. Plover told us she had washed her hands."

He went on to say Officer Clay had found a bullet hole in the wall near the back door. There was also a dent in a curtain rod. He had photographs, which were introduced into evidence, one

99

of each room: living room, kitchen, bedroom, and gun room, which was labeled "storage room."

"Were there blood stains anywhere about?" Juicks asked him.

"Outside and in the house there were drops of blood. On the walk and front steps, inside the front door, then to the left toward the bedroom there were drops of blood in the hall. In the bedroom only a few. In the storage room none. Most of the drops were near the front door."

"Mr. MacMillan, your cross-examination, if you please," Judge Blackington said, with the disinterested air of a person who has seen it all before. My Northcross helper, Strother, got a nervous twitch to his eye as he waited.

"I judge Mrs. Plover was cooperative," Mr. MacMillan said to him.

"Yes, sir, Mr. MacMillan," Strother replied.

"She gave you a confession? Would you call it a confession?"

"A complete statement is what I call it."

"You were the one who wrote it down?"

"She was too—too torn up to write."

"Did you sign it for her?"

"No, sir. She signed it. I also had her sign a statement of her rights, waiving her rights."

"Her helping must have been a convenience for you."

"Yes, sir, Mr. MacMillan. Her father was with her both at the house and at the sheriff's office, and he tried to tell her not to sign anything."

"He suggested that she have an attorney present?"

"Yes, he did. And I told her she could have one. She said she did not want one and she waived her rights, and signed two statements."

"Two?"

"At the house and a more complete one at the sheriff's office. She told me several times what happened."

"Earlier she had showed you where the gun was?"

"Yes, sir."

"And when she had signed everything and showed you everything, you then locked her up."

My friend Strother hesitated, then nodded. "Yes, sir."

"Looks like after such a tragedy, after accidentally shooting a man, after being cooperative, with her father present to take her home—"

"I had no authority to release her, once the district attorney decided to try her," Strother told him. He scanned the courtroom, as if seeking supporters, and for the briefest moment his gaze fell on me.

"Was she going to run away?"

"Not in my opinion, sir. The next day she was taken to court, and that's when you were appointed in this case."

"Yes, I am the lawyer she never wanted." That made me laugh, and the jury laughed, and finally, even Winnette smiled. Yes, she told me she always had multiple orgasms. "Officer Clay, one thing more. It occurs to me that there were drops of blood on the floor, on the front door . . ." Mr. MacMillan said to Strother.

"Yes, sir."

"On the wall." Wearily, speculatively, Mr. MacMillan looked across the courtroom at the jury. "What about on the wife?"

"Oh, yes, sir, blood was on her face."

"Her chin, nose?"

"Right cheek, and on her chin and mouth."

"Where he hit her?"

"I—I think so. Slapped her, she said. I'm pretty sure it was blood."

"Yes. In the same way you assumed the blood was on the other places. I believe you went inside the gun room."

"The storage room?"

"I believe there were nine shotguns, were there? And how many rifles?"

"Seven."

"And were they usable? Serviceable? I mean were they old antiques, or were they usable?"

"They were not antiques. All were thirty-nought-three caliber hunting rifles, except one twenty-two and one thirty-nought-six."

"And were there pistols?"

"Yes, Mr. MacMillan. I saw any number."

"Usable, useful pistols. What number?"

"I don't know."

"Ten?"

"Probably more."

"In holsters?"

"And lying on the table. One was broken down for cleaning."

"I see. These in addition to the P-38 here in evidence. Did Mrs. Plover indicate that there was anything that led up to the shooting?"

"Objection!" Juicks called out. He moved past the bar, toward the judge. "I am going to object to this as self-serving, Your Honor. Let the Defense present its defense at its time."

The judge said, "All right, sustained."

Winnette's Mr. MacMillan walked right up in front of the bar, stood close to the judge as was Mr. Juicks. "Exception, Your Honor," he said.

"Oh, yes, Mr. MacMillan. I would have guessed as much."

"Number five," MacMillan said. "Now then, officer—uh— what is your name?" he said, returning to the witness.

"Clay, sir."

"Mr. Clay, did Mrs. Plover tell you who that day used the P-38?"

"Objection, Your Honor," Juicks said.

"Sustained."

"Exception, Your Honor," I said. "Number six."

"Exactly," the judge said. "I'll let the clerk keep count, Mr. MacMillan, if you consent."

"Now, Officer . . ."

"Clay."

"Did Mrs. Plover tell you why she hid the pistol?"

"Objection, Your Honor."

"Sustained."

"Exception number seven, Your Honor. No further questions at this time, since they cannot be answered at this time."

Juicks addressed the witness. "Was there any mark on Mrs. Plover's cheek, except the blood?"

"I did not see any abrasion."

Mr. MacMillan spoke up from his seat. "Did he look under the blood, Mr. Juicks?"

The jury and visitors laughed.

The judge called a recess, and a bevy of conversations began all about. Winnette turned in her seat and looked for Anne or me, I imagine. Her lawyer stretched. There's something to be said for age, when it comes to lawyers, I decided. Older ones carry a lot of experience, one senses this. This lawyer of Winnette's reminded me of a crane; his neck was slender, his wrists and hands were bony, and so was his face. He was mostly cheekbones and forehead and jutting chin. He was white haired and white mustached and gave the appearance of peculiarity, of specialness, of experience. Now the judge was experienced, too, but he looked worn and tired; he appeared to have folded up and gone into hiding inside his skin, was lurking somewhere behind his eyes, his pursed lips. Of all the men in the room, Winnette's attorney looked to me to be the most alert. Also, he was the best dressed, the most—well, the most significant, the one Winnette would have chosen herself.

And would want to keep, I imagine.

Not fair, Mavis, I told myself. First wives should not diagnose second wives. Even you know that.

Mr. MacMillan seemed to be looking for somebody in the courtroom. He craned his neck once, twice, then arose from his seat and again stretched his body, to be taller in order to see over the throng of departing visitors. He saw me hovering over my two and bore down on me like a big bird. I grabbed each child's wrist, ready or not, and started out.

"Mrs. Plover," Mr. MacMillan called to me.

My two, smarties both, stopped in place as if they had stepped in concrete. "That's you he's calling, Mama," Max told me. "That's one of your names," he informed me.

It was not one of the better ones. Several people turned to stare at me, holder of the dead man's name, possibly another murderer of her husband.

"Mrs. Plover," Mr. MacMillan said in that ever-so-smooth ingratiating manner he had used to pamper the witnesses. "Mrs. Plover, oh, these are the two children, are they?"

"As Winnette must have told you."

"No, not so. Now, Mrs. Plover, repeated telephone calls and letters to your home—"

"I've been away, haven't I, children?"

"Yes, but earlier you agreed to a meeting with me—"

"Out of state, haven't I, children?" I said.

"Now, I take it you're home, and it is necessary for me to talk to you about the deceased, and about Winnette. Her defense needs you."

"Well, you just tell me when," I replied.

"You are listed as a prosecution witness, and it's important to Winnette to call you for her defense—"

"I'd like to make the one appearance, don't you know. Courtrooms make me nervous, Mr. MacMillan."

"Yes, but the judge will not permit me leeway in questioning the state's witnesses."

"You, Kathy, put that bubble gum back into your mouth," I told her and grabbed her hand. "I'm not able to do much for—for the defense, Mr. MacMillan, out of respect to my own husband."

"Out of respect, is it?"

"Considering what Winnette did to him, shooting him in the back, I'd as well be left out of it."

"Oh, my. You are her closest friend and confidante."

"There is such a thing as loyalty to one's husband, the father of these two."

"Yes, and friendship for the living, such a thing—"

"A wife can't testify against her husband, they tell me."

"But your divorce—the transcript of your divorce—"

"If you're asking one wife to tell tales about another—"

"No, not at all—"

"It's all so imposs . . ." I never finished. Winnette was staring at me. She had come close now. She had wandered up the aisle following her attorney while a female guard followed them both, and her eyes were round as river rocks and as large, and the wonder was she appeared to be glad to see me. There was contentment and patience mingled, and a look of sweet charity. Two sheriff's deputies were scrambling to block the aisle door, lest she escape, but she was not in flight, no need for alarm. "Are you all right, Mavis?" she said in that sweet-as-Jesus voice of hers, sweet and not at all suffering.

"Why, I'm sufficing, Winnette. I've been meaning to call on you. They tell me you chose the jail for your new residence."

"I never cared to leave, once I was there. It's not particular with me."

"Not now, I imagine."

"I've messed up everything, haven't I? It wasn't my meaning ever to kill him, Mavis."

"Looks like you have a big show to—look to everday. I was about to say 'to entertain you,' but I suppose it's more entertainment than you really want." She was still wistful, as if she wanted to hug me, as often we hugged like sisters in the old days. "Her and me worked together for years, Mr. MacMillan, side by side."

He nodded understandingly and fastened his two bird's eyes on me. "Then she is a friend; or not?" As he added the final two words, his voice dropped appreciably, as if hesitating, or maybe warning.

"I came to testify, Winnette," I told her. "Was sub-poen-aed."

"It has been my expectation that she would also testify for your defense," Mr. MacMillan told Winnette.

"I used to tell her everything, day by day," Winnette told him. "Of course, I never dreamed I'd be—" She broke off, seemed to be overcome by nostalgia.

"Be standing in the dock," I said, interrupting her, embarrassed by her drooling over me, as if we still had reason to trust each other. "Max, stop kicking, I do need to get these two out into the fresh air." I left Winnette and her bird, left them quick, the aisle being clear now except for deputies and the like, who now swarmed on Winnette as if she were a prize. Make her have a multiple orgasm, all those men surrounding her.

Sorry to be so—crude, but to be sub—subpeonaed to come here to testify in the murder trial of my son's father, my only hus-band—does that strange bird think I have no feeling for Winnette, too? Testify for the state, why, I can't deny the state that. I will put my testimony on the record. Mr. Juicks gave me advice. Well, not advice, but criticism of my initial office statements. "Now if you say this," he warned me, "the jury might judge you to mean so and so, and if you say it this way, they will think so and so. What is the meaning you want to convey?" Mr. Juicks was helpful in opening up possibilities, always stressing that he wanted me to tell the truth, only the truth. He said to me once—he broke out in a laugh and said, "Oh, my goodness, Mavis, don't expect me to believe you took drugs; you'll land in jail telling fibs like that." It was him who was kind enough to confirm about the insurance. When Plover and me was married, there was insurance to the tune of $20,000, with wife as bene—bene— as benefiting, and dear Mr. Juicks confirmed there was such a policy now for her, with my two children to receive it should she be unable. Then, too, there was his and Winnette's—the house and seven acres. It was a considerable little estate, don't you know, what he owned in the world, with also the motorcycle, and all those guns, and whatever is buried around that place.

I went out there alone to his house a recent Sunday to have a look around, and Clara was home, had two cars parked in the yard, and the dogs set up a chorus and one flung himself, that one named Snowman did—flung himself at the fence, at the very place he's already bent it and weakened the post that Plover put in.

Outside the courthouse I got a few deep breaths of air that wasn't tobacco'd, then ate a hot dog at Ellen's, knowing it might give me gas. I had to eat something. The restaurant had about eight booths and eight tables and they was mostly taken. The smell of the place was corn muffins. My two ate the special of the day, which was fried fish fillet and chips, and they drank iced tea, fussing all the while about wanting Coca-Colas instead. "Soft drinks will rot your teeth," I told them. Two sheriff's deputies came in, they and a highway patrolman, and sat in the booth to one side of ours. One of them nodded to me and told me I was to be the next witness, which sent a bolt of fright through me, exactly like electric shock feels, I imagine.

So much to think about. So many claims on my conscience. So many strings on my heartstrings. So many waves, like of the ocean, rising above my head, crashing, becoming salty pools, all part of the rhythm of life, of his and my life on the weekend afternoons a few before she killed him as I lay with him in her and his bed. It was never mine, was it? Never yours, was it, Mavis, once he put the yoke around your neck. "You children was to have inherited twenty thousand dollars once," I told them.

They looked up from their daily specials, their little mouths dropped open, as was their frequent response to surprise. "Assuming your father died, then that was the way. Me, then you . . ."

"We get it?" Max asked.

"Why, you could have it, you and Kathy, so far as I was concerned. It was your father's desire. Now it's her. Or you."

Little mouths open like no other young beasts open theirs, hinged on bone so that they can drop one jaw open, whereas no pup or kitten or other pet can do it. They knew the sum of money was huge, was a lifetime of Brown Mules and other treats. What they didn't know was that a wife who is found guilty of murder or manslaughter of her husband won't get it, and it'll revert to the secondary beneficiary.

Gas. I knew it. I'd be on the stand, too nervous to speak my piece, especially when that Mr. MacMillan got kindly. Gas. Coming up in little, pestering waves, like at Myrtle Beach four years ago when Plover and me first saw the ocean together on our three-day holiday.

"Mama," Max said, "how much you tell me?"

I ignored him.

"Mama, twenty thousand is how much?"

"Not another word," I told him in my you-better-mind whisper.

Mr. MacMillan himself, the Crane himself, came into the café and was peering about. Even the deputies grew quiet.

"Mama, will you get half of the—"

"You shut your mouth," I told him and I'm afraid I hissed, which carried to other tables.

107

The bird approached me, his vestly watch chain was close as my breath. I went on drinking my coffee, sipping at the cup, hiding my face over it.

"Kathy, you and Max enjoying your lunch?" he asked them.

"Yes," they agreed for once. "Mama says if—" Max began.

"Shut up, Max," I said and would have pulled his tongue out if necessary.

"Mummy said—" Max began again, thinking perhaps I had objected to being called 'Mama.'"

"For God sake, shut up," I ordered fiercely.

The entire café fell silent. Quiet. Oh, yes, even yet Max was perched to proceed but was awaiting his chance to get past my guard. Mr. MacMillan smiled at him, at me, then fiddled with his felt hat, withdrew a step or two and turned to greet the deputies. He made his way to a table set for one, a tiny table too tiny for so tall and lean a man.

"Max, do you know what execution means?" I asked, keeping my voice low and ever-so-meaningful. "You hush about any money at all. Smart boys do not talk about money, and they do obey their mothers."

"What—what does execution mean?" His little bright face looked up at me. Food was stuck neatly at both corners of his mouth.

"It's what happened to your father," I told him.

When it came time to testify, I was so nervous I became determined in my ways, seeking to hide it.

"My name is Mavis Huntington Plover. I live in South River on the river, on McKinney Road. Lloyd Plover was my ex-husband, married on June fifth of '73 and we separated—"

"You were a June bride, Mrs. Plover?" Mr. Juicks asked, interrupting me to give me a chance to catch my breath.

I was so nervous—I mean, I was all tension, nothing less, from my spine through all my muscles, and I was gassed up, too.

"Let's see, you and Lloyd Plover divorced in 1975?" he asked.

"Yes. I don't know the date."

"But remained friends?"

"Yes. Off and on."

"Children?"

"Two, and they are in the courtroom now." Both of them stepped out into the aisle to display themselves all the more to the visitors; even the judge and jury strained to glimpse them. Max, so help me God, bowed, which made me on-fire and caused giggling generally. After the spattering of giggles, I managed to get my breath. Winnette did not laugh, though she did swivel her body around to look toward the children.

"In your own words, Mrs. Mavis Plover, tell us when you first met the defendant," Mr. Juicks said.

"She worked, began working the other packaging machine at Silver Spur about this time of month four years ago. I introduced her to my husband, my ex-husband a year and eleven months ago. She courted my husband, and after their wedding—I and my children attended their wedding . . ." It occurred to me that Max might be stirred to further bowing, but fortunately he was still.

Oh, yes, there he came down the aisle, and of course I had to watch, was mesmerized, and others strained in the audience to see what attracted me. Max actually pushed his way onto the bench beside Winnette, took his place beside her, and she appeared to awaken from her concentration to slip her arm around him and pull him against her body. It was unnerving for me, to see my son cuddle close to the woman who had—

"Did you visit their home?" Mr. Juicks said.

"Yes, sir. And my children did, too. During their marriage, including their separation. And Winnette and I worked side by side, each to her own machine, and normally we ate noon dinner together, and we confided in each other, so we were close as gloves."

"Did you and Mr. Plover and Winnette Plover go places together?"

"To my house. To the Family Steak House, but only two times. I tell you, Plover wasn't much for exposing himself. He stayed around home, unless he was away traveling on business."

"Did you do any traveling with him, or with his second wife?"

"Yes, I went—last time I saw Winnette was two weeks before

she—before he died. Winnette and me went shopping in the Asheville Mall. I invited her to go with me. We drove an hour to get there, and three hours we were there, including at the cafeteria, and an hour home, talking all the way, confiding, don't you know. On the way home she talked about—about Lloyd Plover striking her. I recall her telling me how a lady that lived near Kona shot her husband, killed him, and Winnette believed the wife would get out of it. And I said, Winnette, a woman can't kill her husband and escape a penalty in North Carolina. And she said she had herself thought any wife might think about killing her husband. She meant killing, I suppose, Plover." There it was said. The words I had harbored, prepared to say, they were out. The gasp from the courtroom was like a shot, so explosive and instantaneous.

I rested. I let it all settle down. The courtroom was busy with whispers and conferring and rushing out, except as I say for Winnette. It's absolutely strange. The one I had expected would rise to her feet and denounce me, she kept calm as on a yesterday, was merely stroking Max and looking out at the world and overlooking me, all with a mellow remoteness and kindness. My God, she's gone bemused, I thought, she's—how do you say it—bemused is the word, isn't it?

Beside them sat her attorney, his expression like a shiny statue, nothing revealing what emotions were turning over inside, only Lord knows. Must have been confusion from surprise. Even Mr. Juicks had not heard that account till now.

Nor had he heard the next part. "Once when Plover and Winnette were arguing, she phoned me and asked if she could come over to my house, and she said she had taken to wanting to have a pistol handy whenever she was home alone, and whenever Plover was home she felt safer knowing the pistol was available."

Again the rustling, the exchange of comments.

"This was told me after they had separated and made up," I said, "and she had come back to him from her parents' house. There was a separation for two months or more, then she went back to him a month, or maybe it was five weeks after Christmas, about February first, and a week later was when she first pointed her pistol at him, and she told me he went for his own gun and that scared her and she threw her gun aside and ran off."

"This was about five weeks after Christmas?" Juicks asked.

"No, that was when Plover and Winnette went back together, and then it was a month or so later when she held a gun on him, and it was a week after that when she came to my house to tell me her troubles and tell me she'd been wondering what to do about him, for he was starting drinking again."

Mr. Juicks had other questions, most of them over-and-over ones. Meanwhile, I was in a vigorous state of mind, was hot within myself, as muscles will get warm from exercise. At last he came to the end of his tether, so to speak, and sat down, and there was general conferences of all of the people, whispering and trying to evaluate, and over there was the Crane chirping in Winnette's ear and waiting for her replies, and she not noticing, was stroking Max and blowing little waves of breath across his hair, and then there was quiet as the Crane got up on his legs, peering at me, his next morsel. That look did frighten me, let me tell you, and he waited till every sound was silent as ghost steps. He tilted toward me, but in that moment my other child, Kathy, uttered Max's name, then said "Mama," and there little Kathy was in the aisle now, looking. She saw me and she came on anyway, saying, "Max, Mama," and stopped at Winnette's bench, and that one made room for her. So there Winnette sat with my boy on one side of her, my daughter on the other. The courtroom people were seeing it all, and then seeing her envelop both children in her arms, angellike the way she was. Lord knows, she must have been drugged by the jailer or the Crane, for she was out of this courtroom somewhere, wasn't here to notice my testimony.

The Crane kept whispering to her, but might as well be walled, so he swung on me, was saying, "Mrs. Mavis Plover, let me ask you something I'm confused about, so you can clear it up. Did you tell us you are a friend of Winnette's?"

Laughter started at the back of the courtroom and spread, the entire situation was embarrassing to me, me having to sit there and listen to it.

"I am," I said in a loud voice, over the general laughter.

The laughter continued. Mr. Juicks called objections, he was really red with anger. The judge began pounding his desk with his wooden hammer, the gavel, but he was not angry. Finally, order came, and the two lawyers went to the judge, whispered while close together. Somebody in the room lit a cigar, and I began to cough. That's one thing affects me, cigars and pipes. After what I'd call four or five minutes everybody was back in place. The Crane again leaning forward like a spring, exactly like an Alpine skier.

"Mrs. Mavis Plover, you divorced Mr. Plover after how many years of marriage?"

"Three."

"Two years and how many months."

"I—five months."

"So that's less than two and a half years."

"Yes. I suppose you have it better'n me."

"Did you get along well?"

"Objection, Your Honor," Mr. Juicks said, interrupting.

"Sustained," the judge said at once.

"My witness is not the wife who is on trial, Your Honor," Juicks said.

"I said 'sustained,'" the judge reminded him.

"Mrs. Mavis Plover," the Crane resumed again, "in your friendly talks with Winnette Plover, did you discuss your life with Lloyd Ernest Plover?"

"Yes."

"Did you tell her about the times he beat you?"

"Objection," Juicks stormed out.

"Sustained. At least for this time of the trial, Mr. MacMillan," the judge said.

The Crane asked for—if he could approach the bench, and so Mr. Juicks went forward, too, and they argued over something like two cats over a fish, and then they gradually became staid and proper as they walked back to their places. Then Mr.— the Crane, as I call him, said he wanted an exception to the ruling, which was number seven or eight, as the clerk had it set down legally.

The Crane asked me, "Mrs. Mavis Plover, did you ever tell Mrs.

112

Lloyd Plover, your close friend and confidante—"

Objection from dear Mr. Juicks himself, over one word. "She never said 'confidante,'" he told the judge.

"Confidante is a common-enough word to be used without district attorney authority," the Crane said.

"I must say, Mr. Juicks, what is wrong with confidante?" Judge Blackington asked him, as if he really wanted to know.

"I don't like it," Juicks told him, sitting back down.

"Nonsense," the judge said. "Overruled."

"Thank you, Your Honor. Did you, Mrs. Plover, tell your friend and confidante about ever having to defend yourself with a gun, defend yourself from your husband?" the Crane asked me.

Deathly silence in the courtroom, I waiting for Mr. Juicks, but he was pouting and quiet now, had deserted me.

"Please answer the question, Mrs. Plover," Mr. Crane said.

"Yes, I did. You probably have the divorce proceedings."

"And what was Mr. Plover's response?"

"He ran from me," I said, and then greatly enjoyed the laughter. I even laughed a bit, myself. That was all written down in the divorce proceeding of Plover and me, which must have been where the Crane had found it, so how could I deny what I had previously sworn to.

"Mrs. Mavis Plover, in your divorce trial, Mr. Plover was granted what visitation rights with his two children?"

"Limited."

"How limited?"

"None at all."

Again laughter.

"And you and your attorney—did you request of that court that the order be so stated because of Lloyd Plover's drug activities?"

"Objection," Mr. Juicks called out.

"Sustained," the judge said in the same routine way.

"Exception," the Crane said. Then he leaned over Winnette. She shook her head briefly, and the Crane nodded to a bailiff, or some sort of deputy, who came forward to lead my children away, which was a relief to me, but annoyed Winnette, seemed to alert her to where she was.

"Did you become more friendly with Mr. Plover after he began seeing Winnette King?" the Crane inquired.

"Yes, I did," I admitted.

"Did you take your children to visit their father?"

"Yes."

"Did you allow them to spend time with him and Winnette King Plover?"

"Yes." I could see what he was getting at but didn't know how to avoid it.

"Did you leave them overnight alone with Winnette and Lloyd Plover?"

"Yes."

"Did Mr. Plover or Winnette drink alcohol in the presence of the children?"

"Not to my knowledge. I was clear with him and her on that, that they be straight."

"Nor use drugs?"

"I made him promise not to drink or to use drugs in front of—"

"Now, Your Honor—" Mr. Juicks interrupted.

"Yes, Mr. Juicks?" the judge inquired of him.

Juicks was staring at me, seemed to be alerting me to dangers, so I clamped my big mouth shut at once.

"Did you," Mr. MacMillan asked, "leave the children with your close friend and confidante, Winnette King Plover, when you traveled to Baltimore?"

"I—who said I went to Baltimore?"

"Please answer."

"I—yes."

"For three days?"

"It was two days."

"Three days?"

"Two nights."

"And you trusted your friend and confidante to care for them?"

"Yes."

"And you trusted her to keep Lloyd Plover off drugs?"

114

Juicks was upset again, and he and the judge argued while I sweated out the wait, wishing, dear God, it would all end.

Once more the Crane was teetering. "Are you, Mrs. Mavis Plover, afraid of guns?"

"Your Honor," Juicks began, "the witness is not—"

The judge shook his head irritably and Juicks hushed. "Answer the question," he said.

"I am, yes. Now you're going to ask did Plover loan me a gun and did I carry it, and he did, but only to keep in my house. He believed every woman ought to be protected."

"How many guns did Plover loan you?"

"Oh, I don't—one."

"The time when Winnette King Plover pointed a gun at Lloyd Plover, what were the circumstances?"

"Why, she probably told you that herself."

"Was there a special reason for it?"

"I wasn't there. All I know is what I was told."

"Tell us what she told you, please."

"She said or he told me—one or the other—she held a pistol on him." A titter went through the great room, and two sparrows that had flown inside through the high windows tumbled about changing perches, as if they were threatened by it. Then quiet, except now the ceiling fans were revolving, stirring up noises.

"Do you have any idea how much insurance money Mr. Plover left?"

"Why—oh, my God," I said aloud, terrified all in that moment, and wondering, why doesn't Mr. Juicks object. Max? Oh, my God, where is Max?

"Did you find out about it from Winnette King?"

"No, I certainly never talked to her about money."

"Then was it from an officer of some sort?"

"No."

"Then who told you?"

"Yes, I suppose so."

"Was . . . it . . . someone . . . I . . . would . . . know?" The Crane spoke the words one at a time, slowly, turning as he spoke, settled his solemn gaze on Mr. Juicks. His manner caused general laughter, I must say, but as it died down, the Crane swung slowly back to me. "Were you told the amount of twenty thousand dollars?"

"Yes, I've heard that."

"And who was to inherit this?"

"I know what you're getting at, Mr.—Mister—but it's not had any influence over me and don't you think it has. I—if Winnette killed him, the money—" My throat clogged up on me, as much from fury as anything. To think he would imply that I would distort the truth—

Then Max appeared once more in the aisle, and I froze, silent, terrified.

"Yes?" the Crane said ever so evenly. "Please go on. It would go in that case to whom?"

"My children," I admitted bluntly, not that he didn't know all along, "to me and my two." Max once more was approaching Winnette. He slid in beside her and she cuddled him . . . that was all.

When I was dismissed and able to leave, I took Max's hand and led him, dragged him along, and found Kathy in the hallway downstairs eating potato chips and Coca-Colas, which the register of deeds had bought for her. Returning, I led the children as far as the vestibule, because as I left the courtroom the Crane was asking that the judge dismiss all charges against Winnette, and I did want to stay long enough to hear his argument. The judge refused to consider the idea. The Crane then wanted him to dismiss the first- and second-degree murder charges.

"No, we won't do that, either," the judge said. "We will dismiss the first degree. For one reason, she's pregnant. I don't think the state wants to execute mothers, or mother and child. I'll leave murder in the second degree and voluntary and involuntary manslaughter, those three."

That's when I left. "You children had your lunch, you had a whole special dinner apiece," I reminded them. I led them into the sunlight, the fresh air. We heard somebody shout the length of the hallway, "Blackington wants his tea." The swinging door swung shut behind us.

The noise of cars and of a siren far away replaced the courthouse noises, and there was, Max pointed out, a plane high up—natural noises that did not say friend of hers, nor did they affect my children's inheriting, nor my admitted jealousy, for the jealousy grows with Winnette's notoriety and is especially keen now that he is beyond either of us, therefore can never choose me. Go home and take a shower, then let the TV quiz shows bathe your mind, I promised myself.

14

BLUE:

She never appeared to care, not Winnette. Hell, they were talking about her life. She was tot-al-ly unruffled. Now, Anne was ruffled; Anne was crying. In the seat beside me she was biting a corner of my hanky and smearing tears with another and was saying, "That Mavis bitch," over and over, loud enough for people to overhear. Obviously it was Anne's considered opinion that Mavis was a bold-faced liar. Me? I think so, too. It's better to agree with Anne. Would Mavis be laying lies on her because of twenty thousand big ones for the two young ones? Not on your life. Not on Winnette's life, either. That's what got inside Anne's skin. To my mind, the money was icing. That was the white stuff on the cake. Of course there was something deeper than getting money for those children. She could steal money in other ways, or could marry somebody for it, for instance.

Anne and me agreed that evening. She and me were to supper at the big seafood restaurant. Mr. MacMillan himself came in soon after us, and on seeing him everybody who knew about the trial stopped eating. Anne was ordering her broiled fish when she saw him. I had ordered the All-You-Can-Eat Fried Perch. "Broiled fish takes longer," I told Anne just as he came in, and she said, "Maybe it does here, but it's not supposed to," meaning it don't take Anne any longer.

118

Mr. Mac sat down at a table that had another couple already seated. The woman might have been his wife, for she kissed him hello with a polite kiss, one a wife is good for. I mean, he's her husband. Then the other man, much younger, shook his hand in the manner of a respectful stranger, and him and Mac sat down. An empty chair was left beside the younger one.

"That's the doctor she was seeing," Anne told me.

"Seeing about her baby?"

Anne said, "Before Plover set his house on fire."

"How do you know that was a set fire?" I asked, being protective of Plover even yet. Hell, I'm his friend. That's why I told Mr. Mac on the phone hell no, I wouldn't cast aspersions on my best friend, and the truth about Plover was not universally complimentary.

Anne went ahead and ordered broiled fish, so I ordered a start-up of shrimp and wished she'd stop talking loud enough for others to hear. She was hoping to be noticed by Mr. Mac, I imagine. I saw Sam Markle of the King-of-the-Road Company and would have rather joined him and his wife at their table, but he was private tonight, was above us now that he had Wanda Peterson's husband's old job. Anyway, his wife wouldn't be willing to become involved in a murder trial—along with the common likes of Anne Marantha Bailey, for instance. Wives did not kill their husbands in her lofty circle. They ignored them to death.

Winnette came in. So help me, I must be in a dream. She was just over there, already had passed the hostess's station, her and a female deputy. A male deputy and a highway patrolman took stations near the door. Winnette was looking around the room and so she spotted me. I pointed in the direction of her lawyer and doctor, and once she saw them she started toward their way, and the two men rose to greet her. Then the lawyer and female deputy argued about whether this could be called a doctor's conference room—I heard that much. And the lawyer sat the deputy down at an empty table and told the waitress to take her order and put the charges on his bill. So she must have consented, for she ordered the Master-Mixed-Platter, which in this restaurant means about a pound of fish, six oysters, six clams, six big shrimp, twelve popcorn shrimp, a crab shell stuffed with crabmeat and crumbs, toasted; then too, there's hush puppies—those little balls of corn-meal and onion bits, and there's slaw and a slice of tomato and half a lemon.

By now there was not a table that didn't know Winnette was present. Most didn't know her personally, not on sight, but they knew she was the one who had shot her husband. There was one woman moved her table to the back section, maybe seeking to be farther away. That told what must have been on her mind. Any-way, it was a popular speculation, wondering how Winnette was faring, and just who was with her at her table. "All the wives want to see if she's getting along all right," I told Anne.

"She as much as ignored you and me."

"Hell, she has something on her mind."

"One would wonder." Anne was stretching, trying to see her plain-on, or to be noticed by her—hell, I don't know yet.

"Would you call Winnette a celebrity?" I asked.

"Wish I could see how she is bearing up, poor dear."

"You want to change places with me?"

Anne and I changed, acting as if there was a draft where she had been. From my chair she had a straight view. "She's more alert now," she said.

"Got a man. That does perk up Winnette," I said. Hell, it always had, even when she was an unknown. My shrimp cocktail came, and Anne swiped two off the near side.

"Now she's talking to the doctor," Anne told me.

15

DOCTOR ROBBINS:

I had not talked to Winnette privately for weeks. My visits to her cell had been restricted by the jailer and there was no privacy—that's the point. Now, with people staring at us from nearby tables, this was only a mark better.

She was, to say the least, delectably pretty tonight.

It had been Mr. MacMillan's request for me to see her, to try to cheer her up, bring her out of the doldrums, since tomorrow he would need to put her on the stand. On the telephone he had been insistent. For professional reasons already given to him, I had to insist on not admitting to a personal relationship with a patient, especially a notorious one; however, he convinced me a supper would not suggest that, and one did owe help to one's friends. So here we were, I as excited and pleased as ever in my life. Winnette was seeing her doctor, that was the official report, which had convinced the judge to allow her out of her cell.

From across the table I felt her wrist. Temperature was normal, or even a bit on the low side, I would guess. I counted her pulse. Sixty-six. Then I took the opportunity to squeeze her hand repeatedly, yes, and for her to respond. I gazed into her eyes, for professional reasons. I did long to do more, Lord knows, my entire body longed to do more. Here we were together, she just there out of reach except for professional touching, and she wanted to be alone with me, I could sense that. "There was a cure recommended in the Bible, the Old Testament, might work for depression, Mr. MacMillan," I mentioned to him gazing at Winnette. "King David had cold blood, and the elders selected the prettiest virgin they could find to warm him."

Mrs. MacMillan, who appeared to be a bit of a prude anyway, choked on a bite of celery, coughed, got it out of her mouth into her hand.

Mr. MacMillan said, "Medicine was more limited in those days."

"I like those days," Winnette murmured, and smiled. "Not find virgins around here, though."

"Well," Mrs. MacMillan said, seeking to rise to the occasion, "I would think an experienced professional hand would have done better."

"A hand?" Winnette said, pretending surprise, and Mrs. MacMillan, embarrassed, stared straight ahead, then her husband laughed, and all of us were free to laugh, and did, and before long we had a rollicking good table and a good time, and ordered plenty of food, even Winnette ordering boiled shrimp and a salad, and me ordering for her and me a side dish of roe, which I guessed would be liked by her, and which was, although she did worry about all those thousands of unborn fish being lost to the sea.

That, unfortunately, reminded her of her own pregnancy, and all in a wink the joy evaporated and seriousness enveloped us. She told me—she told us all but did favor me in explaining her predicament—that the baby she was to bear in a few months time would be the son of the man she had slain.

"Life is not just or unjust," I told her. "I see death so often, I would favor any life at all."

Winnette seemed relaxed until Mac began to tell me the details of today's testimony, then she bristled a bit. "Oh, Mavis is like that," Winnette said. "One day she's dear, another she's mean and feisty. It's not her monthly cycle, either, for I've wondered about that. She'd do anything to be of help, if we'd only ask her."

Mac was staring at her incredulously, but he said nothing.

No gain in arguing with Winnette anyway. I knew that. She

122

was certain to defend her friend. She would not speak ill of anybody. When her husband had followed my car, intimidating me, and had made office appointments he never kept, and was sitting in my house watching TV one lunchtime, all that unhappy while she excused his actions, worried because he was worried, and in the end chose him because he needed her; it was unimportant, all his threats to me and to her sister and to her parents. Those threats became more and more heated and irrational. They were signs of Plover's pain, his need of her, that was her analysis.

We had our seafood dinners. Nobody ate all of it, and Winnette and I shared a dessert. None of us wanted to go out of the restaurant, that was so. The woman deputy at the next table, she finished and was waiting. I could see her watching, and once again I took Winnette's pulse, as if making sure. "Tomorrow will you need any—any medicine, a sedative, Mrs. Plover?" I asked. "Here's a capsule on the tabletop near my cup."

"I don't take things like that."

Mac pretended not to be listening. Of course, he could hear, but he was looking off toward the far windows, contemplating his navel, I imagine. As we prepared to leave he ushered his wife away, giving me a few moments alone with Winnette. At once I asked if she thought Mavis had told the assistant district attorney about me. The concern seemed cruelly self-serving, but of course Winnette realized my practice, its reputation, was vital to me. No, she didn't think so, or didn't know.

As she left she paused twice to look back, and a more lovely person I've never seen. She was ever so pretty. I was the one who had spent our more private moments worrying about my realm and work, not her future life, which was being shaped for her each day by her friends and enemies.

At the restaurant doorway, Anne Bailey rushed from her own table and made a spurt to talk to her. The attorney was trying to maneuver Winnette and the deputy, and now Anne Bailey, out the swinging doors. Other people's arrivals delayed them. He began turning more attention to Anne, trying to silence her, at least to reduce her overexcitement. The deputy was also shielding Winnette from Anne, and there was Winnette looking only at me.

All in a twinkle, that was all, before the exit was clear and Anne was pushed to the outside, along with the deputy and Winnette, the two MacMillans, and a few hapless bystanders. Then—funny thing—the doors flew open for the disheveled hostess, who swept back in, fighting free in order to take her station, pulling into place her "Fish Are Good for You" jacket. Slowly the buzz of conversation resumed as people began freely talking and laughing, maybe asking who was the desperate woman, meaning Anne, who had been accosting Winnette.

Then the doors flew open with a smack as Anne returned. She was seated by the time the DA came in, he and an assistant, and questioned the hostess. He was discreet, going unnoticed by most of the guests. Then he wandered over to my table and sat astride a chair, the one Winnette had used, and softly inquired if I saw patients in public places, a criticism, a warning. I didn't know. He didn't speak above a murmur and remained only for a minute or so, then made his way into the parking lot outdoors. He left me trembling, let me admit.

16

BLUE:

Whenever Anne concentrates, it's a one-woman affair. No side issues are allowed. Her tongue has to wag for her mind to work, so she is sort of talking to herself, and was that suppertime there at the table reviewing the testimony of Mavis Plover, demolishing it, or at least strangling it to death.

Are they weapons, I wondered, does she ever stab her opponent with those fingernails? One hundred eighty pounds of quivering flesh, with one-ounce claws.

Dirty plates. Yes, do take them away. Anne wanted her leftovers put in a doggie bag. She would perhaps eat it later, once she calms down, she told me. Must take her home and give her a couple of martinis. Gin was the quickest way with Anne. Took four to six ounces. Wham! Then I give her vitamins A and B to offset a hangover—give her a one-a-day vitamin if the A-B pills are at the office. She takes the pills with her whenever she's facing stress. I bought seven bottles at one time at the health food store in Asheville. The cashier asked me if I was from Elida Orphanage. "No, but I'll take their discount," I told her, thinking fast. She said it was only ten percent and wasn't transferable, was only for orphans and for the Salvation Army. "Ought to give discounts to the winos," I told her, or words to that effect. And she was curious about dispensing vitamins to winos, said she wouldn't want the job herself. "Leave the pills on the window ledge when you go home," I told her, thinking fast, "line them up on the ledge so each wino can take one as he stumbles by."

She said the pigeons would get them.

"Will you listen to me, Blue Everett?" Anne said, interrupting.

I sat up straight in my chair, smiled at her. "At least you didn't say wake up."

"What do you mean by that?" she asked me suspiciously, like maybe I was about to share a secret.

"Last night when you poked me in the ribs, you said, 'Blue, you wake up and listen to me.'"

"Winnette's a child, Blue, having to do a woman's work. She's living inside a fairy-story body."

"Must be hard to breathe in there," I said.

"She needs to listen to her mummy this time," she said.

That meant Anne, who saw herself as a mother for everybody, and saw everybody in need of a mother. "He's leaving, too," I told her.

"Did you hear Mavis belch, and her in the witness box?"

"I heard her burp. The doctor's leaving."

"You know why she said all that she said?"

"The insurance money?"

"She hates Winnette, that's why. And you know what the present danger is, don't you?"

"Oh, Lord," I murmured to the tabletop.

"Winnette doesn't seem to realize it."

"One minus one is zero," I murmured, then fortunately the waitress came along with the puddings. The doctor—he must have already paid, or maybe her attorney had paid, for he left, walking directly out the doors.

"Now, Dr. Robbins could help her, but he's scared of being tarred himself," Anne told me. "What about it, Blue? You will testify for her, won't you? Blue? You wake up and talk to me, Blue," she ordered.

17

MR. MACMILLAN:

My wife and I followed the deputy's car back to Cookham and saw Winnette to her cell, a six-foot cubicle behind a solid iron door—private enough but bound to be lonely.

Later Scotty Bett and I stopped at the small, sole grocery store and bought a few staples. In Cookham I feel that I'm being studied by the natives. Inside a store they look you over, not with welcome so much as suspicion. Probably the mountaineer citizens of the small towns hereabouts get tired of strangers deriding them for foreign speech and manners. At any rate, tonight Scotty and I were looked over and were waited on by a closed-face young woman and a male look-alike who kept going out to the gas pumps to check yet again on the totals we owed.

Scotty and I drove home, neither speaking. She had viewed me as a foreigner, too, once I took "a native case," as she had termed it. Not a way to gain social acceptance, taking native cases, especially one which has the smells of gunpowder and sex and narcotics, the rude noise of sirens, closing off a man's breath.

Months ago Scotty had found us a condo at the Emerald Mines Golf Club. She had managed to get us a whiskey locker at the chalet in Misty Mountain. Success loomed. Then to her horror came this mountain girl shooting her husband who was, by my testimony, a drug addict and drug trader.

In Florida drugs were more commonly encountered than here. This mountainous place admittedly is in a backwash of present American culture. This county, for instance, doesn't as yet allow the sale of beer, wine, or any other alcohol, and there are no moonshiners here, either. I know because Fletch and Curtis, two friends from Florida, tried to buy a little moonshine for gifts. None about. There is no train or bus service up this way, no four-lane highways, no visiting artists or lecturers or statesmen, no greater excitement than the carnival tent circus occasionally to be seen just down the highway from Orchid Technical College, where Scotty's full-time maid is taking hairdressing courses. We learned that because she practiced on Scotty Bett and got her hair-dye formula wrong. Scotty was a redhead for one night. I found her to be pretty much the same otherwise, as I assured her next morning.

No local television station. No daily newspaper. No dope allowed. None of the polite Florida tittering acceptance of cocaine sniffing or pill popping, or even of marijuana smoking.

Not much crime up here either, which is another reason Winnette's trial is notorious. No murders in these neighboring four counties in ten years, since a man in his thirties lost his senses and shot his pretty wife and her parents and brother, then killed himself. One Sunday afternoon. He left a pot of water boiling on the stove, the aluminum pot melted and set up a smoke alarm that attracted neighbors. They found under the acrid smoke the last vestige of an immense drama.

One seeking social acceptance did not meddle with such cases, particularly if one is retired and doesn't need fees. One doesn't broach the wall between natives and us outsiders, such as Scotty and me. I regret this because the insiders are much more real to me just now, are defenders of English, Scotch–Irish, German customs ages old, and even though their defense mechanisms have been breached, have been shaken by mass movies and television and new modes, drugs among them, they are quite smart and decent people.

One of the old customs secured a man's rights to do as he pleased within his castle, and a woman's rights to obey. That's where some of the members of the jury would be starting out.

"That doctor is a slouch," I told Scotty. She was stretched out on our living room couch having a strong Scotch with a splash of Perrier. "He's scared to death, but he will testify."

"I didn't hear you even ask him, Mac, and I was sitting—"

"Last week I met with him at his office, since I have none." That absence of an office had become a bone of contention, because Scotty wanted to bounce back to Florida for our winters, and having an office and secretary would hold us here; Scotty was not, never has been a winter person. The fashionable ski resorts nearby at Banner Elk did interest her, but the idea of her and me taking up skiing did not. I drank some of my Scotch and soda, grimaced as always on first swallow, then let out a soothing ooohh.

"I do wish you wouldn't bother," she told me.

"Yes, I know," I said.

"We could travel."

"Yes, I know, Scotty."

"Instead of being here and trying to explain that common slut."

I threw most of my whiskey on her. It simply occurred to me as reasonable and necessary. It was not meant as an insult. Indeed, I then splashed some on my own head, too. It was an anointing. She complained not one word, either. The anointing was enough, said enough. The anointing said: Scotty, you have gone as far as you can go; now try to be delightful.

I slumped down in my usual armchair and felt around for the newspaper. She came closer to me, held her glass up to the light, measuring its icy, amber depths.

"I wouldn't do that," I told her.

"What?"

"I wouldn't do anything, really."

For about half a minute she teetered on the edge of her decision. By then it was all an old idea anyway, and she slipped back onto her couch and finished her drink, and then, of course, another one.

18

ANNE BAILEY:

Blue waited in the car. He was pouting because I was still on to him about testifying for Winnette. He did drive me over here, anyway. Usually at eight in the morning we're just getting out of bed, stumbling about looking for soap and towels and toothpaste, bumping into each other, listening to the radio news while we're trying to piece out the clean underthings and find the hair brush. He wants me to go make coffee. That seems woman's work. Don't get Blue started on what's woman's and what's man's work, not now, for he goes on and on and will make us both late. In this part of the world the old English virtues hold: a woman does the child bearing and child rearing and care of sick and laying out of the dead, the canning and freezing and cooking, the washing of clothes, the making and purchase and mending of clothes, the caring for small livestock, the working of the vegetable and flower gardens, and most work a shift at the textile mill. The men mend leaks in the roof. They cut firewood if their chainsaw will start. They hunt coon and fox and deer. They plow and drive pickup trucks. They also eat hot bread and meat at every meal, and they visit their woman whenever she's in the hospital—they stand in the room or in the hall outside most every night till the close of visiting hours.

This morning, Wednesday, we are already at the Crestview

Restaurant by eight. This is in Emerald Mines. I'm trying to talk Mr. C. C. Pickard, who manages Hudson-Belk Store, who eats here every morning, into letting me buy Winnette a frock. He's busy greeting the Emerald Mines businessmen, such as the insurance people, a banker, and the other members of the power echelon, those who don't have to be at work earlier than nine. I'm asking Mr. Pickard to leave his breakfast and let me pick out a dress for Winnette to testify in. He is eating country ham and eggs and is reading the *Asheville Citizen* and has the *Charlotte Observer* at hand. At his elbow steaming coffee stirs his senses, and he thinks he'll just lend me the key to the women's department. I can get anything in the store I want to, but I'll need to turn off the burglar alarms.

All this is to save his walking one hundred feet. "But it's not what I do of a morning, Anne," he told me, "not at this hour." So I wait. I select a table in the window and signal Blue to come on inside, and we have a country ham biscuit apiece and coffee, Blue complaining about the biscuit being a roll; it's not crumbly or sticky, either, not moist. "Used the wrong type of flour, I imagine," he told me. So he told the waitress, who was one of Cecil Frederick's daughters, told the tourists from Pennsylvania at the next table. Then he commenced laughing, pointing at a picture in a daily newspaper, one taken weeks ago. He showed it to me: Winnette was sitting beside Plover's coffin, and she was laughing. At least she was smiling. It was the most—most damaging picture imaginable and must have been taken at the funeral. "Mavis!" I exploded the word.

"Looks like Winnette enjoys the funeral," Blue said.

"Oh, my dear Lord. Blue, how on earth—"

"Don't you think for one minute this is a North Carolina biscuit," Blue told the tourists. "It's not with the proper flour. Some bread flour, or maybe cake flour. Or all-purpose."

While I was reading about "wife laughs over husband's corpse in Altamont County murder," he's ordering toast and a side order of sausage patties—not too well done—and a slice or two of a tomato "that's not been refrigerated all night."

I pick out a blue maternity dress for Winnette, one with a white collar, rather nurselike in effect. It was the most feminine maternity dress here. What she had worn yesterday was a rig she must have adapted, using a too-big dress, leaving the hem higher in front and making her look left over. Today of all days in her life she needed to look neat, cared for, maternal without being a ragtail plaything, women in the courtroom needed to identify with her.

"I'd put a shawl on her, if she'd wear it," I told Blue. "I'd make her a sort of nurse-nun."

There was a crush of people at Cookham jail. Ten will crowd the place, and there were more by many. It was nine o'clock, and her psychiatrist or psychologist, whichever, was in the cell with her, asking her questions like he wanted to do a book. I knew him slightly, a retired gentleman living in Misty Mountain, a friend of Mr. MacMillan. Winnette's a pretty piece of change and men do get attracted to her; he'd been over there about twenty visits.

Mr. MacMillan didn't want me to talk to her, except to say good morning and go. "You might make her nervous," he warned me, "this is her important day." He had also considered Winnette's clothes and had decided she should wear what she was most comfortable in; however, the psychiatrist looked over my gift and proudly showed it to Winnette. She fingered its new cloth and got acquainted, as a woman will, and she held it up before her body, and directly she slipped the old, stained one off over her head, caring little for privacy, and pulled this one on, the psychiatrist frozen in place—I suppose by his ethics. Then she looked just fine. And looked tailored and clean. I had got a size eight maternity, and it fitted her well enough, and the white collar gave her the puritan look, and her attorney went to see her and actually clapped his hands and came hurrying along the hallway to warm mine, thanking me, and then he let me go see her, led me to her, and I embraced the little thing so close I felt her heart beating like a drum was beating; I held her tight in my arms and swayed and even hummed to her.

"Consider the mystery of it," I told Blue. We were standing in line waiting for the courtroom door to be opened. "Here's a woman who wouldn't hurt a fly, yet the government, a vast organization, is prosecuting her for killing the one man she loved and tried to help."

"I can't find another copy of that newspaper with the picture in it, you know it?"

"Don't you care, Blue?"

"Yes, I prefer sitting at the back, so as if you're going to start crying again."

"Don't you care about what I said about the government?"

Blue stared at me, pleasantly mystified.

"Defense witnesses," I told the deputy, and we were directed like royalty to go to the front, like at a wedding, to set on the bench just behind Winnette's mourning seat, and Mr. MacMillan told me to call him Mac and please to pass notes to him as seemed necessary once Winnette's testimony began. He gave me a pink pad and a new Bic pen, and gave the psychiatrist a blue pad. Girl and boy pads, I told the psychiatrist, who sat beside me. Blue, himself, had no pad, because Blue was sitting off to himself, a few seats away.

The doors were opened. Maybe they were forced open. The press of people was heroic. The crowd flowed along the aisle, filling and overfilling, bantering and bargaining and fussing over seats, a chorus of howls going up. Babies began crying, one woman began crying. Chatting to old Blue-note, I asked what he thought she was crying out about with such hurt in her voice, and he said it might be she had never been given notoriety for killing her husband.

He winked at me, which was the only clue he offered to say he was joking. Otherwise, I'm so gullible I would have believed him. "Who goes first?" I asked him.

"Mac decides. Don't you, Mac?" he said, leaning forward toward Mr. MacMillan. "You still going to lead with Winnette?" he whispered to him, "before she gets scared? I recommend that, for if she goes into that protective coma, she might not come out in time."

19

WINNETTE:

I took the witness stand soon after ten A.M. and my voice trembled, even when I said my name.

"Any nicknames?" Mr. MacMillan asked from what he calls the bar.

"Usually I'm called by the full name of Winnette, not Winney. Even as a child I didn't like to answer to Winney."

"And your parents called you Winnette?"

"And my teachers. But my sister, Clara—I have one sister calls me Winney, time to time."

"Did you grow up locally?"

"Why, I'd think everybody would grow up locally, one place or another." I had not ever intended to be amusing, but everybody laughed, even Mr. MacMillan, and it did please me to think I might have been clever for once in my life. "I grew up near Mans Peak," I told him. "Never went more than seven miles away till I was fourteen, when Papa drove Mama and me to Asheville for the Lamar Lunsford's music festival." I answered a string of questions about age and my marrying at nineteen and divorcing at twenty. "Hal and I simply fell out of love," I told him, "once the dishes were all of them dirty." Mr. MacMillan was easy to talk to, had an encouraging manner, would smile and nod encouragingly, even seemed to bow, and he was polite as any gentleman.

I found myself rattling along about going to Appalachian State University for two terms, intending to become a teacher of history, and how at twenty-one my workmate at Silver Spur arranged for me to date her first husband, Lloyd Plover, who was older and was one of the supervisors of the plant. He and I began dating. By then I had transferred my studies to Orchid Tech and was thinking about teaching English, not history; I was working toward a teacher's certificate."

"And—are you at this time, today, under the care of a psychiatrist, Winnette?"

"Why, you ought to know I am. You put him onto me."

Laughter once more, general and friendly.

"Yes, I arranged it, didn't I?" Mr. MacMillan said.

"A friend of yours."

"For the record, you are under his care and we need to know his name, Winnette."

"Why it's Dr. James Clayton, and he's in the second row."

"Thank you. A formality. Has he given you—are you now under any medication?"

"Yes. He has prescribed Valium, but I don't take it."

"You don't take it?" Mr. MacMillan said, surprised.

"No. I don't take any drugs whatsoever, except aspirin for colds."

"You are or are not under the influence of any drug at the moment?"

"No. Nothin'."

"When did you last take Valium?"

"Dr. Clayton thinks I take it every day, but I never have taken it. He'll probably be mad with me," I said, frowning questioningly toward dear Dr. Clayton.

"He might well be," Mr. MacMillan said, and several jurors laughed. "But I am not, Winnette," he said, warmth coming into his voice each time he pronounced my name.

Dr. Clayton and Mr. MacMillan conferred in whispers, and then Mr. Mac said, "He wonders what you did with the pills."

"I'd rather not say."

"Why not?"

135

"Somebody would go to find them, and fall into a bad habit."

"Did you flush them down the toilet?"

"No. I couldn't."

"Why not?"

"There's only a potty." They laughed, several people did. I suppose whenever a bedpan is mentioned, there will be a certain amount of snickering. "I hid them."

"Very well, let's not continue that line of—"

Mr. Juicks got to his feet, asked to find out where I'd hid them; he'd have a bailiff go collect them now.

I told him they had been rolled away through a mouse hole in the wall, and he told a bailiff to go see about retrieving them.

"Who wants to be a mouse?" I asked, but only loud enough to amuse him and Mr. MacMillan.

Then I began to tell when and where I worked, how I began working beside Mavis, and how she and I talked intimately about marriage and boys and dating, and I asked her to arrange for me to go out with Plover, which she did, and he was breeding and selling Alsatians and they needed to be brushed and to have their pens cleaned and to have a rug apiece to sleep on, which Plover never could believe me when I told him, but I had money of my own, working—going to school nights wasn't expensive—and I bought three throw rugs from the wall-to-wall place and I was helping him find buyers for a litter of white Alsatians that he and I came to—to talk about more and more. I swear to you, the first date we had he didn't say more than twenty words, but once he got to know me he would take off talking on his own. And Blue could get him started, too. Blue is a friend."

"Is he present today?"

"And Ann Bailey. They could. Yes, they're both present."

"Did you and Lloyd Plover date often?"

"Yes. Came to be almost every night. He would drive me to Orchid Tech and come for me there after my classes."

"Did you begin to live with him?"

"My parents raised the dickens, but it's so. We moved in together to a new trailer of our own. This was near Mans Peak, near my parents. We paid fifty-fifty. Plover said he would pay for all of it, but at the time of signing he confessed he didn't want to invest so much cash. I didn't know it at the time, but he had been caught in Georgia one weekend before for possession of drugs—"

Mr. Juicks was so startled he about choked, and so was Mr. MacMillan surprised, so the two and Judge Blackington conferred.

"What drugs were they?" Mr. MacMillan asked me, resuming the questioning.

"Angel Dust I think. He traveled back and forth for two or three weeks after we bought the trailer, but I never knew specifically why he was gone."

"Wouldn't he say?"

"I don't know. Privacy was important to him. Plover was a very private person. He would not let anybody see his toothpaste tube or what men's shaving lotion he used. He volunteered what little he wanted known about himself."

"Was the trailer one you picked out, Winnette?"

"There was no picking out to it. There were fourteen. There were two sizes, wide and not-wide, and he wanted a not-wide. I picked out the colors. I hated the thought of living in a trailer, to be honest. It's not a home to me. All my life, up to Lloyd Plover, I've lived in a house."

"Did Plover sell drugs, Winnette?"

"He did later. Whether back then or not—yes, he must have back then, for he would go off on trips on weekends, and after we married he began to take me. He informed me a wife cannot testify against her husband. I would drive usually, and we would pick up marijuana and Angel Dust and who knows what, always at a drop point alongside a road. Let's say he would have an appointment with somebody. They might be waiting in a car for the pickup, or be standing down a posted trail. You probably know all about it."

"No, I don't know," he told me quickly, and people laughed.

"I didn't know back then, either. I was over twenty-one by a year's margin, but he told me I couldn't be tried as an adult, since he was the older one, so he'd send me to do the exchanges. I was the one told to open any doors first. It was exciting to me. Then at home I would help weigh out the marijuana or Angel Dust, putting small amounts in little plastic bags, the ones with the closure tops. He never did grow marijuana. So far as I ever heard, Plover was not a grower of anything. Simply, he never planted seeds or hoed weeds or farmed. He told me marijuana didn't hurt anybody. So far as I knew back then, that's all he used; this was when we married, that and Angel Dust, which he began using, too, and wanted me to use."

"Where did you, Winnette, find the roads on which to buy the—the marijuana and the Angel Dust?"

"Virginia, near the big college up there."

"Yes. In Georgia did you say—"

"No, he didn't go into Georgia, once he was—had been arrested there—"

"South Carolina?"

"Yes. We went there, too. I helped him, because if I didn't he would go into a pout, or cuss me out till I was smaller than a mouse."

Just then came the sound of a board and nails being pulled free off of somewhere, and this made all of us laugh. "They're collecting the Valium," the judge said.

"If he had any reason to go into a rage, he'd not come out of his sulk for days. It was easier to do as he wanted. After we married he was even more insistent on my doing as he said, and if I didn't he would cuss me out and once he beat me up till I was silly. He slapped me silly with his open hand, or hit me in the belly, kicked me—"

"Before we go into that further, Winnette—tell us first, did you and Plover live together consistently?"

"No, not before we married. I'd leave in frustration, and maybe soon as he sobered up I'd go back. Living with Plover was an up and down experience, let me tell you, and was exciting. Sometimes when we were at the courting stage, he would tell me to leave. He would just say to go and that he'd tell me when to come back. Why he did that or where he went, or what happened wasn't for me to know. Once on a Saturday, he said, 'Get out of my sight till Monday.' That was the message. That time I could

138

tell he was on Angel Dust and alcohol and was past talking to. I left quick whenever he told me to. I never packed nothin."

"Did you drink alcoholic drinks with him or take drugs?"

"I tried everything, but I usually acted like I was taking them, and I'd put it down the drain. Then when he wanted to marry me, he promised me I'd not have to take drugs with him, nor go collect drugs, nor weigh them out, and I wouldn't have to talk about drugs on the phone, nothin'."

"Did he keep his promise?"

"He did. He kept it for the first month. When he combined drugs, he wasn't—didn't do anythin' he didn't want to. Mostly he would cuss me out. I might not'a done a thing on earth—"

"Do you—can you give us an example?"

"One day—you don't want to know the date, do you?"

"No."

"It was just after we married. He had been drinking peach brandy all day. There's a friend makes it even yet, and he gives it to friends. He won't sell it. He told Blue and Plover he's allowed legally to give it away. Plover drank all he'd been given and was also doing speed. It's a drug that will—will pick a person up. After Blue went home Plover couldn't find his address book. It's the one I gave him for Christmas when we were living together, a leather one from London. He kept it in his shirt pocket. I was looking for it all over the house, under the seat pillow, on the sofa, for I sometimes dropped pills away down there instead of swallowing them and didn't want him looking there himself, and under the table and in his jacket pockets. I was hurrying, because he was getting angry and was blaming me, said I'd hid it. He was in the spare room, and I wouldn't go in there where the guns were, but from the hallway I admitted—he called me and I went to the door, Mr. MacMillan, and he picked up an army officer's rifle, a small carbine, and shot it four times. I ran out of the house. I hid in the woods. There had been a car with two men waiting in the yard, and they drove off. I guess the shooting got to them. I hid for hours, and when I returned he was asleep, and when he woke up he never remembered shooting."

"Are you sure he did not?"

"I believed him, Mr. MacMillan. He said I had made up the story and it wasn't true, and when I showed him the bullet holes in the walls, he had to believe me, but he told me he just didn't—couldn't see himself doing shooting like that."

"Where was the address book, Winnette?"

"I don't know. He had it, probably was where he'd left it."

"In his pocket?"

"No, not his shirt pocket. It could have been in a pants pocket. There were other times he couldn't remember later on. I think he never remembered shooting the Alsatian puppy that whined."

On and on I went, unweaving my life stories, my two to three years off and on with Plover, part in love, part in awe; to think so strange a life could be lived, not any more real than dreams. "So much was in a drug or alcohol haze," I told Mr. MacMillan. I was easy with the stories, could talk to him easy. "Then one night coming home I ran off the road into a ditch near the house, and he had to come and help me back the car onto the road, and he was high. He saw the paint was scratched on the passenger's side, and he cussed me out, and once we got into the house, he choked me."

"How long did he choke you?"

"I lost consciousness, that's all I remember."

"And even so, you stayed with him?"

"Yes."

"Why?"

"I wonder, myself. Trying to help him get well. Doctor Robbins said Plover was ill. I asked him if a wife could help her husband when he gets ill in this way. Plover was in the hospital and Dr. Robbins promised me he would not release him till he found out what the devils were that were inside his brain—"

"Devils?"

"That's what Mama said they are. And Dr. Robbins said he would find out for me, but he never cured him. He took blood tests and scanned his brain, thinking he might have a brain tumor, and they couldn't find anythin' wrong. Then when he came home, he had drugs they had actually prescribed for him, and he was off on all sorts of their drugs before I knew it."

140

"Heroin?" MacMillan asked.

"I don't think so. He didn't have heroin."

"In your opinion, what drugs did he use?"

"Pot. That's marijuana. PCP. LSD. Then, finally, cocaine. LSD is halluc—halluciatory. Is that a word?"

"Anything else?"

"Speed. Amphetamines was what he first started on he told me. It wasn't pot he started on, like ever so many people do. He started using pills his mother was taking, or his ill sister. He bought Quaaludes, Valium, Librium, a lot of different trade name downers."

"Did he get them on prescription?"

"Not, not usually. Cocaine he snorted through a rolled-up dollar bill. He inhaled it. He breathed it into his nose first, then inhaled it."

"Did you try it?"

"No. Only once, twice."

"Did he not insist?"

"I told him I wanted to have our baby and the drugs would hinder me."

"Was that something he approved of?"

"Plover's eyes would tell me whenever he was drugged, when he was out of reach, maybe he had got too much, or had taken a bad lot of a drug, or was combining too many drugs. His eyes would actually change color. Whenever that happened I would have to please him somehow or leave, for he would be irrational. Whenever I had to I would leave, but one time he caught me before I got the car out of the yard and dragged me to the house by my coat; I was slid into my own house, and there he stripped me naked and forced me. You know."

"To have sex with him?"

"To have different sex—to have certain types of sex with him."

"Why did you stay with him?"

"I loved him."

Somebody in the back of the room laughed, then a nervous titter went through the room, then quiet at last. Most people never laughed at all. "I was certain love would help cure him."

No laughter this time at all.

"I thought I would learn his moods," I told them.

"And was there still the hope for a baby?"

"My mother said a baby might cure Plover." I shrugged, helpless now at so wasted, wasting a thought, and the same back-of-the-room man laughed again, but this time alone. Was it Blue laughing, I wondered. No, I decided not. One can never tell about him.

"There were times he was better, then times he was worse. He often told me not to leave him, that I was his only handhold."

"And you believed that?"

"He knew he was ill. After he beat me, I showed him the bruises on my own body, and he cried like a child. He never meant them. He had dragged me by my hair and tore and bruised me, was so frightened he called his parents, had me stay there, and I was at their home all day and two nights being treated for cuts and bruises and scratches, so many you wouldn't believe, and his parents both doctored me, and his sister did all she could, too, and then I left them, went to stay at my parents' home, out of sight till my hair started growing again."

I told about finding out I was pregnant, how pleased I was, which had seemed to please Plover, too. "We both saw it as a way to improve our marriage."

"Did you ever hold a gun on Mr. Plover?" Mr. MacMillan asked finally.

"No. Never."

"Never aimed one at him?"

"No. Never. Until the last day when I shot him."

"Did he believe you had held a gun on him?"

"So he told people."

"How was that—did that come about?"

"There was one evening when he was away from the house. He had to go get something somewhere. A strange car arrived, pulled up into the yard and the three men just sat there. They must have been waiting for Plover to make a delivery. They didn't blow their horn, but they drove closer and closer, and revved their motor and kept the highway lights on. Sounded like they were going to drive into the house. From the doorway of the spare room I could pick up a pistol, and I took one and—it was the one kept loaded, Plover had promised me—only one. I laid it on the table. By the time Plover got back, the men had driven away, but the pistol was there, and before I could tell him why, he thought it was because I was going to shoot him, and he waved the pistol around, not at me, but generally everywhere, and I ran into the woods, and he came looking. It was dark, and he had the pistol. I could see him. And the dogs were in their lot barking. He came close enough for me to hear him breathe. Then he went on off, but he let one of the dogs out, and it my favorite, Snow White, and she came to me, and he ordered me back into the house. I obeyed straight enough. This was before I was pregnant. And he came following, once he put the dog up, and he made me confess to all manner of things, such as having the gun on the table to shoot him, and planning to kill him, all the while waving the pistol and making me do—do stunts for him, entertain him." I was tired now, the weight of the memories was heavy as lead. "I was pregnant when he—he beat me. The pregnancy, the baby, has to be remembered. I was so cut, and my hair was bleeding at my scalp, and I was bleeding from inside, so he took me to his parents' house for cleaning up and doctoring. He told me to stay there till he came back, then he left—so much for me, I suppose. Soon as I could I went to my parents'."

"You were frightened?" Mr. MacMillan asked.

"I was, yes. And in pain all over." I was so weary now, as if in a sleep. Even our voices seemed to me to be far off.

"For your life? And for the baby's life?"

"Yes," I heard myself say.

"How far along was the baby?"

"Oh, I don't recall."

"It was just underway?"

"It was after my missing a second—a second—"

"Period?"

"Yes." There was more noise of a wooden plank being pulled

143

free, the nails screeching, from somewhere in the building, and that served to relieve the tension and brought me a ways back to alertness.

"Mrs. Plover, was Mr. Plover working at this time?"

"Which time?"

"The time you realized you were pregnant?"

"No."

"He had been fired from his job?"

"Allowed to resign."

"And he—that is, you were working?"

"When I left him and went to my parents', I was in such a state, missing so much hair, bruised and cut, and my nerves were— irregular. So Mr. Starnes let me go on part-time."

"Before you left Mr. Plover as his wife, you were the only one of the two of you working?"

"He had his business, of course. He called it a business. He would tell me I was trying to ruin his business, that I was hanging up the phone on his customers. Then, too, he would make money trading guns. He could go out on Saturday morning with two pistols and come back by noon with two other pistols and a shotgun, or he would buy a gun for a hundred dollars and sell it for a hundred fifty."

"The trading accounted to what proportion of Mr. Plover's income?"

"I don't know."

"His drug trading was important to him at the time, for income?"

"Oh my, yes."

"Do you know Mavis Plover?"

"Yes."

"She is a friend?"

"She and I are close friends. She was the one who was first married to Plover and understood what I was going through. With her, however, he had gone off more on alcohol, more than drugs."

"Was she beaten by him?"

"She told me she was. When she was pregnant, he shot her in the belly with a BB gun and beat her with a belt—it was on her

144

back, not her stomach. She told me she had once been ordered to sit in the bathtub and he filled it with water and he had held her under the water, to make her promise to do as he told her."

"Which she said was what?"

"With Plover it could have been most anything. I don't know how to say."

"She never told you?"

"You'll need to ask her that. She's here. I see her now, this minute."

No sooner was she mentioned than she tried to hide from sight, and moments later she left her seat, a child in each hand, and her heels could be heard on the stairs as she descended. She went on down to the main floor hall and we heard her heels even there, as she left the building.

The judge laughed, then so did Mr. Juicks and Mr. MacMillan and others, and it seemed funny to me, too, Mavis leaving that way, that noisily.

Once the laughter was done, Mr. MacMillan said to me, "Winnette, let me see if I have it all straight. There was a period of courtship, during which you and Lloyd Ernest Plover lived together off and on.

"The next phase is marriage. You bought a house. You lived together as man and wife, comfortable in the relationship except for infrequent assaults on you by Plover during drug-taking. Then after a painful assault, you left him, lived with your parents, saw a doctor to let your body and mind heal. That concluded the first phase of the marriage. You were at your parents' home, you were about six weeks pregnant—"

"I thought I'd lost my baby, but Doctor Robbins decided I hadn't."

"You had not lost your baby, were again considering giving up your job—"

"And it seemed the idea of abortion got smaller and smaller, the baby not being dead. If it had been dead, as I expected, I was ready to accept that, but after surviving Plover in his worst stormy night, the baby and I were more together, the baby and I were the survivors together. The idea of my doing to it what its father had not done . . ." It was most difficult for me to think this through, even yet.

"You had no money saved, did you?"

"Whatever I had was ours together, and he'd buried it away somewhere."

"You didn't have bank accounts?"

"We had a checking account, but he never used it except to sign checks I drew up for the electric company and Southern Bell. Not much money in it. He didn't want anybody to know his cash flow, as he called it. Of course, that was smart, for he had to pay in cash for drugs, and sell for cash, too. As his business grew—"

"Did it grow?"

"I think it might have, though when he was almost arrested in South Carolina, the sheriff began to watch him. That meant Plover didn't dare carry drugs himself, or go where people were known to use drugs, or associate with drug people."

"Why did you go back to your marriage, to Mr. Plover?"

"I ast myself that ever day since the—the death. I say, it would have been better not to."

"Why did you do it?"

"I'd married him, was his wife. I was carrying his baby."

"Was he threatening you, provided you did not?"

"My sister says she was often threatened, and my father said he was driven off the road. My mother was scared of Plover. My sister was followed, and she got so she wouldn't travel at night."

"Followed by Plover?"

"Sometimes. Sometimes not. He knew how to take out contracts, don't you know?"

"Did he—take out contracts, to your knowledge?"

"He would say how much a contract to kill somebody cost. It varied by place and for different types of people. He was not a criminal in most ways, but had acquaintances—you know, people also in the drug business. He was offered one contract to carry out, but he never negotiated it."

"Did he threaten you?"

"No."

"Anybody else near, close to you?"

146

"My doctor, for instance. He was all worked up about him, Plover was, and Mr. Starnes at the plant. He threatened him. Any man who was at all nice to me."

"Was he worked up because of the baby, or because of you, or—"

"The baby worried him, Anne Bailey told me—that I had his baby inside me. Maybe it was that I had a hold on him. He knew he had not been a proper father to Mavis's two, and he wanted to avoid any further obligation he couldn't do well."

"So why did you go back to him?"

"He ast me to. He came right up to my booth at Hardee's while I was eating 'A Better Breakfast'—my mother burns eggs and bacon. And he didn't even sit down, but stood above me, sort of above me, yet several feet away. I looked up and saw he was not drugged up, so I wasn't the least bit afraid, and he ast me would I consider coming back to him, and I said yes, I'd need to consider it carefully, being married to him and pregnant, and he ast me to name my terms, any terms I wanted, and I became engrossed in that."

"What were they, the terms?"

"I had so many I don't recall all of them. No more drinking or drugs at all. That was the main one. No more shooting guns. Have to put all the guns away. No more going away without explaining. And no more hurting the dogs. And so forth. I had a frying pan with a Teflon coating and he wasn't to use it, for he had scratched it twice mixing the dogs' platters in it."

"And what was his response?"

"He said, tell me what else you want. That surprised me and was a promising sign, don't you agree? And after a while, when honestly I couldn't think of anything else, he said well all right, then? And I said maybe. Lord knows why. But it was my house, too, Mr. MacMillan, it was my furniture and rug and dishes and hope of a home and a sane husband, and he had hopes for all that, too, and without my going back neither one of us would have the hope left."

"Did your parents advise you to go back?"

"Lord, no. Papa's here, ast him. Papa said never to come visit, said he'd mark me down for lost and unfound. My sister, Clara, cried like a baby and begged me not to. Mavis said not to go, that she would consider it an insult personally. Anne told me not to go. My doctor—I still was being treated deep inside myself, and Dr. Robbins's nurse in the office, and Mr. Starnes at Silver Spur . . ."

Mr. MacMillan was now this side of the bar, was several steps closer to me. "So you were cut off from all supporters, were you, Winnette?"

"I was—so lonely I couldn't have sung even a hymn. That was another item on the list, Mr. MacMillan, that I wouldn't be required to sing."

"You did go back fully expecting this time to work out the marriage?"

"Yes."

"And Plover was agreeable?"

"He was."

"You and he made up."

"Like love birds we were."

"He welcomed you."

"Yes."

"He loved you."

"Several times."

"And made love, the two of you. I understand. He got rid of the guns?"

"He showed me they were all unloaded and locked up, and he had a lock on the spare room door, and the bullets were gone. He told me he had to have one pistol to protect me with, since he was dealing with lawbreakers, people crazy on alcohol and cocaine and uppers and downers. He assured me he would not use that one pistol in the house. And he swore never to strike me again."

"So really, Winnette, as time went by he did not do what he promised."

"No. For a while he did keep the bullets locked up. They were not in the house. He couldn't keep them in the car, for he was stopped twice in Yancey County and searched, and he was afraid what they'd think of all those bullets and shells, like maybe he was a Nazi Party, or a Klan, or something else crazy, way out, which he was not. Plover was not for or against anything. You can ast Blue; he's sitting back there. Plover was a supporter of what's accepted as modern. He was a loyal citizen of whatever the country is. He wants to be liked."

Several people laughed, and the judge twisted in his chair, annoyed with them, frowning threats.

Mr. MacMillan said, "Your Honor, she's tired, and I'm tired, and since it's eleven-thirty could we take a break before we go into the final questions with her?"

I listened to them, half-asleep from weariness, weary to my own grave seemed like to me, tired of recalling the drumrolls. It had been my claim that Plover had dreamed the dream of home and family, too, but had he? At least, occasionally. Now and then. Never, not in the way it was with me—my breath and bones for which I would suffer any scars, bruises, pain. Hunger for home was fierce with me, but was it ever fierce with him? It was myself he wanted, not a home, but even in that he liked to humble me, to see himself reflected in my fear. My consenting. My humiliation. Then see me grateful for his releasing me. Sitting there on the hard seat, I decided I had lied in my testimony, but only in being more considerate of Plover than the truth. He had never been able to be a good husband or father, for he was strung from the old catguts, was too slack a man, saw tenderness as unmanly and was afraid of it. No, he never took the guns away and never had intended to, nor did he do any other promises well. Also, I had not told the full truth about going back to Plover. Some of the truth had to do with a desire to be held the way he holds me, and the way he makes my own desires flow, my heart to pound, my muscles to tighten into tension and then, all at once all over my body, flex and let go. I wanted to be owned again, possessed by a man uncompromisingly male. God knows, I didn't want to be pistol whipped, but I did want Plover again, to be his. Maybe I would not be his wife so much as his woman. That was a matter beyond me. I wanted Plover to be mine again, even in the way he required, which is for me to be his without restraint, self-sacrificingly, my own body accepting his, my life accepting his, agreeing to harbor and nurture his, him, and ask of him the pleasure of giving myself to him. I had not said that, was ashamed of it. So, in a way my testimony had to be forgiven in part. But that was only one of my secrets.

They were still arguing about whether to stay out for lunch, as Mr. MacMillan wanted, or come back in fifteen minutes for a brief session, then break again at one o'clock, this time for lunch. The judge finally decided. He sent the jury out for lunch, with the admonishment not to talk among themselves or to others.

None of the jurors looked at me; as they left the courtroom they appeared to be on a plane apart, or were unable to admit their power over me.

Mr. MacMillan was asking the judge about where he and I could eat lunch. The local restaurant was not private enough for the judge to let me go there. Somewhere outside the building, Mr. MacMillan begged, somewhere in the sun.

"Yes, but she can't leave the yard of the courthouse," the judge said.

I watched the judge during all this, but he would not look at me.

Once in recess, would I became visible? I am a piece of luggage to be disposed of only under the law. I am not to him a human being who eats her lunch in a café, but a legal entity. Does an entity eat lunch? Does it eat food or devour its own number?

My father came as close as the lawyer's bar and offered to bring me a bacon, lettuce, and tomato sandwich, knowing how I favored them. "With mayonnaise?" I asked him, and he hurried away to get it, pleased to have a chore. Dear Papa, I never knew him to wrong anyone. He harbored his dissents, too, was not given to arguing. When Plover and I took up living together, he objected reasonably, briefly. Mama scolded me, too, and she went on and on about it, even though I had told her this was the way many young people lived today. Papa never said another word to me but must have bit his tongue. Sis said he asked her not to follow my example. "I can't stand it if you do, too," he told her, which she accepted as his confession of love, father to daughter.

Mr. MacMillan selected a place on the courthouse side steps, in the full sun, for him and me and the woman deputy, and Mr.

MacMillan even had to move over to give His Honor room to use the steps. His Honor stopped to chat about the breeze, the fact that sunlight can cause skin cancer, the fact that his grandmother had worn a bonnet or wide-brim hat whenever she had gone out of the house. "And she never drank alcohol," he told me, even then not looking directly at me, the helpless accused, "not till she was past bearing age, then she lapped it up pretty heavy. Nowadays you read medical reports about alcohol affecting babies, even if drunk at time of conception." He was talking to me, but only in spare glimpses did he look at me, as if he wanted to remain outside my influence, or even from knowing me, so that in the final hour he could without qualms say to the bailiff and deputies, "take her away, whoever she is." He was talking about Altamont County having the lowest percentage of alcoholics in the country. "Then, now, we have this dope coming in."

Max saw me first, and he and sweet dumb little sister Kathy came to join us, too. Several teenage girls approached tentatively, guardedly, and from twelve feet away asked Mr. Mac if I would give them my autograph. He said it was all right under the law, it was up to me. I didn't know what on earth to write, so I just wrote my name and home address, as if maybe they would want to write me sometimes. One girl asked me to sign the newspaper picture of Plover and me, and I refused. It was that strange picture Mavis had taken at the funeral, more or less by accident. Mr. Mac saw the picture and clouded over like a summer storm and asked me where it had come from.

The woman deputy gave Max a harsh look, but harsh looks don't influence Max. He went so far as to ask a man, a visitor, to borrow his umbrella, and with that he shaded me, stood beside me exactly like an Indian-from-Asia in colonial days. Embarrassing, but pleasing. And what a creative, dear gesture. It proved that Mavis hadn't alienated me with Max and Kathy. I sat in the shade eating the sandwich Papa brought and signing my name and address on lined school sheets, on napkins, on scrap slips "borrowed" by the girls from the register of deeds' office. His Honor returned, striding swiftly, coughing bits of food out of his throat, spitting and casting a glancing smile and nod at Mr. Mac. I began to gather up our trash. Mr. Mac had eaten nothing. He had asked his wife to bring him a milkshake, if one could be found, "with a raw egg in it," he had told her. But two other women detained her in conversation and she never got as far as being out of sight; I knew there were no milkshakes hereabouts, anyway. Mr. Mac and I went up the stairs to the main doors, walked side by side, he touching my arm by accident, drawing his hand away quickly, then to my surprise he took my hand, stopped me, looked kindly at me and told me please not to hold back while telling of my last day with Plover.

We reached our bench, where Max already sat. "Did you give the gentleman back his umbrella?" I asked him.

"Mr. Crawford's is all it was," he told me.

"Where's your mother?"

"Hiding in the library, Kathy says, across the street."

"Where's Kathy?"

"I don't know."

By one o'clock people were seated and waiting. Judge Blackington took his high place, the jury filed in, and I was ushered forward to the witness box. In my mind was the fluttery picture of Max hovering over me, shading me with the plumbing contractor's umbrella. He's so unlike his father, I thought.

So like his mother, shading me as long as she could bear the pain. To thine own self be true, And it must follow, as the night the day, Thou cans't not then be false to any man. Polonius. *Hamlet,* Act one, Scene three. I played the part in the eleventh grade for Mrs. Goforth's class, which only had five boys in it. She wanted me to say the lines with force, and so I did, for no doubt Polonius believed in them. Not I. Never made any sense to me. And now Mavis was hiding across the way, nursing her wounds, including self-inflicted ones, but all the while she was being true to herself. I had told Mrs. Goforth that Shakespeare wrote a number of parts for clowns, and maybe Polonius was a version of one of those; Polonius's other lines were also babblings, seemed to me. She was offended by the suggestion.

"Better turn on the ceiling fans," Judge Blackington ordered.

Mr. Mac came just in front of the bar to address me. He said my name using special kindness, but Mr. Juicks objected to his coming even that close to the witness box and asked the judge if attorneys could approach the box—was this Florida he asked. So Mr. Mac retreated, took his place near where little Max and now Kathy sat huddled.

"Mrs. Plover, Winnette, please do tell us what happened on the day of the fatality, Winnette."

"All of it?"

"All of it," he said.

"There's some of it that is shameful," I admitted. I was particularly wary of what the children might hear.

"You let the court worry about decorum, Winnette."

He began by asking about my house, what pieces of furniture, was there a bed in the storage room, such easy facts he wanted to know, and pretty soon we were chatting along, Mr. Mac and me, and the courtroom was away off out there, seemed like, was a foreign element that was allowed to witness us. "A mattress lay on the floor for Max and Kathy to use," I told him.

"What else was in the room?"

"Rifles and shotguns, and a dresser drawers full of pistols in socks. I never went in there, except to vacuum, and whenever the children visited I'd put a fitted sheet on their mattress. I had extra sheets for their mattress. Theirs was a double, and our bed was a queen. Their bed had its own Cannons."

"Cannons?" Mr. Mac said, surprised.

"Cannon sheets," I told him.

At once people all laughed, even little Max and Kathy, but it was a supportive sound, came as welcome to me. Then Mr. Mac asked what—activity had preceded the shooting, and I was willing to try to tell him. He had no idea how difficult—I had not told anybody the most of it, and was about underway when I was stopped and another attorney conference—an argument ensued, and at its close I was asked to step down.

20

MR. MACMILLAN:

There are risks one has to take. She was in fine fiddle, ready to go forward with the testimony, when a slip of paper was handed to me saying the Chapel Hill doctor had arrived. I had subpoenaed him. He had another court appearance this afternoon and wanted to leave in half an hour. He had come all that way, some four hours by car, and it was simply good manners for me to put him on the stand at once. After all, nobody knew how long Winnette would require.

She took her seat without a murmur, and appeared to become interested in his testimony. He was a kindly and dignified person; the two traits are not often associated in officials these days, although once they were. His qualifications were unimpeachable, including Ivy League education and studies here and there in legal medicine. He had his doctorate in pharmacology, and thus far in his life this dapper fellow had performed autopsies on 14,950 corpses. That one fact was so astonishing to Winnette that she rose to her feet, the marvel lifted her and the two children. All of us stared in open astonishment at the dear doctor, as if he were straight off of Mars.

He told us in utterly competent fashion about the drugs he had looked for in among the organs of Lloyd Ernest Plover.

"Among the barbiturates are phenobarbital and Nembutal. We

examine for Doriden and other drugs. Methaqualone, and in addition other organic bases similar to it and to other drugs. Cocaine, we look for, that and its metabolites. In the case of the tests on the late Lloyd Ernest Plover, results were negative except for cocaine and methaqualone. We determined there was half, that is one-half a milligram of methaqualone in the blood sample; methaqualone has slang names, among them ludes and sophor. As for the cocaine, I could not determine the amount, and it might have been a metabolite instead of cocaine. The living body will retain cocaine for about one hour. During that time it changes into its metabolite, which name is benzoyl ekonine. Eventually the benzoyl ekonine disappears. In other words, the living body throws off cocaine rapidly."

Mr. Juicks, once he questioned him, wanted him to say cocaine was found in prescription medicines. I suppose this would make Plover legitimate, but the doctor wouldn't agree, except for certain eye drops, which amused me thinking of our Mr. Plover using eye drops.

On my next round of questions I had a bit of sport with that. "Doctor, how many eye drops would be required to leave a half milligram residue of cocaine in a man's body?"

"Even if he bathed in it, Mr. MacMillan, he would not reach—"

Mr. Juicks asked for a meeting. Yet again we gathered at the bench, we happy three, where this time Blackington feigned indifference to Juicks's current pain. "Oh, hell," he murmured, "this is a Thursday, it's two o'clock, getting on. One more workday to go. I imagine the jury is also thinking about plans for the weekend."

The witness testified further that if a person such as L. E. Plover took of methaqualone in a dose of 300 or 400 or 500 milligrams, then in an hour the amount would be down to about what we found. "The finding does indicate that he was before death using the drug, but no test will reveal how much was taken."

"Is methaqualone an upper or downer?" I asked him.

"It's a sedative, a depressant. Today most people use Valium instead, or Dalmane."

Juicks could not dare accept Plover as a drug user, in spite of all the evidence. His questions showed he thought of him using one sleeping pill—something on that order.

"By the time of the examination, it's true that equivalent was what remained," the doctor told him.

Juicks wondered if this sleeping pill might have been prescribed for Plover by some doctor. Juicks seemed to want proof it had *not* been prescribed. By the time he was through, two-fifteen, a break was called, and it was two-thirty by the time the witness had departed, the fluttering of papers had ceased, and I was able to ask Winnette to take the stand once more.

She was now somewhat distant from reality, was nostalgic, no doubt having been dragged into considerations of Plover's drug taking. Once she was back in the witness box, I began by asking her if he had supported her in the house redecorating activities. I asked if he was handy about the place, as men often are. I asked her about the kitchen curtains, their patterns and color, seeking out matters of interest to her which would relax her and give her confidence; I was seeking the chatty relationship she and I had enjoyed earlier.

"Where did you shop for such items?"

"I went to sales and drove with Anne or Mavis out to the discount warehouses. I remember buying at a yard sale a log-cabin quilt, which Mavis and I draped over the doorway to the spare room; I would place a stool on its bottom hem, to help hold it in place, and this was to keep the draft down, for we didn't heat or air-condition that room except should the children stay overnight."

"Was there a back porch?" I inquired, turning my back on Juicks and his signs of irritation.

"Yes, but it was mostly for the parts to the motorcycle, and for muddy boots and such, and had only one chair on it."

"As I recall, you and Anne were cleaning on this Saturday morning, while Plover was working outdoors."

"He was working on the dog lot with Carvel Morrison, who was hired for the day. Plover usually went away on Saturdays, but was taking time to help fence a dog lot, as promised since before I came back to him, and Anne Bailey and I went out there to see how big it was to be. They were laying out the fencing. You see, I wanted it long, for running, and Plover was not caring, so I ast him to make it bigger by at least ten more feet, to make it twenty-five feet, and that set him off to cussing, and I asked Anne Bailey back at the house did you notice the slur in his speech. I said it was noticeable to me and was a bad sign. You see, Mr. Mac, at the dangerous times his speech would slur and then, too, he might begin to stutter once the drugs were tightening on him, and his eyes would glass over. As I saw it, the drugs would tighten on his brain, keep closing until he couldn't think straight, nor remember."

"Then he and the worker—how long had they been working?"

"Over an hour about."

"And Plover, in your opinion, was taking drugs. Do you know what kind?"

"No. Being a dealer he had various kinds, and he would try them out."

"And some would not be pure in manufacture?"

"I'd guess they were not always pure. They were whatever came to him."

"What time did you and Anne Bailey—"

"Visit the dog lot? Oh, ten o'clock. Anne's here, and she would recall. We had been cleaning away and stopped for a cup of coffee, except Anne takes tea, so I took tea, and we were in the kitchen stirring in the sugar when Plover came in. He used the front door even with his muddy boots, even though we had just vacuumed, and I ast him what he wanted to drink, if anything, and he never answered. So, I gave him a kiss on his cheek and pressed against him, joking with him, trying to get a smile, but he ignored me. He went back outside, and I decided it was worrying time for me. It was testing time, to see if he would become dangerous, if my—my efforts were worthwhile."

"Had he not taken drugs during the period between your return to him and this day?"

"Plover mostly took alcohol during that time. I'd see him drinking, and maybe a maintenance dose of drugs. He might need something merely to be average of a day. It was beyond me as to

157

that, but this morning he was going on over the line, and it only ten or eleven o'clock in the morning."

"I see."

"So Anne and me talked about going to her house, but she said Blue was there and wouldn't cooperate with us against Plover. So we talked about finishing up the cleaning and going to Marion to shop, but before we decided what to do, Plover came indoors once again. He was the least bit staggering. You know how a drunk man might need to place his foot just right, out before him. I didn't smell any alcohol, but he looked like a person who has been drinking and doesn't feel well. I asked him could I fix him some canned onion soup. He likes that when he's coming off a hangover from drinking, but he never replied, so Anne and I went to the clothes dryer to see if the children's sheets were dry yet, and when we got them out and put back on the mattress, and got the quilt back over the doorway, he was still in the kitchen, and when we came in there he went—"

"Where was the washing machine?" Mr. Mac asked.

"In the bathroom."

"Go on."

"He went into the bedroom, our room. I told Anne we better escape while we could and to park her car on the road and I'd run out the back, come through the woods. It was my plan to stay away overnight. She was arguing with me about running out this way, when he calls me back to the bedroom. Anne advised me to tell him the time of day, so to speak, remind him of his promises. So, anyway, I went back there and he was propped up on pillows. He pulled me onto the bed beside him and seemed to want to be—comfortable with me, and he said he appreciated my washing the kids' sheets, and I said they had needed it, and he said I had been a second mother to them and they needed that, and they needed a father, too. He said he wasn't going to be like his own. He said he wished he had learned more in school so he could be a desk man. He said he knew I had tried to please him, and that he wanted me to know he realized this. He never said he loved me, Mr. MacMillan, but he did talk around saying it, and he was gentle with his rubbing and holding me, which was pleasing to

158

me. Then he said he wanted me to get Anne out of the house so we could make love. I found her in the living room waiting for me to tell her what to do, and I told her to go help outdoors for half an hour, then we'd go to the trade lot in Marion, so she went outdoors, and I locked the front door and hurried into the bedroom and took off my clothes and managed to pull off Plover's jeans, and we were preparing to make love when the telephone rang. He got up and answered the telephone. All he got to say was hello. That's all I heard him say. The telephone is there in the hall, near the bedroom doorway. Some man's voice was talking to him a blue streak, and then the voice hung up, and Plover came back, cussing a blue streak, and he slapped at me once I tried to embrace him. He said I had betrayed him. That was the word. I had put his business in jeopardy, was forcing him to use the streets. I had told people what he had been doing, so now the cops were onto him. 'They'll be digging me out of here any day now.' He got up and began pacing the room and cussing, and he kept saying the same things. I told him I didn't understand and hadn't done it, and he said, 'I'll show you.' He picked up my panties and tried to find the crotch and he poked his finger through it and ripped it out, as if he had a finger in my—my—in me, and another finger in my—it's not easy to talk about this—"

"Your rectum?"

"And he pulled it all out, the division. And he threw the torn panties aside and went into the spare room and came back with his pistol and said he would splatter my damn brains. He held the gun against my forehead. He waved it around. He was acting like a desperate drunk man and was gasping for breath he was so angry, and he said to tell him the truth. He said he wouldn't kill me after all, but to get out of his house, then he said no, he would go, instead, would leave me, that was the way, but he would kill me later, within so many days. 'What day is this?'

"Saturday," I told him.

"By—by Saturday. Is this Saturday, is it?" he asked, stuttering and slurring words.

"Yes."

"Then by . . . Saturday, Sunday . . ."

"Monday comes next," I said.

"By Monday you'll be dead. Now if you tell me the truth, I'll move out and everything will be OK, but if you don't, I'll move out and by . . . by . . ."

He forgot Monday. I didn't dare help him again. He began walking about; of course he was still naked. He cocked the pistol and aimed it at me, then he waved it about and raved that I had betrayed him and was putting his business on the street. Then he sort of forgot about me and worried aloud about somebody coming along directly. My stomach growled and he noticed me and told me he remembered promising not to hit me, but this time I had gone too far. So then he slapped me across the side of the head. He slapped me on the other side of my face, this time using the knuckle side. This was the only time he had struck me since we remarried, or whatever, and never had he hit me twice that way. I wondered if even living till Monday was going to happen to me. He then told me to lean over the bed with my—my fanny in the air. My ears were ringing and I was scared to death, but he came to hit me again, and I did as he wanted, and he pushed the barrel of the pistol into—my—rectum, and I cried out in pain. You wouldn't believe, and then he played with my—my clitoris, you know, and me shaking from being so in shock, and then he put the end of the barrel against my—my—well, I don't like saying it. My clit and rubbed it till I ast him please God to stop, and then he pushed it on into my—into my—me, and I cried out into the covers and prayed to God out loud, and he began to work it back and forth and told me he wanted his baby to see just what sort of mother I was, me doing so-and-so—he said the word—to a gun, and I tried to crawl forward and get free of the pistol, and it went off. I knew I had been shot inside. I had been shot and my baby and I would die. Then I realized I had not been shot, only scared to death, and he said he wanted my sister to know how he had made love to me, and he wrestled with me, trying to get the pistol back inside me. I was on my back, and he began slashing my face. "You lie still," he told me, and once I did lie still, he tried to get the barrel in, could not find the opening, so he had me push—push the pistol up inside myself. Its barrel was warm from the shot. He told me to push its barrel deeper till I heard the baby cry. Somebody began pounding on the front door, and he told me to keep moving it back and forth and he backed up to the bedroom doorway and shouted toward the front door to stop the racket, and then he was leaning over me again and spit fell on my breasts.

"Fuck her," he shouted suddenly, meaning whoever was knocking and leaning on the bell, and he swung his big powerful body erect, leaving the pistol in me. He said he would tie me to the bed, but he didn't tie me; he got confused trying to get a sheet free to do it with, and he told me to leave the pistol where it was and he'd be back, and he went into the other hall, pulling on a towel, and I got the pistol out of myself, which was painful as new burns, and put on my skirt and was pulling on a bra as he returned, and when he started for the pistol, I did, I did, too, and was closer to it and it went off and I screamed, "Oh, my God, did it hit you?" And when he said it had not hit him, he started for me, and I told him to stay back. "I want to get out of this house, so you let me pass." I was trembling so much I could scarcely hold the pistol out. He said, "You are going to have to take what I give you; I've just found out how you can make love." He swung toward the spare room; he pulled the quilt down and stumbled up against the stool and kicked it out of the way and as he fell against the door, opening it, the pistol exploded yet again, and I saw the round hole, the bullet in his back, and the blood appeared. "Plover," I said to him, "honey, tell me, are you all right?"

21

I was sitting only a dozen feet away. She had spoken conversationally, and once she finished talking there was not a sound in the courtroom. Sometime within the next minute, the boy Max must have left the seat beside me and gone to her; he even got into the witness box and laid his head on her lap, was with her when she gave a little toss to her head and politely apologized for having to tell such an awful tale. "I wish it could have been avoided," she told me. Hers was a ladylike recovery from the throes of embarrassment. No, not quite, for she had not appeared to be embarrassed, nor did she gloat. She had spoken plainly and with the rhythm that mountaineers sometimes fall into, a singsongness with an old-world moaning imposed. She had been—what is the word? She had been competent, quite objective in manner. She had uttered the most fateful, dreadful words simply, and I dare say any effort to enhance them would have detracted from their impact.

"Winnette," I said to her, "you must put the boy, Max, out of the witness box." Once she had done so, I asked her, "Did you then call for an ambulance?"

"I screamed for Anne. Plover went into the living room. I followed him and was trying to open the front door. I saw him bleeding, and Anne was pushing on the door, and Carvel ap-

162

peared, had already come to help Anne get inside, so we were all there near the doorway, and Carvel said, 'Get a towel.' He was talking to all of us. He was really saying he didn't know how to get a towel in my house. When I got back with the towel, Plover had his arm over the man's shoulders and they were moving to the front door, and when I approached with the towel, Plover swung at my head, hit me and dazed me. And I was knocked flat onto the coffee table and the floor. I remember saying, Do we need an ambulance? And Plover said he didn't want the police, so not to call one. He staggered outdoors and I began to call out, begging him to let me call an ambulance. Here I had just shot him on my own, but was begging him, and I had blood, his blood on my face, in my mouth. I phoned the ambulance. I called Papa to come get me. He had told me please not to phone him except if I wanted him to come get me. By then Plover was lying in the front yard. So I prayed Papa to come get me and went out into the yard and knelt down beside Plover across from Anne, who was doing the breathing for Plover. I did it in her place, she assuring me Plover was all right, all right."

"When the ambulance arrived, what did you tell the attendants?"

"I don't recall."

"Did you talk to the police officers?"

"Yes. I told them I had shot my husband and showed them where the gun was. I had hid it to keep it from Plover. One of the officers was a kind man and asked me if I was all right, myself. I had blood on my face he said, and I told him that was where Plover had hit me. Blood was on my hands, too. So I went into the bathroom to wash."

"Where did you get blood on your hand?"

"Helping him breathe. Later one of the police officers did a paraffin test, and he said I shouldn't have washed my hands, and I told him I hadn't known not to wash blood off of myself. He wrote down what I said and told me, ast me to sign it, and so I signed it. Then they took me to the jail and booked me."

"And next morning you were taken to court for setting of bail?"

"I didn't want any bail, or any lawyer at all, but I—" she hesitated, seemed to be flustered.

"Go ahead and finish," I told her.

"But, I got you," she said, and everybody laughed. Winnette began telling about the funeral arrangements without even being asked.

"Plover's father came to the cell. He was pleasant to me, said he had known Plover was sick. That was the very word he used. He ought to have done more himself, he told me. Then he ast if Plover's body ought to be given to science, and I said plain burial was my first choice, Plover not being of a scientific turn, and he said it was the same with him, and would I mind if Plover was buried at their church's cemetery. No, I said, meaning it was all right with me. It was a surprise to me, Mr. Mac, to think I still was to be ast, after shooting his son. Then he ast me to choose a preacher, and would it be all right for him to choose one or two himself, there being several who had called on him once the story of the shooting was in the newspaper. He said there'd doubtless be a throng of people come. So I agreed. He was to pick out two preachers, and my parents' preacher would do for a third, if he wanted to participate. And he said I must come to the service. 'Oh, no,' I said. He said he wanted to take me into the church on his arm, and I said, 'No, thank you,' which upset him. So I agreed to attend the church part of it, and on the day announced—you were present, Mr. Mac?"

"No, I wasn't there."

"Plover had brothers, but they'd moved away, and I'd never met them. I knew they might want to revenge his death, that being a mountain trait, isn't it?"

"I'm told so."

"One reason I wanted to be in the cell was not to endanger my parents and sister by any more confrontations."

"I see. So you went to the church service—"

"First the deputies drove me to the funeral home, and Plover was in the closed-up coffin, with about a thousand flower blossoms all about. His parents arrived and were the ones who wanted the coffin opened, but I went on into the office to write a check for everything. I wouldn't look at Plover, I told them no thank you. At the church there was a crowd, people all over the yard, and they were saving a place for me. There were reporters and—what do you call them? The people with them?"

"Editors," I suggested.

"Photographers. And many others had cameras, and the Asheville television crew, and as we drove up in the rented limousine and got out, I was supposed to be sorrowful, of course, and Papa Plover and his wife were sorrowful, were so downcast, both of them, as if they'd never hope to see sunlight again, but I was too scared. I was waiting to be shot and was surprised to make it to the vestibule, and then he and I walked solemnly down the aisle to our front pew, people gawking. I recall there was the singing of Avonda Stapleton, who claimed to Papa Plover to have gone to high school with Plover, and three little girls sang about heaven. Well, since that's where Plover is, there had best be special attention paid by the angels, let me tell you. Then the eulogies were delivered, my Papa's preacher reading his part out of a book. I think it had been written long ago for somebody else, for it used the word 'woebegone' and referred to God save us from the storms. It also referred to Plover being first in war. So far as I know he hadn't gone to war, had never fought anybody outside the county, except highway patrolmen. And having 'filled to overflowing the cup of life.' I leave it to you to figure out what was in the cup. Then Mildred sang again, and Plover's mother and sister sobbed out loud, and I knew it was my duty to sob, too, but all I was worrying about was what his brothers might do. After the service I went straight to the limousine and got a corner seat, but here came his parents and all the brothers and sister of 'the dearly departed,' as Plover was being called, and everybody was cordial, and so I went to the graveside with them, Plover's oldest brother's wife inviting me to come visit them in Chicago. She made her husband, Billy, to give me his business card, and she stopped on the trail to write the home phone on it. There were mostly scripture readings at graveside, and the coffin was not lowered, it was left in its bower of flowers. It must have been that a hundred people filed by my chair to shake my hand. Then when

I finally was ready to go, Mama ast me to come home with her, but I excused myself by saying my medicines were in my—my house, and maybe tomorrow. The limousine had pulled up to the gravesite, and I was in the corner place, when Plover's brothers ast me to come for a family shot. They actually used the word 'shot.' Then one of their wives corrected it to 'photograph.' And so— they told the funeral home men to open the casket. Plover was to be in the shot. I said no, never, and almost fainted, and the funeral home man said they had not brought the key. That made me smile to myself, to think a coffin needed a key on the outside."

People laughed. At last we were able to laugh. All of us in the courtroom, myself included, had not dared laugh before, afraid to miss some of her soft flowing words. I was unsure whether Winnette herself viewed the predicament as comic or tragic. I suppose it had to be viewed as a mingling of both, but this was the first opportunity she gave us to laugh, and some did, the judge, too. Then quiet—everybody had to be particularly quiet because Winnette was talking softly, as if to me only, and nobody else.

"One of the sons of one of the brothers was the one who knew there was no key. He merely went ahead and opened the coffin lid. I saw him do it and hurried away. But once it was open, the family lined up behind, leaving a seat for me. I was told to return and was unable to look down, so I tripped, but I collapsed onto my chair, the same one, the same one, and so it happened that I was not more than four feet from his face, Plover's face was just there within reach, and the morticians had costumed him in a business suit with a white shirt and necktie, all of it starched and new, and he had a clean handkerchief in his suit breast pocket, and his face was plastic-looking, the skin had been drawn so tight it was shiny, and his lips were parted enough to see his teeth, which gave him a foxy appearance. Of course, he was asleep, contentedly asleep here under the oak trees, with flowers all about, and I laughed, Mr. Mac, I began to laugh, and that's how someone got the picture of me laughing over Plover's corpse in his coffin, which never should have been made. I never should have done it. The surprise of seeing him again was what did it."

"Who took the picture?" I asked her.

"I wonder. A brother, maybe. Did the newspaper say?"

"Did it? I don't think so."

"Of course, I never should have gone to the graveside." She paused, then after a twist of her shoulders, a slight nod, she said, "That's not the whole of what I should not have done."

22

MISS RACHEL FAMOUS TURNER:

If a person had never sat on a jury, he or she might not know how difficult it is to keep the details straight. A jury has no notebook, no secretary, has no desk to write on. A jurywoman cannot even write on her wrist or arm, like the William Hart twins used to do in my classroom. Actually, they preferred their arms to lined paper. "Well, are you going to turn your arm in, close of day?" I asked one of them. I think her name was Susan. *S-o-o-s-a-n* she spelled it whenever she felt sassy. "I'll go home with you, Miss Famous," she told me, "and you read my arm at your liege." At my liege. Her word—at your liege—is Shakespearian English, but it doesn't mean leisure. That was a mistake.

The judge droned whenever he talked. Couldn't help but notice. If he were a student of mine, I'd tell him to sit up straight and speak out. The words were too familiar to him. I tell my classes not to mumble and not to listen to the radio, either, which is clear talk, talk, and vulgar music. It causes measles, I tell them. That makes them laugh. Those telephone listening things cause hair nits and nitwits. The nitwits are relegated to society's people-dumpsters, where they sleep out their days in failure. I tell them you will be the four *O*s, obdurant, officious, oxnate, and plain objectionable. One year a Horton girl raised her hand and informed me there was no word *oxnate* in her dictionary. I told her that added distinction to the word. Most any common word could be found in dictionaries. She repeated that it was not there at all, therefore it was not, and I said she appeared to have the same faith in dictionaries that some folks have in the Bible. Some of the children got the point of my argument, but others did not, could not. Perhaps the mind does not develop in some, as in others. At any rate I told them the word obviously did exist or we wouldn't be discussing it. We used it ourselves. That tickled a few of the more mature ones, but confused some, and downright irritated others. Generally there were those three responses to my efforts to awaken their minds. "Do you ever hallucinate, class?" I would whisper to them.

"Oh, my, no, Miss Famous," they would reply.

"You would think of doing it, would you?"

"No."

"Never?"

"No. Never."

"Even if it meant you could see Santa Claus?"

That might stump them. They might begin to suspect that hallucinate was not a sex sin, was not even as crude as masturbation.

Our modern heroine, Winnette, left on the bench listening to the court announcements as droned by Old Judge Sleepyhead, himself, had hallucinated, all right. She had reason to wake up long before she did. The idea she could change Ernest Plover from devil to human being was naive: *n-a-i-v-e.* She needed a dose of realism from fifth grade on, something to race those frilly, self-sacrificing notions out of her. She was brought up by caring parents who taught her to be self-sacrificing. If she had been in my class—more's the pity she wasn't—she would have heard my solid defense of selfishness. Also, my opinion that changing people once they are adults is "mite nigh impossible," as my grandfather would have expressed it. He would amend that: "Jesus can—maybe." I don't know of any way I will amend it today. And here we have an example of a woman reared to be of help to others, and the tender bough broke finally. She did to Ernest Plover what she had stored up for years past. Now, I would say be selfish to a class of students. Murder is never justified under the law, of course, but most people who get murdered deserve some punishment—excepting street crimes. A failure of the law—much like a failure in the dictionaries—is always possible. It is not a weakness in my character that I will not allow laws and dictionaries to decide my thinking.

Mr. Juicks became so intense while he was cross-examining Winnette that he was red as a radish. Even his ears were flaming. He could not seem to accept that Winnette was telling him she and her husband had bought marijuana in five-pound lots, and she now testified she didn't know from whom they had bought it.

"Mostly from such as a picnic trash can," she explained, "beside the road."

"And did you serve the money on the picnic table?" He was too sarcastic for his own good, if you ask me. Abel Juicks—middle initial C—was in my class for half a semester. His parents moved into the area during Christmas vacation, where his father got a job helping to manage Christmas tree growing and selling. Was born in Shelby, Abel Juicks was. Was smart for details, but easily confused. He hated exaggeration. Poetry is exaggeration, for one example.

Juicks was insisting Winnette tell him who bought drugs from her and her husband. They bought drugs only from him, she explained.

"If you helped buy drugs, as you testify, and you weighed it out in small lots, and you handed a given lot to a buyer who came to your door, and you took the money, would you call that selling drugs or not selling drugs?"

Winnette smiled, bemused, unruffled, unworried. Now that's another word that's not in the dictionary: unworried.

"I was doing what Plover told me to."

"That does not make it nonselling."

"If you were married to Plover, you'd learn to do what he said, Mr. Juicks."

"I have not been married to Plover," he admitted heatedly.

"No, for if you were the way with him that you are with me, he'd'a beat you silly."

We laughed. The entire courtroom, even our foreman, who was retired pastor Davis, who didn't find many moments while in retirement amusing. Fred Juicks got a mite more red, if possible. Anyway, he was flaming. Even so he continued berating her, wanting the names of customers, which she claimed not to know. He threatened her with prosecution on drug charges, and she told him all right, but she hoped he'd just lock her up and not put her to trial. She preferred a jail cell to a courtroom.

All this time her lawyer was reading the morning paper. He had it wide open and was totally engrossed, or so it appeared. His was an effective way of saying he found Mr. Juicks's questioning to be unimportant. He used the pages of the newspaper adroitly, too. If Fred Juicks asked Winnette a telling question, Mr. MacMillan would carefully turn the pages, trying obviously not to make a racket. Mr. MacMillan usually held it double-paged open, held it high and wide hiding him from view. So far as I could tell, there was nothing Fred Juicks could do about this, either, though he had to notice.

She admitted to using speed two years ago. She thought she had used PCP twice, a year or two ago. She had used LSD. She was speaking so casually that one simply had to believe her; she was not denying, nor did she show agitation, although young Abel Juicks did so. Here he would come with a dark charge, and it would float away on her quiet reply. He seemed to me to be battling a cloud. I imagine her husband had had something of the same experience.

Young Mr. Juicks asked about the testimony of Mavis Plover, "the preceding wife," I once heard our fellow juror, Reverend Davis, term her. Now, Mavis was once a student of mine, as were three of her brothers and sisters, but it would require total recall for me now to distinguish among them. On the stand Winnette denied ever telling Mavis she carried a pistol, or that she ever held a pistol on Lloyd Plover. "Maybe Plover told her that. I have no idea what all Plover told people." She said she didn't recall about a woman in Kona killing her husband. "Maybe Plover told her I had told him that. Mavis tries to keep everything straight, but that's hard sometimes."

"Did you not tell her this only two weeks before you shot your husband?"

"Did I see her within those two weeks? Let me think. I wasn't any longer at work, which is where I usually saw her."

"When was the last time you saw her, Mrs. Plover?"

"I'm wondering. She and Max and Kathy came to supper, and Max and Kathy spent the night. That would be four weeks before, Mr. Juicks. I don't recall seeing her at all for a month prior to the shooting. Would that help you at all?"

Indeed, Winnette was trying to help him, it seemed, even as he tried to hang her. That might have been her downfall all along, her helpfulness. The child must have been born without a temper of her own. A show of temper might have pleased Plover. I can imagine him day after day failing in his honest efforts to rile her, make her flare up at him, he laying in wait trying to irritate her, discover her selfishness, only and always to meet her willingness, helpfulness, considerateness, all the indulgences and permissiveness taught her over her childhood by well-meaning souls, who should have taught more of that to Plover and less to her. One might conclude her agreeableness made Plover all the more overbearing, and made her a pent-up powder keg that exploded.

Small bones. That went with her attitude. Frail. Compact. Easy to throw about or ball up or stretch out. Fey. *F-e-y*. "Wishing for death," is one definition of *f-e-y*. Does wishing for death suit her at all? She wears almost no makeup, maybe doesn't need it, because she does have some color on her lips, her cheeks. Appears to be rather sad one minute, then all in a few seconds she brightens, comes into flower, opening her lips and eyes in a smile, welcoming her persecutors to warm comforts. She wears even now the promise of forgiveness of Juicks. Small feet. "Feet are a woman's weapons," my grandmother used to tell me. Oriental outlook, perhaps. I saw Mother kick livestock, that was all—billy goats, rams, the meanest of Papa's hunting dogs, the calf, the colt. I've seen her stomp snakes. One blow of her boot was sufficient. The young thing on the witness stand opening her life story for

us has tiny feet, so maybe that has made her cater to defenseless-
ness.

Mr. MacMillan asked for more details about seeing the two
children. Was Plover required to send Mavis child support? He
was. Did he do so? Yes, once Winnette was present to write out
the checks, he would sign them, she testified, then she would mail
them at the time she mailed the telephone and power bill payments. He had no visitation rights, and he rarely ever saw his
children until Winnette began to invite them over. Not seeing his
children had bothered him, she believed, might have made him
use more narcotics. Since he was into drugs, Winnette and Mavis
always stayed in the house with the children—at least one of
them did; however, during the separation, Mavis might have left
them there alone with him. Winnette had been told she did. On
and on, uncovering other facets of Plover's life, of his two wives
and his two children, of his drug habits. Dwell on the drug issue,
Mr. MacMillan appeared to like that.

"Did he use or sell any of these—or all of these, Winnette:
diazepam, chlordiazepoxide, which is Librium, lorazepam, also
known as Ativan, oxazepam is also known as Serax, alprazolam,
also known as Xanax; the amphetamines were methamphetamine,
street names meth, crystal, whites, speed, brand name Metham-
pex, dextroamphetamine, brand name Dexedrine . . ."

Winnette was attentive, polite. She thought Plover had used
some of them, most of them, all of them. What she had to go on
was conversation, memory, throwaway containers. She testified
over and over that she had not used drugs outside Plover's presence, except once Blue had given her Quaaludes at his and Anne's
house. She said Anne had not taken any. They were in a prescription vial. "I told Plover I did not want to use drugs or be around
drugs, or buy or sell drugs, or have them inside the house."

"Did he keep them inside the house?" Mr. MacMillan asked
her.

"He'd hide them in the yard, but occasionally in the house. He
would put them in canning jars, inside the house." Repeatedly she
testified that he had sworn not to hit her, provided she would
return to live with him. "He promised me he would quit the drug

173

business and find a job. He was a supervisor at Silver Spur before he was allowed to quit . . ." Over and over, on and on the repetition went.

The doctor, Dr. Robbins, who has that nice office building and a major, really a fine practice—well, he was scared to death. Called to the witness box, he was pale as a ghost. Mr. MacMillan asked him to tell the court what sort of bruises and cuts Winnette had suffered in the last encounter with her husband and his P-38 pistol, and he was utterly beyond coherence. "As to the most personal matters, I judged the barrel of the pistol had torn her rectum and vagina—apparently the former more than the latter," he murmured. "The little aiming device on the front of the barrel might have done most of it, I suppose." Mr. Juicks merely had to cough, to clear his throat, to make Dr. Robbins jump in alarm. When he was asked how long he had known the defendant and how well he knew her, he was vague and appeared to be critical, unhappy about the association.

In contrast, the psychiatrist, who was living summers near Misty Mountain and had practiced mostly in Ft. Lauderdale, was not at all intimidated. Calmly he listed his credentials, and calmly he itemized more than a dozen meetings with Winnette, all in her cell. "I became infatuated with the case, itself, I stress. But she confided in me only guardedly. I prescribed Librium, but the druggist had telephoned to say he was out of that and might he substitute Valium; therefore, she has been taking Valium, or so I assumed until yesterday." Yes, he had heard her testimony, all of it. "Psychologists and psychiatrists do not always agree, as the court realizes, even though a science is involved. The science is evolving." On and on he went about his science, while I wanted to know if Winnette was guilty—was legally responsible or not.

"There are, as of this very year, differing theories about psychiatry in America, England, and elsewhere," he told us. "The schools of psychiatry are Freudian, Sullivanian, Adlerian, and Jungian. Psychiatry can also be subdivided into psychoanalytic, biochemical, and behavioral. They are quite different schools of thought. There are differences in the theoretical understanding of phenomena and—this may interest you—there is little difference about the appreciation of phenomena. The cause of any phenomenon is where differences of opinion lie, as to whether it is biological or psychoanalytical or that the hormones cause the mood change, or childhood upbringing, or present influences, or drugs . . ."

On and on, leading up—was it leading up to whether or not Winnette . . . people were not any longer listening.

". . . different psychiatrists might disagree about what causes the phenomenon, but there would be considerable agreement about describing the phenomenon. . . . Another psychiatrist and I might disagree on the brain mechanism responsible for a particular mood or shade of feeling, but as to describing the phenomenon there is little difference. If there were, our science would just now, today, be total chaos."

Instead of mere chaos, I thought.

". . . there are areas in clinical psychiatry where there is interrelated reliability, and these are considered scientific to some extent. Of course, it is not precise. Our work depends on information from the patient or the patient's supplies of information with one proviso. A psychiatrist is trained to deal with information both intentional and unintentional . . ."

Winnette just might be convicted before this one told us what he thought about her. As for her, she was surely, at the least, daydreaming. What were her daydreams? Of fields of white-belled snowdrops growing in birch woods, of leafless dogwood trees in bloom in April? Of the white lace of the service tree, first of the trees to bloom hereabouts? Of the ten-thousand-acre gardens of rhododendrons awash with lavender? Or was it of a man's hand rubbing the soft flesh of her thigh, moving slowly higher, with the sound of a gun cocking: c-o-c-k-i-n-g. Interesting word in this connection.

". . . unintentional information can come in the form of body language, slips of the tongue, behavior patterns, dreams—although dreams as valid indicators are under reconsideration just now. These body-language clues are given much weight in understanding what a person is portraying, revealing, saying about themselves . . ."

It was late on this Friday—by late I mean four o'clock—when he did appear to have wound up his spring, for he then launched into reading a written statement that seemed to pertain to Winnette. "If the jury should find that Winnette and her husband were alone in their house on this certain afternoon, and Winnette believed he was under the influence of some drugs, and if he had a gun; if the jury should find that she was, her body and person, were assaulted by him, and that she asked permission to leave the house and was refused permission; if the jury should find she got possession of the pistol he had used to threaten her and to assault her earlier; if the jury finds he started to enter another room where other guns, and only guns were stored, my opinion about the state of her mind is that she was terrified. I think she was terrified when she shot her husband."

Well—I must say, everybody could agree with him, but whether being terrified is reason enough—well . . . The other members of the jury also were mystified. One by one they began relaxing, sitting back, permitting themselves little grimaces and burps, were sneaking glances at their watches, especially some of the men, this being a fox-hunting weekend coming up. We had climbed a mountain with this gentleman and he had left us stranded on a barren peak. The point of it all had disappeared. No hope of help. Well intentioned, no doubt. Probably wanted to help her. I do believe he meant to seek to justify Winnette's action, but he had fallen victim to—to himself. A pity, really.

23

MISS RACHEL FAMOUS TURNER:

It was three-thirty Thursday, and there was more testimony to come. For one, there was a sheriff's deputy who was called to testify, which for some reason, vague to us, we on the jury were not allowed to hear. He was nobody in the world but Lloyd Ernest, whom I've known for years. While Lloyd was on the stand, Mr. MacMillan asked him about an arrest made sixteen years ago. Now that is indeed digging back, long before Winnette even knew Plover. Apparently he was arrested for disorderly conduct at a ball game, and it required three officers and three other officials—

We never got the whole of it for Mr. Juicks was all over the place objecting. The judge put us jury people out and we were isolated with one another, twelve eggs in our twelve-foot-by-fifteen-foot carton, to wait well out of earshot. Once we were returned to court, Lloyd was allowed to say to us only that he had been a courthouse employee for twenty-some years and knew Lloyd Ernest Plover, and knew him to have a reputation as a dangerous and violent man. Nothing about the arrest or arrests as a youth were allowed. The testimony was purified. Or was blanketed, silenced, censored. As for myself, I would have given a new coin to have heard about Plover's youth.

We heard instead about Winnette's make-believe, unbelievable marriage, this time from her friend, Anne Bailey, who was sure that Plover was a dangerous man. She did very well while being questioned by Mr. MacMillan, but she became confused under Mr. Juicks's insistence for dates, days of the week. She even got years wrong. Later she finally admitted she had taken drugs, herself, she and her friend, Blue, whom she was obviously trying to protect.

The sister was a better witness. She was crisp, decisive, rang true. A hairdresser, she was quite a nice-looking woman of about twenty years. Indeed, she looked like Winnette. She testified that she had witnessed Lloyd Plover snorting cocaine.

Mr. Juicks objected. I don't know just why. By now none of us on the jury was surprised by cocaine or anything else Plover might have snorted. Mr. MacMillan continued, asked the sister if she had seen him snorting cocaine in Winnette's presence, and there was another objection.

"Well," Judge Blackington said, peering about sleepily, pausing in his random gazing to study his watch, "objection sustained. Motion to strike allowed. Gentlemen of the jury—and two ladies, disregard the witness's last response."

"Exception," Mr. MacMillan intoned, all part of the routine, the legal business I didn't understand.

"One night we were at Wrightsville together. This was—they were married by then," Clara told us, "and we were at the motel, I in one room and they another. Around three in the night Plover woke up and told Winnette we were all going home. Apparently he couldn't sleep, so nobody was to sleep. Winnette woke me. We tried to talk him out of it. For one thing the roads were icy, and for another it was cold."

"Why were you at the beach in cold weather?" Mr. MacMillan asked her.

"To buy a gun collection, but we couldn't find the man. So I told Plover we were sleepy, and he told me if I wanted to stay awake, then to take some of this. He gave me cocaine. Winnette began to beg him not to give her family dope, but he did, and I refused it, and we left in the middle of the night, in a storm and drove seven hours." She had examined and treated Winnette after

Plover had dragged her by the hair, pulling much of her hair out. "He'd left bald places which scabbed over awful." She testified that Plover had made sexual advances to her, once had asked her to meet him to buy a Christmas present for Winnette, but really had planned a tryst, which she managed to get free of.

Her father was an even more effective witness, I felt. A gentle soul, he identified himself as the father of two beautiful daughters, both present in the courtroom. He took note that Winnette had gone to church while living with him and graduated tenth in her high school class of 240. She got her driver's license at age sixteen, and he gave her a car. He said he had no idea Lloyd Plover was on drugs, nor that Winnette ever used them, and he was surprised if either daughter had much tolerance of them. He believed she had got along well with her first husband. Lloyd Plover was a different matter, and he had hoped she would soon be free of him completely, "Soon rather than late."

He said on the afternoon Lloyd Ernest was shot, she had cooperated fully with the officers and had ever since. "I never thought I would see one of my daughters in a jail, but I've visited her in the one here in Cookham of late, and she's same sweet girl. Of course, her failings have about killed her mother. The doctor won't let her come near this courtroom. She can't testify. She would like to. We're still getting telephone calls. Some of the calls threatened my life and hers. One man said he would kill me, any of us, who says an unkind word at the trial about Plover. Well, I'll settle that score right now. He was a cruel and unnatural animal, and I wish to God in Heaven it had been me who had killed him, and not my daughter."

Powerful words defiantly proclaimed, and one did have to take notice. His thin voice had filled the auditorium with passion.

Then quietly, an eternity later, he uttered these words: "My trouble is, I could never kill anything, since a boy." Then he said, looking at Winnette, "Same as my girls."

Hands clenched, head bowed, she was listening or praying or had closed out his words; I couldn't tell.

On the jury was a man named Carter—he did look a little like President Carter—who invested funds for clients, most of them out-of-state, and soon as our jury was given a rest break, he rushed for the one telephone, which was in the hallway near the deputy's chair, and occupied it throughout, the other eleven of us going without. As the jury was filing back into the legal cathedral, as Reverend Davis termed the courtroom, I spoke to this Mr. Carter. "Do you need money?" I asked him.

He looked at me askance, his mouth puckered, his teeth clicking. "Of course not, thank you very much."

"You have enough to piece out your life?" I asked him. "How fortunate."

"I certainly do."

"But not enough to stop worrying yourself about getting more?" I had no right to assault him this way, but it was amusing to catch him on the spearpoint, for he wanted to be thought of as wealthy, while obviously he was delirious, desperate for dollars, much like a pauper.

The median IQ in the nation is one hundred; that is about right, one must assume, for juries. If our jury's median was one hundred, Mr. Waitland, our half-deaf member, was in the bottom half, well down. So, I fear, was Mrs. Pender. Or is it Miss Pender? She wears no ring, I notice, but it is unlike a Pender to remain single.

There were five men on the jury whom I classified as fox-hunter types. Good Joes all, they could be counted on to sit contentedly by a fire all night, tell stories, listen to their dogs howl. Two of the fox hunters I had taught in school, if indeed they were ever taught—one did remain peculiarly quiet in my class. There was dear Reverend Davis, who would not harm a fly on Sunday or degrade an Episcopal catechism.

The other male jurors were less well known to me. One was in life insurance; dyspeptic and pale, my guess was he had an illness. I had seen him about a nearby town for years, always gray. The tenth juror, according to my numbering, was the owner of the Five Flags Motel and Restaurant, a Mr. Gaus, a recent immigrant from the north, maybe even from as far as Canada, who had built a beautiful thirty-room motel as a retirement hobby.

Then there was this Mr. Carter, number eleven, who had been a broker in Gainesville for years.

Who on earth is the twelfth? Have I forgot one member? Let's see, there were five good old boys, there was Miss/Mrs. Pender, there was deaf-and-dumb Waitland, there were Insurance, Motel, the broker, pastor.

Oh, yes.

And me.

24

MR. ERNEST:

My name is Lloyd Ernest—same as the dead man, except in my
case, that's the whole of it. Mr. Ernest, in other words. For
twenty-seven years I've worked for the county, and in fact was
one of the men who tried to subdue the other Lloyd Ernest at a
high school basketball game in about 1970. He was drinking
heavy. It took six of us to get him into jail. Then there was a later
ball game, and he was arrested and locked in one of the locker
rooms till he simmered down. Then there was a ruckus when he
was refused admittance to a music festival in Asheville, and some
of his friends joined in and seven boys were taken to medic. In
Winnette's trial I never got to testify as to any of it, because the
DA's office said he wasn't on trial. Also, I'm not now even in the
sheriff's office; I'm titled courthouse warden, and mostly I clean
up, get the air conditioner to work, hire window cleaners. You can
see yourself what a job it is to clean those courtroom windows
from the inside, much less the outside, they being more'n average-
ladder high. And one Superior Court judge, Murphy, whenever
he comes up here to officiate, looks first at the floor and next at
the windows, and he crows mighty loud if there's a smudge.
Those two and the ceiling fan are his three visions. I'm in charge
of all of them. He threatened two times to lock me up.

I was told to take men to Lloyd Ernest Plover's house and dig for drugs. This was on the Thursday of testimony, it was mentioned Lloyd buried some things under his stoop. Earlier, the woods was mentioned. I couldn't get diggers promised till next morning, Friday, everybody watching the Thursday's testimony, hoping to see Winnette again. She's a sweet girl. There wasn't a man working at the courthouse who didn't take to her. There was not once she passed by without smiling in a sort of secret special way, and at every doorway she wants to go last. She'll motion for me to precede her, for instance. She's a calendar picture, that one. I would set her up above the page for June, when the Roan fields are full of rhododendron blooming. Or October, when the leaves flare out in colors. My favorite is the yellow maple.

My papa planted two acres in Sourwood, back when I was a boy; this was for his bees. He had an acre left over, so Mama asked him to plant maples in it. He fussed and winked and wriggled, claimed it'd be a waste, but he allus did what she asked him to, loved pleasing her, and he planted yellow maples, with one fringe of red maples. That piece of ground was 250 feet by 200 feet. Now, that was about forty red maples around the fringe, and about one hundred in the middle. He took care of them, mowed the weeds, him and me. And after five years, he took Mama up there to see it. Now, I wasn't allowed. None of us seven young'ns was allowed. They went alone together. They was gone two hours and all we children knew was both come home crying. Nothing in the world but satisfaction.

The diggers were Sam and Cole. I took both for I never knew how much we were to dig for, and I took the pickup, Cole riding in the back, he being younger. Also we had picks and shovels, a pothole digger, and the county's metal detector. We had a time finding the house, so it was about eight-thirty that morning, Friday, when we rolled into the yard of a house that fitted. Winnette's sister came outdoors after we called who we were. The dogs were penned up, but were barking and jumping, so us diggers had to talk loud. She never knew a jot about where her brother-in-law would have buried anything, and there we were in a swept yard, with dog lot and old sheds and the four-room house, which had an open crawl space under part of it.

183

Sam and Cole tried detecting, then started digging under the porch, actually a small stoop, while the sister and me sat on the steps, her talking about going to work as a hairdresser for her first customer at ten, a Mrs. Wright. The Wrights were mining people, well-to-do. "Need to get all the feldspar out of her hair," I told her, "and the mica." She kept her legs well together, was prim and modest, I'd say. Of course, can't tell everything by one session. They tell me her older sister, Winnette, married first at nineteen; sounded like this one was that old or older. I'd marry her myself, you can believe.

Sam and Cole broke a mason jar in the ground and had to collect the pieces. Inside the jar had been plastic pockets full of powder, and these they put in a bigger plastic bag, and I wrote a big "1" and the location and time of day. With renewed vigor they went to scratching again. "I hope your Winnette don't get sent up," I said to this sister, Clara, risking my opinion with her. "State prison for women is not polite. Them as goes to federal prison might as well be visiting a hotel, but she would be sent to a state prison."

"What are the federal ones?" She was close and being confidential, her voice soft as a darkened room, even with me.

"Tax lying," I told her. "Drug smuggling. Kidnapping. Over the years sent fifty men, one at a time, from here for whiskey running, and some preferred the penitentiary to home. Nobody wants to go to a state prison, especially if they're women. You have at least to knife somebody, or drowned their baby child, or shoot your mother."

"Winnette's not like that," Clara told me.

Hold those legs together, baby, I thought. She wasn't trying to hook me; although I live on hope. They tell me some of them will take out after an older man, want his hide on her wall for trophies. Well, sir, this here woman on step number two can make a fool out of me any time she wants to—off duty, of course. And so can Winnette. "I'd not be the least bit afraid of going to sleep in the room," I told Clara over the dog barks.

"What room?"

"With your sister," I told her.

184

She looked over at me, strange as an extra Saturday.

"Hit another'n?" I called out. Sounded like broken glass to me. "Now you'll need to more use the metal detector, try to pick out the metal lids," I told them, holding open a second bag.

We had made the yard into a war zone by the time the jury's bus and the sheriff's car arrived. Must have been glad to get fresh air and sunshine, for people were wandering about smiling and laughing, looking at Sam and Cole use the metal detector. We had found seven jars thus far.

"There's Winnette," the sister told me, bounding off the steps like a pronged rabbit, going off rushing across the yard dodging pits and sticks. She had to stop ten feet from Winnette, warned off by the deputies. Sisters can't even touch, seems like, under the law of the accused.

Winnette came to her, regardless, embraced her warmly, kissed her forehead, her cheeks, came leading her toward the house, walking around holes and dirt. "I never knew there were so many places," Winnette told me, greeting me, leading her sister and the first of the jurors into the house, a squad of lawyers and deputies attending, and here was even the judge arriving in a car, and there came two TV vans and the car from the newspaper. Everybody tried to get into the house, where Winnette was the one talking, showing off her furniture and knickknacks, telling where and when she had got her drapes and why she didn't have a bulb in the overhead fixture in the living room, because of glare. I was able to hear most of it. Pride, that was the way she told it. And where the blood had been, her sister telling about washing it clean with Ajax and one of Plover's shirts. The rest of his things she had given to the shop at Northcross School. Then the people were out in the yard again, listening to the metal detector, watching Cole uncover yet another mason jar. By now we were able to see they were planted in a straight line from dog house to house; then, too, there had been two under the house stoop. Sheriff Goforth looked into four of my bags and declared cocaine in two of them, marijuana in one, and "God only knows" in one. Then Winnette from the porch asked if we had let the dogs out, which we sure as hell hadn't, being damn frightened of German police, and so help me, she did, she let the two females out, and there was people running in ever direction, scrambling over one another, including the judge, and she told the mother dog, the biggest and oldest, to sniff a jar, and then that there dog, she ran over to the edge of the woods and began to dig, and then the other female dog got a place of her own, and soon my men were outclassed, and that there TV camera was taking the dogs' picture uncovering mason jars, with Winnette proud as punch, giggling with every success, bubbling over, and so it went for fifteen or twenty minutes, till there were eleven quart and twelve pint and one half-gallon jars, plus two broken ones, on the steps, enough dope to supply the Spanish army, and me out of plastic bags, I mean entirely, and using a crayon to number jars with. Sheriff Goforth figured it was worth at a minimum fifty thousand dollars wholesale, and many times that on the street.

Winnette seemed not to care one way or the other, except she insisted on rewarding the dogs with platters of food. She also fed the big male in the dog lot. Everybody was laughing, having a great time, almost like a picnic, and my men and me, we left finally. Those were clever, her dogs, and they were trembling all over on seeing Winnette. They never jumped up on her, either. I knew two German police that could sniff out where cigarettes had been hid, but I never knew any that could smell through closed jars, and them buried, but I'd guess memory done it.

Miss Famous Turner was one of the last of the jurors to leave. Her and Mr. Carter had been inside fussing over use of the telephone, and I recognized her for having had three of my children and now one of my grandchildren in her class, so I said hello to her and walked with her to the car, careful not to mention the trial, except once we were to ourselves I did tell her of my respect for justice as it is, has to be. I said, "Won't it be better when young Miss Winnette is back home and able herself to take care of her dogs, they love her so."

She never replied, and she never missed a step. She moved right on toward the van.

Well, I could lose my job talking that way to her, a juror, but all of us enjoy Winnette. It's difficult not to tell a jury that. Winnette was trying to be decent to a difficult man, she was trying to be a good wife, that's my opinion, and I'd like to see her given justice. If there's one strong person on this here jury, it's this woman.

25

MR. MACMILLAN:

The judge was rambling on. I sat beside Winnette and held her hand, even gave it a judicial, judicious squeeze during the several references to murder. Juicks and I had done our final appeals to the jury, and the judge was spieling along, charging the twelve.

". . . if the state proves beyond a reasonable doubt, or it is admitted that the defendant intentionally killed Lloyd Ernest Plover with a deadly weapon or intentionally inflicted a wound upon Lloyd Ernest Plover with a deadly weapon that proximately caused his death, you may infer first that the killing was unlawful and second that it was done with malice, but you are not compelled to do so. If the killing was unlawful and was done with malice, the defendant would be guilty of second degree murder. Now then, having defined second degree murder, I will define voluntary manslaughter, the unlawful killing . . ."

I had never held a client's hand before in my forty years practice, but my holding Winnette's did seem to comfort her, to make her less trancelike, vulnerable. She needed—if anybody ever needed one—a friend.

". . . I so instruct you, gentlemen of the jury, and ladies of the jury, that a verdict is not a verdict until all twelve jurors agree unanimously on the decision. A majority vote is not of any count under our law. Even a ten to two, or eleven to one. I instruct you to consult one with another, to deliberate, and I instruct you to reach an agreement, but only provided you can reach it without violating the judgment of individual members. Each one of you twelve must decide this case for himself, even while you as a jury, a group, consider it. In reaching—in deliberating toward an agreement, you are instructed to reexamine your own views and, if you're in error, change your views accordingly. At the same time, you should not surrender honest conviction you hold solely because of your fellow jurors or because you as a jury need to reach a verdict. Once you have reached a verdict, you are to write it on the verdict sheet; that is, have your foreman write the verdict in the space provided—bailiff, where is the sheet? Give it to one of the jurors now."

He handed it to Miss Famous Turner, who was holding out her hand for it. She had taught school long enough to appreciate the volunteer class member, I suspect.

"You see, there's a blank or two for your foreman to fill in. Once you retire to the jury room, you are to elect a foreman who can lead your deliberation, and once the decision is reached, can date and sign the sheet. Then knock on your door and the bailiff will lead you back in here to pronounce your verdict to us all. Now, it is two o'clock. I instruct you to retire to your jury room to begin the deliberations."

Off they went, twelve human beings to decide the fate of this young woman beside me, a woman a bit older than a child, a lot younger than a mature person, a rather unimportant person on most counts, a failure in most of her efforts, a person adrift, shallow in much of her thinking, yet a human being with charm and the capacity to feel pain.

"How long does it take them?" she asked me. The little boy, Max, his head in her lap, was asleep, and she was careful with sound and with moving about so as not to awaken him.

"The jury? An hour minimum. Between an hour and two days," I told her.

26

MISS FAMOUS TURNER:

I had the sheet, and I kept it, even though Reverend Davis asked to see it. Of course, he wanted to be foreman. I took my place at one end of the rectangular oak table, and he took his place at the other, and the remaining ten pulled up their metal chairs to either side, the chair legs making a fearful, grating racket.

"Well, here we are," I said, taking hold, "and we must elect a foreman."

"Yes," Reverend Davis intoned. "So we must."

One of the fox hunters nominated the insurance broker, which so surprised dyspeptic Jim himself that he broke the point on his pencil. The insurance man said, "Reverend, why don't you do it." And Reverend Davis, without fluster, said he had been pleased to accept all the responsibility assigned to him, since his mother began doing so many years ago. Then the broker said ideally a lady ought to be foreman, considering the nature of the case. Mischievously his gaze swept to me, then on past me and settled on Miss/Mrs. Pender, whom he put in nomination. Obviously, he was getting back at me. So, rather than have her, a dummy, I supported Reverend Davis, who accepted once more, and once I gave him the sheet, the form, he assumed the chairmanship.

At once he suggested we put on the blackboard the four possible judgments. He asked me to be the one to write the possible verdicts on the board, since I had blackboard experience, which brought a quip from one of the fox hunters, the silent one who was in my class just after Vietnam. He was the one called Caesar by his classmates, a terror out of class he had been. In any event, he spoke up, said, "Yes, she could always use the chalk." Rude, but that made it all the easier to ignore.

"Second-degree murder," this Caesar called out loud, as if picking his choice. "Put that down first."

Whatever is put at the top of a list gains prominence; therefore, I wrote "second degree" at the far left of the blackboard, then accompanied it with the others alongside.

Second	Volun.	Invol.	NOT
Degree	Mansl.	Mansl.	GUILTY

By printing them in this manner, I was able to give suitable prominence to "Not Guilty." Also, I made its letters bolder, larger.

"Very well," Reverend Davis said, rearranging, jostling little slips of paper he had torn from a notebook, then testing his pen. "What is your desire, gentlemen?"

This introduced a long minute or two of silence, broken when I suggested we vote on whether Winnette was not guilty, which might make all the rest academic. My objection to anything academic was noted by the broker, causing even the insurance man to smile. Then one of the fox hunters said he didn't come on the jury to have it ended in a jiffy. That one was staring studiously at the blackboard, and he said he had lost track of the difference between involuntary and voluntary manslaughter.

"If she's not guilty," I said, "it won't matter about the definitions."

"If it don't matter, why'd you write them on the board for?"

"Yeh," another fox hunter said.

"Are we voting yet?" Miss/Mrs. Pender asked, her voice daring to rise slightly above a whisper.

Reverend Davis agreed that each term ought to be definable, and Caesar told all of us he thought definitions were at the heart of a teacher's trade, another remark deserving to be ignored. There then followed chalk exercise number two, with my writing under each term a few key points.

Second-degree murder. I wrote, "with malice," and at once the insurance man wondered aloud about malice, which was all the cue Reverend Davis needed. He recited at length—for five or ten minutes—about the nature of malice. "... not only does it involve hatred, but it goes beyond that, extends to the point where—now for example, Esther had malice toward those citizens who were persecuting the Jews, and she asked her lord, the king—she was his mistress, as you ladies might not know, might not want to know—asked him to let her kill her enemies for two weeks. She was granted this and exercised her right for two weeks, then asked for two more weeks. That's malice, one example. Then there's Herod, who ordered all the male babies to be slain. Imagine the parental suffering . . ."

On and on, so help me. Reverend Davis had an opportunity to do what Reverend Davis did best, and he was off and running, graduating from Esther to Herod to Pontius Pilot to Saul of Tarsus on the road to slay Christ—i—ans, as Reverend Davis pronounced it, when a ball of light struck him and he was converted. Reverend Davis's own face took on a celestial radiance as he reached this holy ground. "And God cleansed him of malice, and God—"

"Shit," Caesar, the fox hunter, allowed, loud enough to bring an appalled silence, which went on until broken by that fox hunter himself, rearranging his body on his chair and saying, "I was only wondering about the difference between second-degree and involuntary manslaughter, for Christ sake."

"Yes," Reverend Davis said, his voice vibrating in his chest.

I took advantage of the silence this time, which was still enough to cut, and wrote a few more notes on the board. "Malice" was required under "voluntary," while "passion without malice" was listed under "involuntary."

Another question or two from the fox hunters put all into confusion once more, and when Reverend Davis began another discourse, the broker, who probably was eager to get to a telephone, asked that we return to the court for help, which we did, the insurance man claiming that in the instructions the judge had left out involuntary entirely. In any event, at three-fifteen we were in the jury box once more.

Judge Blackington: "All right, who is your foreman?"

Reverend Davis cleared his throat, then gave his name for the record.

"I understand you might have a question for the court. Is that correct?"

Reverend Davis said it was quite so, and had to do with malice as to involuntary and voluntary.

"You want me to define those again? Is that correct?"

"Correct. We're like the lamb lost in the storm who is losing sight of the flock," Reverend Davis told him.

Judge Blackington considered that thoughtfully, his expression unchanging. With a shake of his head he freed himself from figuring it out. "Simply put, gentlemen, voluntary manslaughter is the unlawful killing of a person without malice and without premeditation or deliberation. Now then, involuntary manslaughter is the unintentional killing of a human being by an unlawful act not amounting to a felony or by an act done in a criminally negligent way. Does that suffice as to the definition of the two?"

Psychologically, that reply left us with the sense that we ought to choose between those two, they having received the emphasis, so I spoke up from my seat and asked the judge to help us with our definition of self-defense.

"All right," he said at once, nodding, his way of assuring me my question was in order, Reverend Davis's gasp notwithstanding. "As to self-defense, let me simply say that a killing would be excused entirely on the grounds of self-defense, provided it had appeared to the defendant to be necessary to shoot the victim in order to save herself from death or great bodily harm. The defendant should at the time be a person of ordinary firmness. And thirdly, provided the defendant was not the aggressor. And fourthly, that the defendant did not use excessive force. By reasonable force we must conclude that the force was reasonable, appeared to be necessary at the time to this person of ordinary firmness. Does that answer your question?"

Nobody replied. Everything wasn't clear to us, but I understood self-defense. After the look Reverend Davis shot at me, I certainly did not dare speak further, and he chose not to do so, so there was no response, until His Honor said, "All right, you may retire and resume your—your deliberations." This was at three-thirty-two by my watch.

27

MR. MACMILLAN:

Waiting for a jury to return is one of the more painful attorney tasks. Anne Bailey came by my bench, brought Winnette a bag of wool yarn and knitting needles. This was especially thoughtful, I felt. Also, she brought a small book of Keats poems, which she wanted returned sometime.

"Should we arrange for their supper, Mr. Juicks, Mr. MacMillan?" the judge asked us. He had returned from his chambers, his partial hairpiece off-placed. He hovered just there, nearby.

"I'd say the steak house, if they'll let the jury have the private dining room," Juicks suggested.

"Yes. No, I meant should we keep them in session this evening, or return tomorrow?"

"I'd say yes," I told him.

"Yes, what? Feed them? What say, Mr. Juicks?" he called.

Finally the decision was to feed them. "Any word as yet, how they're getting on?" I asked Judge Blackington.

"You'll know as soon as anybody." Even now, a few feet from Winnette, he appeared to be buried under routine, boredom; he was talking about Winnette's life, but was not even looking at her, much less sympathizing with her plight or admiring her endurance.

Suddenly, he did look at her, he was looking at her strangely.

To my astonishment, she was motioning with her hands, using her own head to suggest he see to his hairpiece. This sent him scurrying off to his chambers. "Oh, hell, Winnette," I murmured critically.

"It was crooked," she explained.

"Yes, but you must remember he is not human." I had to smile. "Anymore than you are."

4 P.M. Knitting. Winnette talking to her mother. The woman looked older than forty-two and obviously was under sedation; her eyes were dilated and her speech was blurred.

4:30 P.M. Winnette's sister, Clara, came by, lingered for about half an hour.

5:15 P.M. Her father came by, fell to talking about her car, for which he could buy a rebuilt motor for two hundred dollars, and he could put it in himself, provided the Ford place would let him use their hoist and tackle.

Winnette was having none of that. "I've been enough trouble already," she said.

Amazing, I thought to myself. Her reply has to be one of the outstanding understatements of all time.

5:30 P.M. The jury is called back into the courtroom. The press members stir, the visitors swarm up the stairs from the hallway and street downstairs. New visitors are present, people who came here after work at Herndon and Silver Spur, eager to get a glimpse of Winnette and her trial. The courtroom was soon filled.

Judge Blackington: "All right, gentlemen of the jury. And ladies, too. It is now time for the evening meal, and we have arranged for you to be driven to the family steak house. They have a closed-off space there. However, before you leave, without— would the foreman identify himself once again?"

Reverend Davis held up his hand.

"Without telling the court how you on the jury stand, if you do have a numerical division, would you please state that to the court. Now let me be clear on this. Just the numerical division is all I'm asking."

"Your Honor, we've not voted as yet. There's been an unparalleled effort made to get clear on the definitions."

"All right, then, please go to supper, and don't explain. I understand from the bailiff that you are satisfied to work for a few hours tonight. Is that correct?"

"Yes, Your Honor. He said till nine o'clock."

"Or nine-thirty. All right, that's fine."

"When we come back after dinner, we would be grateful to hear the four different parts of the judgments defined again, if that's not too much trouble."

Judge Blackington, frowning, revealed his disappointment with him.

"Some of us are not sure of it," Reverend Davis admitted.

"Well, make the request when you come back. Now, please go to the steak house and have a nice supper as a group and, as you recall, you are instructed in accordance with my earlier admonitions, you are not to talk with anybody outside the jury about this case, and you are not even to talk among yourselves about this case except when locked in—in the jury room during your deliberations. Of course, you are not to talk to the defendant or witnesses, nor to the attorneys—who are—which steak house, sergeant?" the judge asked.

"The one in Emerald Mines."

"So, you attorneys stay clear of that place till—till seven-thirty. Eat somewhere else. Now then, are you going to accompany them, sergeant?"

"Yes, Your Honor. And Sergeant Wilson."

"All right, you two sergeants come around and place your left hands on the Bible and raise your right hands. All right, do you and each of you swear that you will keep the persons of the jury in a convenient place for supper when in your charge, and you will not suffer any person to talk to any of the jurors, neither shall you speak to them yourselves except by leave of court—"

"Yes, sir," Sergeant Wilson said.

"No, damn it, wait for the 'so help you God.' "

"Yes, sir," both Sergeant Wilson and Sergeant Godwin said.

". . . neither shall you speak to them yourselves, except by leave of the court . . ."

"Yes, sir," Sergeant Wilson said, interrupting yet again, which so amused everybody that the judge waved him on.

"All right, gentlemen of the jury, and ladies, you may now be excused to go with these two sergeants, and you're to return to the same seats at—let's say—seven o'clock tonight."

The jury filed out, silent, reverent. The judge told the clerk to make out an order for the state to pay for the food and to list the two sergeants by name. Then he realized that I was standing. "Yes, sir?"

I said, "Respectfully, I further request that the court instruct the jury that Mavis Huntington Plover is a witness who is interested in the outcome of this case, and that the jury should scrutinize—"

Juicks was on his feet. "I don't believe, Your Honor, that is necessary under the rules—"

I continued: "She knows she will benefit substantially, she and her children, if the defendant is convicted of anything in regard to the—to Mr. Plover's death."

"I understand," Blackington said, and breathed heavily for a few seconds, then apparently proceeded quite to forget my requests, to let it merely die away, at least for now.

"Your Honor," I said, speaking over the hubbub in the courtroom, "I suggest respectfully that the jury does not realize it is required that the state prove my client was not acting in self-defense; if the state does not prove she was not, she must be found not guilty."

Blackington, shaking his head, said, "Too many 'nots,' Mr. MacMillan, for me. Just now I've put the court at ease and mean to retire. Any such request can be written out."

I wrote out my request on the back of a plumber's bill, the only sheet of paper at hand.

State vs. Plover 86 CRS 26339
Defendant respectfully requests, in light of the jury's requests for additional instructions, that the State has the burden of proof as to every element beyond a reasonable doubt—and specifically that the State must prove that defendant did not act in self-defense.

Further—that involuntary manslaughter is a felony.
7-7-82
Harold MacMillan
Attorney for defendant.

My plumber's bill was returned. It bore the entry dictation of the clerk, with time and date, and the judge's scrawled opinion: Jury has gone to dinner. They have been in deliberation for two hours already. Request denied except as included in charge. Go Eat. Blackington.

Winnette and her guards, along with her sister and I went to the seafood place and ordered a quick meal, and it was there I noticed Winnette's nervousness was growing perceptively. At first there were only small signs, her lack of appetite, lack of interest in conversation, her preoccupation with her own world, the tremble of her fingers, her hand shaking so much that she turned over her water glass. She closed her eyes tightly and sat there barricaded from all the world, even me and her sister, her hands now pressed against the table, one of them in the splashed water, her lips moving—no sounds issuing.

A woman appeared above her. She had approached from the back-window side. I recognized her to be that Mavis Plover, herself.

"Honey, you don't have to cry, do you? Don't act like a baby, Winnette."

Winnette looked up at her, startled out of her trance. "You having your supper?" she asked Mavis.

"I always come here Wednesday nights. You know that. You want a fresh glass of ice water?"

"Yes, I do, Mavis."

Mavis took a clean glass off another table, and a pitcher from yet another, and poured as she approached us and plopped the glass down before her. "There. Is Winnette having a rough time?"

Winnette drank deeply. "I'm having a rough time, Mavis."

Then Mavis went away, as suddenly, rudely as she had arrived, that rich fellow—the trucking man—joining her at the cashier station near the door.

Winnette ate some of her supper.

"That woman is not really your friend, Winnette," I told her.

"No, she's not," Winnette agreed. "But she does love me."

28

BLACKINGTON:

Serving on the bench requires stiff hindquarters, as well as negotiating ability. Families of deceased and accused grow heated and often irrational. It is common for the two lawyers to develop persecution complexes, and to come to dislike each other. Usually, later the lawyers make up and the judge is forgiven, but the tumbling about and rumbling of relationships continues among members of the bar, especially in rural counties. Now, the cities are worse, not better, but here in the mountains there are only a few attorneys, and they butt heads every session of the Superior Court, and meet each other socially afterward, continuously.

This new DA has not learned to give even a little bit. He need not have gone for first-degree murder, even though he did have supporting testimony of premeditation from one witness, Mavis Huntington Plover; that woman, damnit, as the first wife, is bound to be jealous of the second one, and also she's the mother of children by the deceased and they're going to gain the money if Winnette Plover is shown to be guilty, even if only of manslaughter. MacMillan is upset over my not reminding the jurors that Mavis Huntington Plover's testimony is suspect; however, this was testified to. It is not my obligation to review all the crannies of the testimony. I told the jury they were to weigh all the testimony and use common sense. If one tries to think for the jury, a revolt can occur. A jury is willful as a teenager, is determined to be independent, and it values its new powers highly. Just now I have here in my chambers notes from MacMillan and Juicks objecting to aspects of my charge to the jury, as well as several earlier rulings. Each fighter is swinging with all his strength, Juicks for his record, his career, MacMillan to save the defendant. Yes, and to reaffirm himself. He sent me a note early on, advising me of his availability should I need to assign an attorney. That's not generally done. In the case of a retired Floridian who is a new arrival to our bar, it is a bit more appropriate, is excusable to seek a case assignment from the judge. It is not the sort of maneuver one would publicly admit to.

Too bad the accused's friend Anne testified without effectiveness. Too bad her Blue was not called to testify. I assume Mr. MacMillan sought him. Nor was Winnette's first husband, who is living now I understand in Tennessee. That's not far to travel. MacMillan told me the man had not even told his new wife he had been married earlier and did not want to share the first wife's public shame.

A felony conviction will follow this Winnette Plover all her life, will shadow her legally. Every month in the woman's prison will change her attitudes and image, too. She will have to work out compromises with fellow inmates, the toughest pack of women in the world. Better to let her, and her unborn baby, leave this courtroom unfettered, but that privilege is in the lap of the gods right now. The twelve gods. And the ire of the Plover family.

Early on, Plover's father sent me a letter, mentioning God seven times and justice nine. He would be content, and so would his three sons, with simple justice. Simple justice is all he wanted. Probably he felt duty bound to see to his son's proper revenge, should the state falter. I've not met him; the sheriff watched him and his sons during the first two days. He said they were as pleasant as could be. They have not been present here in the courtroom, apparently. Might be in the hallways downstairs, where so many people congregate and exchange views of one sort or another, including revenge.

Up until a year ago when I got talked out of it, whenever the doorbell rang, I'd answer with a pistol in my hand, for one never knows what felon or witness or father will be there, or with what intent. My wife now has put the pistol in the hall table's drawer, close by. She believes that's safer all around. "After all, Sid," she told me, "the gun might go off and you'd shoot somebody."

I had shrimp and oysters for supper myself, served in my chambers, and was feeling perky now. About seven the jury returned and directly seated itself in its dozen chairs. "All right, Mr. Foreman," I told the preacher, "you recall you said before supper—by the way, was supper up to your expectations?"

"Yes, Your Honor. If I'd have only eaten half of one of those baked potatoes, my stomach would like me better."

"Did you dare to eat two?"

The foreman shook his big head of hair and we all laughed.

Oh, to get the jury in a jocular mood, which will inevitably favor reaching a decision soon. "Do you as a jury have questions of me, besides the potato? Let the record note that all twelve jurors are properly seated in their respective seats. Their dinner napkins removed. That last is to be stricken, clerk."

"Your Honor," the foreman said, "some of them said they weren't clear on some of the definitions from second-degree down, so could you go through them one more time for the—for them?"

"All right, I will read the definitions one more time." I noticed that the defendant was stiff as a board; she was staring ahead with unseeing eyes, two blurs, unfocused. "First, however, let the attorneys please come to the bench." The two men negotiated the bar and came close enough for private whispering. "Is she all right?" I asked MacMillan.

"She got tensed up at dinner," he told me.

"Did she take any—anything?"

"She ate part of her supper."

"Drugs?"

"No, I never saw any."

"Anybody come near her?"

"No. Her sister and me, and the woman deputy."

"Did she go to the ladies room alone?"

"No. I've never known her to do so, come to think of it." He smiled. Juicks laughed softly.

"Your Honor, I hope you'll mention the fact that Mavis Huntington's testimony is suspect," MacMillan said.

"Well then, let's get on with it," I replied to him. This was his third such request. Once he and Juicks were seated, I went through the entire litany once more. "Second-degree murder is the unlawful killing of a person with malice. Voluntary manslaughter is the unlawful killing of a person without malice and without premeditation and deliberation. Involuntary manslaughter is the unintentional killing of a person by an unlawful act not amounting to a felony or by an act done in a criminally negligent way." Twelve unknowing faces gazed back at me, not a smile or sign of brilliance on a one. "All right, you may retire to your jury room and resume your deliberations." The time was seven-twenty by my watch. I made a note of that fact and under the note wrote: Defendant appears to be dazed, is close to breakdown, I'm afraid. Her attorney and sister are talking to her. What to do? What to do? Did I define self-defense?

Or did I forget it again?

29

MR. CARTER:

Before going to dinner we had been polling ourselves, and the teacher's idea was to start with the not guilty, but several men wanted to start with the murder end and work our way down. I really was surprised. So we began with murder in the second-degree, but only three men, including the one who appears to be deaf, voted for it, and he didn't know what he had done, but while we were getting him sorted out, the bailiff called us forth before we had a tally. Now, after our supper and a few phone calls, we progressed to the next one, voluntary manslaughter, but some of the men had defined it in various ways. The teacher had notes, so she read off her notes, stressing the word malice and without premeditation. "Well, she did not premeditate, and I'll tell you why I know," I told the group.

"Why?" one of the men asked me.

"Because she doesn't have mind enough to think ahead." That insight amused several of them.

"Can we eliminate voluntary manslaughter then?" the teacher asked, and I do wish she had not, because—well, there is one other juror who dislikes her, and he bothered to speak against it for no other reason. Then our deaf man spoke up, merely insisting she was guilty. "Well, we all agree she's guilty," I told him. "It's how guilty is she."

"She killed her husband," he told me, sharing the bloody secret with me.

After that we ignored him, left him on the platter for later dissecting, generally agreeing we could beat him into submission, that he would settle for any punishment he could inflict on her.

The teacher now began defining involuntary manslaughter vs. voluntary manslaughter. She seemed to find them more or less similar.

Well, first the motel man told her he had always believed involuntary was mere negligence resulting in somebody's death, which did not, he agreed, quite fit this case. "But who the hell knows what the judge meant?" he asked.

I agreed with the motel man. Winnette was not merely negligent; accidental was not suitable. In agreement was the other man who disliked the teacher, whose name was Caesar, and then so did several others, nodding heads all around, so we were on a roll, as gamblers say, when Reverend Davis once again began talking about morality, and we had to call for a vote to silence him. As I saw it, the difference between voluntary and involuntary manslaughter— "the difference being," I said, "that in the former one she accidentally shot him, and in the later she intentionally shot him."

"That is not the distinction," the schoolteacher informed me, arching.

"Call for a vote," I said.

"I second it," the motel man said. Hell, he had work to do, more nighttime duties than during the day. Others of us also needed to be free. So, anyway, the motel man and I pushed for the vote, and Reverend Davis, rather than have a revolt, began insisting on a vote, too, so we voted by lifted hand, and it was the women and the confused deaf man for the lesser, the accidental, unintentional shooting, and all others for the more serious one.

"Hell, she meant to kill him," Pert said.

"She was defending herself," the teacher said.

"That's the verdict named not guilty," one man told her. "We've not voted on that." He was angry, really furious. "Winnette meant to shoot him and that means involuntary, not voluntary."

"You have them reversed," she coldly informed him.

"What the hell did you vote?" I asked the swing voter of the decade, having to shout in his good ear. He couldn't hear me.

"I will vote with the majority," Reverend Davis replied, assuming I was asking him. As for my deaf peer, he only stared daggers at me.

"That's three for involuntary and—let's see here . . ." Reverend Davis was stumped by mathematics.

"Not quite so, is it?" our teacher asked, seeking for a change to appear reasonable. "We have not voted for not guilty."

"Exactly," I said, which surprised her. "Now we twelve only need to vote on whether she's not guilty or is guilty of involuntary manslaughter."

"What happened—uh—" Reverend Davis pastored the situation as best he could. "Uh—where is the voluntary manslaughter?"

"We just defeated it nine to three," the teacher told him.

"So we did," he said, and sighed, and actually made a note of it.

Perfectly obvious we now would vote on not guilty, but the teacher began explaining that a wife protecting herself from grave bodily harm could legally use force—

"A pistol?" one of the men inquired sarcastically.

"Plover had no pistol, not when she shot him," another said.

"He had already assaulted her," one said.

"Yes, and if she had shot him while he was armed," the motel man began.

"But she could not," that Miss Pender said. "She was—was speared. You don't know what it's like."

"No, and neither do you," the motel man replied, which made most of the men smile. I did not smile. I was seeking a vote. Only a vote, in order to avoid chaos.

"She shot him so she could leave the house. That's what she said," one of the men said.

"She had threatened to shoot him," another said.

"She had not," the teacher said, arching toward him.

"Listen to the testimony," the man said, surprised by her attack.

"Vote," I suggested. Repeatedly I suggested it, and finally it was agreed to. By then one issue was clear enough. Either she had been acting in self-defense or she had not. The vote was as one would expect, eight for manslaughter—one or the other, and three for self-defense, the foreman hesitating. In fact, precious seconds found him still mulling aloud over the two choices, at the close of which he cast his vote "for mercy's sake." He voted with the women in favor of self-defense, which is not guilty. That amounted to eight to four—two women, the foreman, and the deaf man, who was voting out of confusion and bafflement, or obstinacy and a penchant for absurdity. At this precise moment, as if a bailiff had been listening, the door opened and we were called back to see the judge. If we had been allowed another ten minutes, the momentum would have carried us on to decision— either that or locked us in.

30

MR. MACMILLAN:

They appeared to me to be wildly animated, as if every one of them had his or her feathers ruffled. At nearby booths several people expressed surprise at so unexpected a change from their modest, daydreamy demeanor of awhile ago.

"All right now, Mr. Foreman," Judge Blackington was saying, "it is eight-twenty, an hour has elapsed. Do you have a report to the court? I want merely a numerical division and nothing else, if you will, please, sir."

"We stand six to four, sir," Reverend Davis told him, "and I'd say there are people on both sides that mean—"

"No, no. Only the numerical figures. All right, then, thank you, sir." The judge adjusted his body to the big chair, sniffed inward meaningfully. "Six to four is ten," he said.

"I mean eight to four, sir."

"Very well. Let me convey these further instructions to you all. Your foreman informs the court that you have so far not agreed on a verdict. The court emphasized that it is your plain duty to do whatever you can to reach a verdict. You should reason the matter over together as reasonable people and reconcile your differences, if you can do so without surrendering conscientious convictions. No jurors should yield his own convictions for the purpose of returning a verdict; however, it is your plain duty to reach a verdict. Therefore, I will ask you to go back inside there and deliberate some more. You can now go back. If you have questions, any of you, you can have your foreman convey those questions to the court, if you please."

31

He reached across the jury room table and slapped my hand, chiding me, all the while fussing and fuming about needless delays. The latest vote had pitted Miss Pender, the deaf man, the foreman and me against the galloping horde, and some of the horde were considering voluntary manslaughter themselves, on us, although others were amused, seemed to be reveling in a new spectator sport. The motel magnate was the loudest. One would conclude, as I told him, that his motel needed his personal attention before nine-fifteen. "What is a woman's life reputation compared to getting lodgers in another five beds?"

"She damn well did shoot her husband," he shouted at me. "She can't be not guilty. She shot him!"

"She shot him in self-defense, which is not guilty."

"Shot him in the back in self-defense?" one of the fox hunters asked me, then winked.

"He was going to get a gun," I reminded him.

"Might wait till he'd got it."

"That is nonsense," I told him.

"She fired twice," another man reminded me.

"Was perhaps justified," Reverend Davis said, "considering her pain and suffering. The way he used the pistol, himself—"

"Shooting is justified, Reverend?" the insurance man asked.

"If not quite justified, then excusable."

"Understandable."

"Yes, exactly."

"But not excusable."

"Well, we must go," the innkeeper murmured aloud, our reminder of urgency. "Can we settle on—on something that admits a crime?"

"Not guilty," I said.

"The next one up the ladder." The insurance man said, "What? Involuntary what was it?"

"Meaning what?" one of the men asked, which drove me to distraction. One more definition and I would explode.

"Wouldn't want to be the one to tell that dead man's family his murderer went free," the broker began.

"Stop using that word!" I stormed out at him, my nerves on fire. "Murderer she is not determined to be."

"Not yet," a fox hunter corrected me.

"Would you call it an accident?" the broker inquired facetiously. "Shooting her husband in the back—"

The deaf one was mumbling. The words sounded like, "She went back to him."

Now one of the fox hunters began to hum.

"After all, the first shot was fired by Plover," I reminded them. I was in a state of anger so fierce it could have been cut with a knife. A teacher's role is not one of compromise. Mine has never been one of compromise. A teacher requires assurance, truth, facts. When a decision is made by me, it is accurate, honest, irrevocable.

"If we vote again, we might be deadlocked again," our foreman said. "Shall we vote again?" he asked, looking about hopefully. "Yes, indeed. All in favor of not guilty, hold up your hand."

Miss Pender and I and the foreman, three, the deaf man was blinking.

"In favor of guilty to some degree?"

At once four voted for it. Then other hands went up. Then to my astonishment, the foreman held up his. "I'm going to swing that way. It's almost nine o'clock," he explained to me. "So, what—what did you say, Miss Famous?"

"I see I've been talking to myself."

"Please forgive me for changing my vote, but let me explain. If we do nothing but balk we tie our own hands; she'll have to stand trial again. All over again. She'll have months of waiting, then the new trial with witnesses' testimony, a new jury, and they will decide, not us. The judge, His Honor, said it was our duty to reach a verdict. Now, our duty is—is clear, though the way to it is—is not."

That was the most intelligent argument he had delivered thus far, I must admit. To have that young woman go through a new trial was unthinkable.

Miss Pender whispered she could conceivably vote for the lesser manslaughter. Her thought was unwelcomed by me, and I said so to her. I had realized she was crumbling. Her part of the wall was about to go.

"Yes," Miss Pender said, "I'm willing to reach a decision, to change my vote, if others will."

"You will not," I told her.

"You are not to boss me," she shouted.

"You are not going to desert Winnette—"

"I vote—I vote with the jury," she told me defiantly, "for whatever the words are, for that manslaughter." And she collapsed back into her chair and stared misty-eyed at her hands, which were gripped into a single ball on the table before her.

"I demand a vote," the innkeeper said.

The door opened and the bailiff called us out for another lecture. We stood at once, to obey, but the innkeeper insisted on first voting, and himself called for the vote and held up his hand. All held up their hands except me, some voting to have a vote, merely that.

"It's not a vote unless called by the chairman," I said.

"She's not voting," the broker announced, pointing at me.

"I vote not guilty," I told them, "always."

Weakness—this was the first time in years I experienced weakness. At the moment of strong assertion, I was most frightened. Oh, there had been moments in childhood, when tremors afflicted me. I can recall in junior high being beset by pressures which lay beyond me to endure, it seemed. Back then a tremor came to my neck which—well, the tremor was beginning once more, so that I had to press against the back of my neck with the palm of one hand.

"Take your seats, if you please," His Honor told us, frowning at us. Frowning at me, particularly, I felt. You can't tell me they don't know what goes on in the jury room. Dear child—look there at her, look at Winnette. Is it within my power to send that mild and pretty woman off to prison?

"Mr. Foreman of the jury, I want you to give me your latest vote."

"Nine to one, sir."

One woman gave out a yelp, whether of victory or defeat or surprise, I don't know.

"Can't be ten jurors," the judge reminded him.

"Nine to three," our foreman corrected himself. "Or eleven to one."

What a bungle, a plain embarrassment. The judge jotted notes on his desk. He appeared prepared to ask further but must have decided only mine fields lay in that direction.

"Yes. Now then, let me stress your duty." He did so in a five-minute talk addressed to me particularly, I felt, about the need for our system of justice to function, for trials to be held that reach a verdict, for justice to prevail. To be sure it was to be tested by each link in the chain. A chain is no stronger than each and every link in it, he told us, looking at me. However, if the chain fails to serve, it matters not about each link, that is irrelevant. Then he repeated—word for word it seemed—the very same talk as delivered earlier, and when he asked Reverend Davis if there were any questions, and our foreman said no, I held up my hand.

"Yes, ma'am?" the judge said. "Have you told your concern to your foreman?"

"Not all of them," I replied.

The judge had to smile. "Very well. Give me your questions then."

"Please once more define not guilty, the legal term."

214

Once more an audience commotion ensued; it swept across the big room like a welcome, relieving breeze. Even the girl smiled, and she smiled at me. The very words, simple as they were—

"Yes. Well. Very well, Mrs.—Miss—"

"Famous Turner."

"Yes. The teacher. Well now then, not guilty is the balance term for the three others. It means the state has not proved that the defendant meant to kill her husband. That is, the proof must be given beyond a reasonable doubt that she did not act in self-defense—"

"Who must prove she did act in self-defense?" I asked.

"Nobody has to prove she did act in self-defense, but it is up to the state to prove she did not."

Mr. Juicks was calling for a conference, and he and Mr. Mac-Millan and the judge talked for several minutes, with me all the while reciting to myself: the state must prove she did not act in self-defense, prove she did not act in self-defense . . .

Their conference over, the judge sat still and silent for a long moment, then murmured something to himself, then to us. "In that case, then the proper verdict is self-defense—I mean is not guilty."

"And how does that differ from involuntary manslaughter?" I asked.

Mr. Juicks was on his feet again, but the judge waved him aside. "No, no, no," he said in his direction. "Miss Famous Turner—now then, that is the next step up. It signifies, let's say, that the defendant pointed a pistol at her husband and it went off, or that she shot him in a—what we call a criminally negligent way, causing his death. That is involuntary. Will there be anything further from the jury?"

"No, sir," Reverend Davis said quickly, followed by some of the other males in swift agreement.

"All right, then, you have been—this third time return to your deliberation. What time is it?"

"Nine o'clock, sir," the clerk replied.

"Can we aim toward nine-thirty? I hope so. Now then, off to your chamber."

I found not a person on the jury could answer me as to what was the proof the girl had not been engaged in self-defense. She had shot him in the back, but he had been getting into a room full of weapons and nothing else, and without an outside door. As to this latter point, we had to have a copy of the floor plan, and once it was brought and showed no outside door from that bedroom, from the storage room, certain of them stopped claiming proof that she had not been defending herself. The insurance man and Miss Pender returned to my side, then the innkeeper capitulated, and the foreman. Finally all except three, my ex-student Caesar and some of his friends; although we had not taken a new vote, I judged the majority would be in my favor, so I ceased, I simply required of myself to remain silent, realizing that I was a red flag before certain of these bulls.

The vote, once taken, was seven for not guilty and three for voluntary and two for involuntary. Then to my horror Miss Pender again suggested we all compromise on involuntary, and all I could do was watch in sorrow as that vote was taken. Nine to three. The chief of the three was me, and I knew there was no way back now. It was this compromise or a new trial for Winnette, which held greater dangers; even so, I said my two words of victory and defeat, "I disagree." They sent the entire jury room into disarray, with men and Miss Pender shaking their fingers at me, pounding the table, declaring me incompetent, saying they did not want to meet on Saturday, no nor Sunday, either, but wanted to go home now, that they had tried to be reasonable, while me the fiend, the devil—

My ex-student fox hunter brought the assault to climax. "You're the one ought to have a God damn pistol put up your twat."

Silence then.

Absolute silence while I tried to recoup my own senses. I must have looked at him, uncloaked him down to his heathen nakedness, for he wilted. Of course, some of the others were horrified, too. He had left himself defeated.

That was the peak of animosity toward me, and toward the helpless, hapless Winnette. There were men aboard who could

216

not tolerate the fox hunter's bombast, who felt called to disassociate themselves. I had to say not one word. The insurance man, the innkeeper, the foreman, insisted on fairness, and although this was fairness toward fellow jurors, it slopped over to all others, was a general attitude, including finally Winnette Plover. I think some of the men voted with me as a form of apology. Whether such rancor and personality quirks and shifts belong in a chain of justice—well, I am not as impressed with the jury system as earlier, even though in this case it supported my own views.

The vote was eleven to one, the "deaf" man unpersuaded "for a spell," but before the next vote he was asked his opinion, and he delivered a message about Frenchmen having *crime passionales,* where a woman is physically guilty, even though innocent of heart, and why, he wondered, couldn't we here do as well.

Driving home that night, the insurance man beside me, we had the further victory of finding the broker and innkeeper's car beside the road, their car having run out of gas, and I gave them a lift into Emerald Mines. All of us were giggly from exhaustion, and had praise for Winnette, who on Reverend Davis's announcement had leaped to her feet and made an acceptance speech so infectious because of her emotion that it could not—not one word—be understood. Only after effort was the judge able to regain decorum, and after her lawyer and sister and Anne got her off her knees and gave her their own large handkerchiefs and napkins.

The broker had a house on the north hill overlooking the his-and-her shopping centers—I call them that because one is owned by a realtor, the other by his ex-wife; meanwhile we had dropped the innkeeper off at his too-well-lit lobby. As for the insurance man, once we reached his home he sat in the car for a minute or so. Even after his wife clicked the porch light on, he waited. "I thank you," he said

"Thank me, for goodness sakes?"

"I am a terminal fellow, Miss Fancy—Famous."

"Oh, my . . ."

"Yes. So it's been told to me."

"I'm sorry."

"Six months, and not happy ones to go."

"Oh, my. I'm sorry, Mr.—Mr.—"

"Still a secret, mind you, but my wife and me share it."

"No. No, I wouldn't mention—"

"I'd rather you didn't. But I had a chance to vote out of charity. The Bible calls it charity."

"In Corinthians."

"Not something I could do otherwise, Miss—Miss—"

"Isn't it amusing," I said, "neither of us knowing the other's name, and we've been through so much together."

32

BLUE:

The courtroom was a blaze of light and tears for hours, and seeing Winnette happy again was a splash of life, even to me, like in the old days. Well, even in the old days she wasn't radiant, like now, hugging her papa, who was the happiest man on earth, and sister and mother. In the old days there had been a wariness about her disposition, as if she might be trespassing. Here and now she was exonerated, she was crowned queen. I mean, she was aloft.

Nobody was more pleased than Anne and me, but Anne began to harp on me not having helped. "Don't you dare look victorious, yourself. You were on his side all the way." She even slapped at me in her anger, which she had never done before.

"Well, the women have got the bit in their teeth, have they?" I said to her. She never hit me, mind, was careful to miss me. Well, in fact I never favored Plover over Winnette; being neutral was my way of favoring both, agreeing with Winnette that she was in the right to try to help him get competent. He was dragging a lot of old ways, some of them inherited, I'd say, tatters from one century to another, manners which were being knocked over, and this floored him now and again. He wanted his own world, mind, and there was a time up here a man could have that, could live in his cove, in his cabin, be his own man, have his own family to himself, as he saw fit. Now it's all invaded with schools and governments, trucks and planes, radio and TV and movies and magazines, frowns and opinions and criticisms, highways and airports . . . Plover never dared to fly because the one time he took a try at flying, him and me went to the Charlotte airport, and he wouldn't yield to another man's system, not even an airport's; he wasn't a person happy to pay over all his cash money, or stand in lines, or allow people to question him or look into his suitcase or x-ray him. Some uniformed woman found he had a pistol on him, which he did. Hell, Plover had carried a pistol while traveling even to town, had since he was a boy. "Now, you get to hell," he told her, told them all, and we left without even seeing the airplane.

He went from alcohol to drugs, and that bound him to the mast for sure. It was his own boat, but he was sinking. She kept him from drowning, and he had to love her for it, but resent it all.

Had to love her—look how pretty she is, like a dawn sun she's so happy. Even hugging that lawyer.

"You bitch," Anne was saying.

At first I thought it was to me she was talking, and I was inclined to set her straight, but I saw it was Mavis being treated. Oh my Lord, Mavis was in enough of a state of fraught, couldn't keep her expression set, and couldn't grab Max for trying to corner the other one. Max was as tearful with joy as Winnette, and Mavis was trying to collect her family and keep herself together, and I suppose the cords broke inside her and she cursed at Anne, furious like a tiger, she boiled over, mind, all boiling inside her, and it took a deputy and me to keep her off of Anne, and it was Winnette who tried to comfort Anne—not comfort Mavis, I noticed. Nobody tried to comfort Mavis. Hell, she had scarred herself with a blotch on her heart that'd never come off. Even I never tried to calm her. She got her kids and stumbled away, her feet making clomps on the stairway.

As I said, neither Winnette nor me helped her—we being the peacekeepers ordinarily.

That there Assistant DA was a-settin' in his car as me and Anne left. His lights were out but a street light showed him frowning.

"He has nobody to go home to," Anne told me. "Lives near Boone."

"There's plenty around, if he'll pick one," I told her. "Look how I come out, myself."

She didn't even smile, anyway not for a minute, then she laughed and took my hand.

As if she owned me.

33

MR. MACMILLAN:

Loneliness can result merely from being without last week's spate of excitement. A prince in the royal circle on Friday, I was nobody on Saturday, with the same newspaper to reread. One does miss power and prominence.

Also, it is possible I missed Winnette. Here, too, there was a void in my life that needed filling. She was in no sense an intimate, but she and I had been partners in a life-and-death struggle.

By Monday morning my nerves were on edge from my wasting away, and I went ahead and telephoned her parents' house, asked for Winnette, my luncheon invitation memorized. I felt giddy as a teenager on his first—making his first such invitation.

Her mother, weeping, told me Winnette had persuaded her father to drive her to Marion so she could go away by bus for the weekend, visiting school friends in Tennessee, but the mother had just discovered her clothes were gone, all the best ones, and all her shoes, so she must be leaving home. "I went to get what needs washing, Mr. MacMillan, and found everything is gone, except her medicines, so I phoned the two doctors—"

"Two?"

"Her doctors."

Driving down the twisty road to Marion, I rehearsed my speech to Winnette. My driving became as risky as my thoughts. "It's surprising even to me, Winnette, at my age to find myself infatuated. This is risking making a fool of myself, and I'm certainly married securely and up to my ears in joint property, but is it conceivable that you could locate nearby and let me help you make arrangements for yourself and your baby, and you help me find—rediscover my sense of vitality . . ."

Twenty-six-minute drive to the truck stop that served as station. Sweaty from anxiety, I did arrive in time, for I saw her sitting at a window table, one bathed in sunlight, talking to her father, and she saw my car jolt to a stop and me jump out, for a big smile came over her face and she waved, then threw a kiss to me, which damn near devastated me. Somewhere between sanity and helpless desire, I hurled myself inside, flung myself into her booth and began my apologies, realizing her father was now sitting only a dozen feet away at the counter, and had turned to stare at us, the man clearly intrigued.

"Papa and me—we been arguing," she told me.

"Winnette, I don't want you to leave."

"You ought to talk to Papa about that. He's mad as a hornet."

Being classified with her father brought me a step or so closer to sanity.

"He saw I bought a ticket all the way to Denver, and he's sitting by himself," she told me.

"Winnette, I'm—I'm not your father, and I don't mean to be, but I do offer to help—to take care of you and your baby . . ."

"Oh, I know what you mean," she said, and her eyes went misty, welcomed the thoughts, and she took one of my hands between her two small ones and pressed it. "If I were older, Mr. MacMillan, it would be possible, but I've—have to play out my own hand. I told Papa, well, you don't call what I've been doing living—"

"It would be a wonder, a pleasure to make up to you what that husband deprived you of—"

"I've turned two husbands over, and the first one was sort of blank, and the next one had skulls and crossbones on him, and now I have to go off to myself, find another one."

"I want to help you with the third."

223

She seemed to know, to sympathize, she was grateful for my concern; however, she was not going to be caught just now, not by me. Sunlight was bathing her and gave her a natural radiance. She shook her head, revealing gentleness even in rejection. "Wish me well, will you?"

"Yes, with all my heart," I said. Then, desperate, I told her I wanted her to go to my home in Florida. "It's on the water. Live there without charge till you've found a place of your own." I would go now and buy her a new ticket—

The gentle shake of the head. There was perhaps a wisp of regret, or could it be shame for me, in my persisting even yet? She mentioned her own house on the river, as she called it, the nearest to a home she had ever managed for herself, "a nest with briars in it," she said ruefully. "It's not even the River Road, Mr. Mac. It's—a—common man's name, Tom Smith Road, but I called—"

"Does it go to the river?"

"No. Not for a mile or so."

"I see." Dear girl. "So your house is not on the river."

"It's natural for me to want a home, and for it to be pretty and have a porch. It didn't have a porch."

"A mile away, you say?"

"His and mine, such home as we had, and it—no, it's only called the house on the river."

"Because you so much want it to be beautiful?"

"Is that wrong?"

"Not for you."

"Why, we need romantic notions, if you ast me, or what's a woman for?"

I put money into her hand. She returned it, told me her sister had money for me, enough she hoped to be a proper fee.

Both of us were startled by a car steaming across the gravel parking lot, skidding to a stop; out of it bounded a middle-aged man who scanned the yard, searching for—for her. He saw her and hurried to the restaurant door, Winnette waving at him, beaming her innocent smile. Before I was quite oriented, Doctor Robbins was at our booth, was beside her, urgently talking to her, using some of the same statements of want and desire to help that had made a fool out of me.

From my stool, sitting beside her father, I watched Robbins as he made his appeal, and as she ever so kindly refused him. I didn't hear all, and none of her words, but it was done neatly, considerately. That much I could tell.

Her bus arrived. The doctor and I vied for possession of her two suitcases, which we stowed aboard while she said good-bye to her father. Then she went to the doctor, and kissed him, not on the cheek as she had her father, but on his lips; then she came to me, and I began to stammer an apology for this intrusion on her life, but she hushed me, a finger sealing my lips. Then she kissed me, and hers were the softest lips mine had felt ever. Quite remarkably soft, actually.

I watched her climb aboard her bus, my mind reeling with humiliation, pride, affection for her, fear for her. The doctor and father were beside me; the father was sniffing. The bus pulled out, the three of us side by side, waving. The father asked if we would think to have a beer with him, which was accepted, and we took three stools at the counter. He told us she had always been going away, had run off from home as a child of three, not in protest, for the home was comfortable, but poking into experiences, even dangers. It had been an awful experience for him, these last months, and his wife had aged years. But thank God for the other daughter, the secure one, the steady daughter. She was God's blessing. "Of course, it's the stray sheep that one wants to find and help, ever' time."

All the while, the doctor was in a dismal trance, not even listening, the best I could tell. Twice he got up to go, perhaps to try to follow her, then sat down again. Once more he was getting ready to leave when my dear friend, the psychiatrist, arrived out in the parking yard. We all saw him walking about, no doubt looking for Winnette. On coming into the restaurant, on seeing the three of us on our stools, he paused for a moment to reflect, then without a greeting returned to his car and drove off.

Dear child. I actually spoke aloud to her on my way up the mountain. Dear child, be on your way. You are quite right to leave

225

us, all this residue. It is too much to rearrange. Good-bye, sweet girl. Better, surely, will be the next card.

Her sister had my fee in a paper bag, which some of the people hereabouts call a poke, one of these people's old English words. Her sister came to my house, complaining that she could not find my office, with the poke, my fee, and I peeked inside, ever cautious of fees in pokes, and saw a quart canning jar. Dirt was on the jar.

"My dear girl, it isn't narcotics, is it?"

"No, sir," she assured me.

"I—can't accept—" I tore the bag down one side to reveal the glass. The jar was full of money.

"They never dug in the dog lot," Clara said. "That's where Plover buried the money."

Packs of twenty-dollar bills, the sort of packs one gets at the bank. They come in thousand-dollar lots, and in the lower half of the jar were five such packs, and one was folded at the top.

"She left one jar for your fee, Mr. MacMillan, and one for me, provided I wouldn't marry till I'm twenty-three." Clara smiled wistfully, then winked at me. "I asked her if she meant I have to be chaste, too? And she said heavens no."

I laughed, as much from giddy surprise as delight.

"And she took the other two jars with her, one in each suitcase."

So there Winnette went, innocent as dewy down, into the bosom of the country, innocent little woman, a trail of kindness and assaults behind her, and two quarts of twenty-dollar bills in her possession. Clara and I laughed, we both had a fit over it. Clara had the same pretty laugh, and for that matter, the same feminine appeal of her sister; she might even be prettier under all those jeans and oversized blouse.

I wondered aloud if I might come by her house—Winnette's house some night, bringing the food, of course, and if the two of us might cook our supper, and the notion brought about the same smile, I swear, as Winnette's.

34

From the *Rocky Mountain News,* Denver:

BORN to Mrs. Winnette King Plover a daughter, Clara King Plover, 7 lbs. 11 oz. at University Hospital. The father, the late L. E. Plover, businessman, passed away recently following a shooting accident in the North Carolina mountains. Mrs. Plover is a student in the University of Colorado Health Sciences Center.

FIC   Ehle, John
EHL
          The widow's trial

$17.95

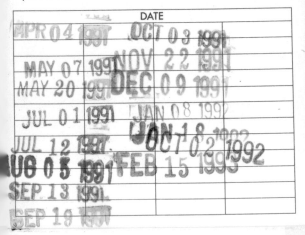